all that Drama

all that Drama

Tina Brooks McKinney

A

SBI
PUBLICATION

A Strebor Books International LLC Publication
Distributed by Simon & Schuster, Inc.

Published by

Strebor Books International LLC
P.O. Box 1370
Bowie, MD 20718

LCCN 2003116580
ISBN 0-7394-5083-2

Cover art: André Harris

Manufactured and Printed in the United States

dedicated to the ones I love

I would like to thank God first and foremost for allowing me to finish my dream. This book would not have been possible without the love and support of my family. I especially want to thank my husband, William McKinney, for believing that I could do this and for putting up with my late nights at my laptop. Many thanks and praise to my children, Shannan and Estrell, for their love, faith and confidence in me.

I want to thank my friends, Kathy, Kim, Vanessa, Lindsay and Angela, Scott and Erica. Without your support, I might have given up on this book a long time ago. Thanks for the endless readings that you all did, I really appreciate it and this book is for you, too!

My other friends and family, this list is numerous and I don't want to leave anyone out. Special shout-outs to Angie and Valerie, my long-time childhood friends, the real-life Sammie, Regena Barnes, Diane Turner, cousins Laura, Tarcia, Donna, Mike, David and Kevin and the rest of my Baltimore family.

Special thanks to Zane and Charmaine and the rest of the Strebor staff, to my Strebor authors who showed me the way and my road dogs: Harold, Shelley, Darrien and Allison. I would also like to thank my boss Kelvin Walton for his understanding and support. It's on now!

And last but certainly not least, Ivor and Luetta Brooks and my sister, Theresa. Love you all!

chapter 1

I f I knew yesterday that I would be fighting for my life today, I would have done things differently starting with last night. First of all, I would have gotten laid for real. I would have been fucked until my feet curled over and my back refused to stand straight. I would have gone downtown to a club, scoped out two fyne brothers, possibly cousins, took them home and fucked the daylights out of 'em. Sounds freaky but you would be surprised at the thoughts that flow through your head as the blood oozes out of your body.

Prior to today, the very thought of being with more than one man never appealed to me, but after all that I have been through over the last couple of months, the sheer freak in me has arrived.

If I had a chance to do things differently, I would not risk picking up someone with either a tiny dick or one that was rendered useless after a few minutes, so, nothing less than two men would be acceptable.

"Oh God, what about my children. I don't want to leave them alone," I moaned even though no sound escaped from my lips. The fact that they did not come to my mind first does not by any means lessen the love that I feel for them. Hell, I wish I would have thought about them first but shit, let's be real; I'm bleeding here and can't control my thoughts or dementia at this point.

At least they have my mother who'll continue to watch over them and make sure they do well in school and whip their asses if they don't. I can't help but to cuss at the powers that be that got me here, but *bear in mind, I was not about to cuss at God since I might be meeting him soon.*

Vivid images flood my head. I flash forward to all the special moments that will occur in my children's lives, their proms, dating, marriage and then children, my grandchildren.

Whoa, hold up, what the hell am I thinking; I am not even ready to think about either of my children dating or getting married, much less fucking! My injury must be worse than I thought.

I have a pre-designed plan for my daughter which is to lock her up at the onset of puberty, not letting her go until she turns twenty-one. If she only knew, she would be chanting, "Bleed, Momma, bleed."

For my son, I want to do everything in my power to keep those scrawny chicken heads away from him. I want him to grow up to be a real man, one who is self-reliant and self-supporting. *Did they hire someone to try to knock me off?*

Ok, I am pissed now. *How the hell did I wind up here? Yeah, I did my shit, but was it worth this?* Sammie came out of the house and lifted my head onto her lap. She gently rocked me encouraging me to hold on. I had so much to tell her but I could not speak.

"Hold on, Marie. Hold on," she cried, dropping more tears into my already full eyes.

The blinding light that I saw in the distance was getting brighter and kept drawing my attention. When I first arrived on the porch, I turned my head to keep it out of sight, but I kept checking it to make sure it did not come any closer. *Damn, where is Five-O when you need them?*

My mind sought to gallop along a path of fantasy of which I had no control. I simply refuse to go softly into the light!

chapter 2

Sammie Davis was accustomed to chaos in her life. Lord knows it was so common to her it could have been her middle name. If things weren't stirred up, then she was not happy. For Sammie, it had always been that way and it drew me to her like a bee to honey.

Me? I can't live that way. I am too used to law and order. But when I do get the urge to creep on the wild side, Sammie is my freeway of choice. Truth be told, I'm an undercover drama junkie. I want to hear about it, I just don't want it anywhere near my back door!

I met Sammie on the most embarrassing day of my life. It was the first official day of spring and the temperature had reached 70 degrees. I wanted to wear something very colorful to celebrate the arrival of the season. I chose a bright pink skirt set that accentuated my shapely legs. I purposefully left my coat hanging in the closet.

I am an avid commuter. I prefer taking the subway to work because I hate to drive. The morning I formally met Sammie, in my haste to leave the house I grabbed my old maternity slip. It fit securely when I left the house and did not shift when I climbed into the car, but as I was rushing to catch the train, the slip chose to show its tattered condition. Not realizing what was happening, my leg movement became restricted. I was in trouble. Sammie stopped me from kissing the concrete by snatching me up by the scruff of my neck. Sammie didn't laugh, as I would have done after witnessing the steps I had just performed. Maybe her heroics were a normal course of events to her, but to me, she was a savior.

I was relatively new to the Atlanta area and I have no sense of direction so I could not tell you whether I lived west or north of the city. But I can tell you, with exact detail, about every woman's hairdo on my stop and how she acquired it. I can tell if it is sewn, glued, stapled or borrowed 'cause hair is my thang! I can't do shit with my own but I pay a handsome wage to have it done. Mine is God-given and chemically altered. When it comes to hairstyles, Sammie is the queen of the weave. She kept me constantly guessing what the hell she would do to it next. One day, she showed up with this yellow hair that was woven into a birdcage. I was totally outdone because Sammie's hair always matched her outfits no matter what color she wore. I always wanted to ask Sammie who did her hair but she intimidated me. Now that I'd made an ass of myself, I really didn't know what to say to her.

I had noticed Sammie as she started appearing at the Indian Creek train station about six weeks before the incident. She had a presence that commanded your attention as she confidently strolled to the train every morning never appearing to be rushed. On the other hand, I arrived at the station hell-bent on catching a train and willing to knock somebody on their ass if they got in my way.

No matter what the weather, Sammie always appeared in the shortest of skirts and the highest of heels. One thing that stood out about Sammie was that she didn't have the usual baggage like other women carried. We carried canvas bags, grocery bags, dog-eared novels, tennis shoes, Walkmans and bottled water. But not Sammie; she never carried anything other than a tiny clutch, which was always coordinated with her outfit and her hair. I envied that clutch because there was no way my shit would have fit in that tiny little bag. Her bag was so tiny that not even my cigarettes and lighter could be squeezed into it, and I wouldn't dare leave the house without them. Silently, we boarded the train. Sammie took the seat next to the window. After a moment's hesitation, I sat down beside her. Despite Sammie's flamboyant yellow attire, I could not help but to steal glances at the sheer coordination between her hair, mini skirt and the clutch. Her black leather shoes even had yellow lines running across them. I always wanted to wear yellow but did not have the confidence to do so.

Feeling embarrassed, intimidated, and a bit of an idiot, I could not muster up the courage to say thank you. She just looked out the window as if nothing had transpired. She was so damn cool! God, I wished I could be that cool! We continued to ride in silence for the next two or three stops.

The sun had not risen so it was still dark outside, but Sammie continued to gaze out the window. I wanted to say something witty to Sammie but old fears and insecurities captured my tongue.

"That was the funniest shit I have ever seen in my life," Sammie declared.

"Excuse me, what did you say?"

"I said that was the funniest shit I have ever seen in my life," she said, trying to suppress her boisterous laughter. "You were about to eat the concrete big-time!"

"You're right," I uttered a small giggle still torn between humor and humiliation.

"And, what really blew me away, you left the shit in the middle of the sidewalk. That's what I can't get over!" Sammie said with her hand covering her mouth trying to physically contain her laughter.

"What was I supposed to do, pick it up and claim it? I don't think so!" I replied in a huff.

The train was approaching Georgia State station, near the mecca of downtown Atlanta. It was also my queue to begin gathering my stuff. The slowing of the train matched my thought process.

Picking up on my distressed state, Sammie said, "Girl, it was not that serious. You tripped; that's all. At least I think that's what your ass was doing!" No longer able to hold back, she exploded with laughter.

Her laughter was what I needed to make me loosen up. Once we settled down, I introduced myself.

"Hi, I'm Marie Morgan and normally my clothes don't attack me." Sammie laughed again and I joined in. *Whoopee, I've finally found my witty retort,* I thought to myself proudly. "I just grabbed the wrong slip this morning. I didn't feel it until it tripped me up and you saved my ass."

Together, we departed the train and began walking down Peachtree Street. My job was about three blocks away and I was glad that I had worn tennis shoes instead of high heels like Sammie wore. I set the pace and surprisingly Sammie kept up with me.

"I just wish I could have seen your face as you were going down! Girl, when you started wind-milling your arms I didn't know if you were trying to fly or fighting off a fucking bee," Sammie said, chuckling all over again.

"You know what's the worst part? I thought I was looking too cute this morning when I left the house! I was switching my ass off like I was walking down the

5

runway in a spring fashion show. Then I realized I was about to miss the train and all hell broke loose!"

Explaining the situation was like lighting a fire under her ass 'cause she started laughing, saying, "Not to mention raggedy slip breaking loose!" I was beginning to get tired of being the butt of a bad situation. I glanced at my watch.

"Look, I really need to hurry 'cause I don't like to be late. You want to meet after work for drinks?" I asked, speeding up my pace.

"Sure, where do you want to meet?" she asked.

"Hell, we could meet at Five Points. What time do you get off?" I was almost running at this point.

She yelled back, "I get off at five o'clock."

"Me, too," I yelled back over my shoulders.

If I had thought that our meeting at Five Points would have changed the course of both of our lives, I don't believe that I would have bothered to show up.

chapter 3

As promised, Sammie was waiting for me when I arrived at Five Points. I was looking forward to unwinding over cocktails. Work had been a bitch that day. Thank God it was finally Friday.

Sammie waved at me as I approached. I grunted and said, "Come on, I need a good stiff drink." Sammie turned and followed me as I stormed past her. I decided to try Fat Tuesday's 'cause they usually had an awesome happy hour. I wanted to get drunk and see some cuties at the same time.

"Who the hell peed in your coffee?" she asked, attempting to match my pace.

"Girl, it was a day from hell. My mind just was not in it and I could not wait to get the hell up out of there."

"Well excuse me, Ms. Morgan," she huffed.

I stopped in my tracks and whirled around to face her. "Damn, I don't even know your name and I'm going off on you."

"I understand, girl; don't sweat it. Let's go get our drink on! My name, by the way, is Sammie, no 'y,' with an 'i.e.,' Sammie Davis and before you start with the jokes, let me just say that I am not ready to talk about that with you. Just call me Sammie and we will be okay." She took the lead down the escalator as if she knew where we were going.

Shit, she shut my ass up. I was ready to ask a million questions when I heard her name. Not wanting to risk a physical altercation, I quietly followed her. Working our way through the nine-to-fivers we entered Fat Tuesday's and scooped up the first two seats we saw at the bar. We both ordered strawberry daiquiris.

Looking around, Sammie said, "This place is really nice. This is my first time here," she continued. As I scanned the crowd, I noticed that there were not any black men in the growing crowd yet. Sammie must have read my mind and asked, "Don't the brothers come here, too?"

"Yeah, but they don't show up until after six." I took a sip of my drink and glanced over at Sammie.

"Where are you from?" I asked.

"From all over really. My brother was born in North Carolina, my older sister was born in California, and I was born in Germany. I was a typical army brat living in a lot of houses but never having a real home to claim. Living wherever Uncle Sam sent us."

"So what brought you to Georgia?"

"We moved to Atlanta after my dad retired from the military. This is my mother's hometown. But I moved to California with my husband when I was eighteen."

"You're married?" I asked, shocked that she had married at such an early age.

"Yeah, something like that," she answered, not bothering to elaborate any further on the details of her life to someone she barely knew.

"What about children? Do you have any?" I inquired.

"I have a boy and a girl but they have always lived with my mother here in Atlanta. I just got back from California about two months ago."

"How long were you in California?"

"Ten years."

"You left your children in Atlanta for ten years!" I exclaimed with a hint of judgment in my tone, not able to comprehend how a mother could be separated from her children, and by choice.

"Look, I was young, dumb and in love. It's a long story and this is not the time or the place for it, okay?"

I threw my hands up. "Hey, no problem. Been there and done that." I continued sipping on my drink and asked her if she wanted another round.

"Sure," Sammie replied. "I know that you have kids or you wouldn't have had on that maternity slip. How many kids do you have?" Sammie asked.

"I have two: Kevin who is four and Keira who just turned six last week."

"What about a man?"

"Legally separated," I exclaimed proudly.

"Legal or not, separated is separated in my book," Sammie responded. "Were you born in Atlanta?"

"No, I'm originally from Baltimore."

"So what brought you to Atlanta?"

"My dad passed away and I moved here to be closer to my mother."

"I'm sorry to hear that. When did he die?"

"It's been a few weeks but it still hurts. My father and I were very close."

"My dad died also several months ago," Sammie acknowledged plainly.

The bar started to get a little louder and the crowd began to swell.

"I need to make a potty run," Sammie announced, sliding off the barstool. "Where is the bathroom?"

"In the back to the right," I said, pointing in that direction. I watched Sammie move through the crowd and had no trouble following her progress since she was a bit taller than most of the patrons.

Sammie took her time coming back from the bathroom and I was already on my third drink.

"Damn, girl, you ain't wasting no time, are you?" she said as she eyed the fresh drink that was sitting before me alongside the two empty glasses.

"If you had a day like I had, you would be drinking like a fish, too," I answered back defensively.

"What do you do?" she asked.

"I'm a paralegal with White, Miller & Stevens."

"Go on with your bad self," Sammie replied, finishing up her second drink and signaling to the bartender that she was ready for another. I chose that moment to go to the bathroom myself. When I got back to my seat, Sammie was deep in conversation with a guy whose head only came to her chest. She quickly finished her conversation as I inched onto the stool. As I did, I noticed her put something down her bra. She did not say anything about her new friend and he promptly left as if dismissed on cue.

"Now, where were we?" I asked.

"You were telling me about your job," she said.

"Oh, right. What about you, what do you do?" I inquired.

"I am a jack of all trades. Right now I'm temping at Equifax. I really don't like those boring ass desk jobs but I needed something. We are staying with my mother right now and it ain't working out too good."

"I know exactly what you mean. When I first got here I stayed with my mother. Mom and I were cool but I was used to having my own space."

"I know that's right!" Sammie responded.

I stole a glance at my watch and realized that it was getting late. "Girl, I am really going to have to cut this night short. My mother is watching my kids and I am sure she is ready for them to go home. I need to stay in her good graces especially since she keeps the kids for me while I work."

We paid our check and were headed to the door when another guy grabbed her around the waist.

"Take care, Sammie. I will talk to you soon," he said. Sammie just smiled at him. For someone that was "married" and new in town, I noticed that Sammie sure attracted a lot of male attention. But this was just the beginning.

chapter 4

Sammie married the first man that asked. At the tender age of eighteen, he took her from her parents' house and moved her halfway across the country to California. His name was Jessie Alexander and he was six years her senior. Jessie took Sammie to California because he wanted to mold her into a super-model. She stood at 6'2" and her beauty was unequaled. She looked like an Egyptian Queen and her movements were as sleek as a jaguar's. Jessie loved showing her off. His aspirations for her were motivated by his greed for money. Jessie was a hair designer by trade so Sammie was like a giant black Barbie doll to him. He did her hair, her makeup and even chose her clothes. He also scheduled numerous appointments with various modeling agencies trying to break into the fashion industry.

Despite his best efforts, Sammie never received those high-paying jobs mostly because her heart wasn't into modeling. She just went through the motions to keep Jessie happy.

Jessie was a pretty boy. He had light green eyes and clear caramel-colored skin. His eyes were slightly slanted and he had very long eyelashes to which he secretly applied mascara. His hair was longer than that of most women, and he wore it either in a bob or a ponytail. He was conceited, arrogant and egotistical. He was unaffected by the looks he received from his daring hairstyles. Most people thought that he was gay because he was a hairdresser and because of the way that he carried himself. He stood about 6'2" and was rail thin, weighing perhaps 155 pounds soaking wet.

Jessie was frustrated that Sammie was not making the money that he believed she could make. He had invested a small fortune building up her portfolio on one hand and exploiting her on the other.

During the day Jessie promoted her beauty and at night he exploited her body. On her twenty-first birthday, Jessie found a small strip club in a remote section of town that catered to an unsavory clientele.

"Jessie, why are we celebrating my birthday here?" Sammie inquired, not quite comfortable with all the women in various stages of undress.

"Uh, I just thought it would be different, that's all," he mumbled in response.

Sammie tried her best not to look at the women but everywhere she looked all she saw were tits and ass. A waitress came within shouting distance and Sammie stopped her.

"May I have a gin and tonic, please?" Sammie ordered, while looking at Jessie for approval. Not that she really needed his approval to have a drink; she just needed to know if they could afford it. Jessie nodded his consent.

"Look at her," he said, pointing to a lightskinned woman on the stage. She had bent over at the waist and was sucking her own pussy. She alternated between fondling her breast and sucking herself, which was driving the men wild.

Sammie glanced in her direction and quickly averted her eyes.

"What about her?" she inquired, studying the tablecloth as if seeking answers to life's most difficult questions.

"She can't hold a candle to you, baby," he said. Sammie fully looked up at him for the first time since entering the bar. He called her "baby" and it had been some time since he had done that. She looked to the stage to see if she could see what Jessie had seen.

"Look, she can't even move like you. She looks all stiff and unnatural!" he said. The waitress placed Sammie's drink on the table and she quickly drained the glass. She signaled for another refill. Jessie did not even notice that the waitress had been there since his eyes were glued to the stage and it had his full attention.

Jessie held up a bill and the woman on the stage came over to the table. She did a special little dance in front of Jessie and Sammie turned red. She could not stand to watch the woman but it was even worse watching Jessie as he slobbered all over himself. He tucked the bill in the front of her g-string and the woman went back to center stage. He turned his attention back to Sammie with a *what do you think* look in his eyes, obviously expecting a response from her without asking.

"She's all right," Sammie said, not knowing what else to say to describe the other woman.

"She could learn a lot from you," Jessie said.

"Is that a compliment?" Sammie asked, not sure how to take his remark.

"Yeah, if you don't know nothing else, you sure know how to shake that ass," Jessie said, eyeing her midsection.

She no longer felt like she was being complimented. Jessie continued to ignore her for the rest of the night.

Over the next few months, Jessie continued to take Sammie to the strip clubs at least three nights a week. He never told her their destination until they pulled up in front of the dimly lit bars. Sammie eventually learned to tolerate it. However, she still felt uncomfortable openly staring at the women. She tried to imagine them with clothes in a fashion show but could not get past the tits and ass on display.

One night they arrived at Paradise. The club was real crowded when they got there but a table had been reserved for them in the front row, close enough to the stage for Jessie to get his hands on any of the dancers if he wanted to and did. Sammie saw the same dancer that she had seen the first night Jessie had brought her to the club. She was talking with the manager. They were both looking in her direction and she began to sense an uncomfortable feeling in the pit of her stomach again. Sammie knew the woman's first name was Kim but that was the extent of her knowledge.

She looked over at Jessie and he had a shit-eating grin plastered on his face that usually meant he was up to no good.

"I want you to do this for me," he said. His voice was gentle but it had an underlying tone that said, *if you don't, bitch, there will be hell to pay.*

"Do what?" Sammie asked, leaning closer so she did not misunderstand or misinterpret what he was saying. She also wanted to get out of the eyesight of Kim and the manager. The hair at the back of her neck began to stand up as she noticed the maniacal look in Jessie's eyes.

"You know damn well what," he snapped. "Don't pretend like you don't know why I have been bringing your ass here. You're not that stupid," he jeered.

His evil side surfaced and Sammie swallowed a knot of fear that formed in her throat and threatened to close off her airway. She knew what he wanted but she was unwilling to give it to him.

"Please, Jessie, not that," she pleaded.

"Shut up! You're sniveling," he shouted back. "We need the money, plain and simple."

"But we can make it some other way. I'll get a full-time job," she declared.

"Doing what? Your dumb ass didn't finish high school! You ain't making shit with those modeling gigs I managed to get you either," he announced.

"Jessie, I have never done this type of stuff before. I can't," she said as tears welled up in the corners of her eyes. Just then Sammie noticed Kim making her way to their table.

"Bitch, you better not embarrass me in front of Kim. You're going to dance and you better make it good," he growled at Sammie, slamming his hand against the table to emphasize his point. The force of the blow caused Sammie to jump.

"Are you ready for the spotlight?" Kim asked, grabbing Sammie's hands and propelling her out of her seat. She winked at Jessie as he patted her on her partially clad behind.

"What the fuck?" Sammie interjected, looking to Jessie for understanding of what was expected of her. What she was getting loud and clear was that Kim and Jessie had developed some kind of relationship.

"I, uh," Sammie stuttered still confused.

"Don't be shy, girl," Kim said. "We all acted like this the first time. Jessie tells me you're a natural and born for the stage! For tonight, you can borrow some of my things but after that, you will be expected to bring your own." She turned and pushed Sammie towards the door. One final look at Jessie's stern face told Sammie that she had no choice in this matter. He did not smile as she walked away. His face was frozen like a block of ice, wearing a menacing sneer that was meant solely for her.

Kim led Sammie into the back dressing room. She cried inwardly. She knew she had little to no choice in this matter if she didn't want to receive an ass whipping from Jessie when she got home. It was evident that he had arranged this before they arrived at the club.

"Don't worry, honey," Kim said, trying to console her. "The first time is always the worst. Just pretend that you are home alone with Jessie and no one else is in the room. He told me how hot you make him when you dance for him," Kim went on.

"Jessie told you that?" Sammie asked in a state of shock. First of all, she had not danced for him since they first moved to California and second, now days he acted bored. She wanted to ask her just how well she knew Jessie but thought better of it.

"You have a great manager," she said with a broad grin. "I wish I had someone like him to look after me."

"Manager?" Sammie choked. "Is that what he told you he was to me?" Sammie asked, unable to contain the fire she felt upon hearing her own husband refer to himself as only her manager.

"Yeah, sugar. Count yourself lucky," she said with the utmost sincerity. "Some of us are not blessed with good management."

If she only knew, Sammie thought to herself. She wanted to correct Kim on the true nature of their relationship but she was not ready for the big beat-down that would ultimately follow if she did.

chapter 5

To the best of Sammie's knowledge, Jessie did not make it home last night. When her set was up, she quietly left the club and took a cab home. This was happening more and more on a regular basis, but Sammie refused to think about it and instead relished her temporary freedom. This was her only down time.

Over the past few years, Sammie had fought against dancing in those sleazy clubs. She had pleaded with Jessie to allow her to attend open auditions for modeling jobs but she no longer had the body for it. Dejected, Sammie became accustomed to the smoky dimly lit room.

Alone, at last, she leisurely stretched and belted out a hearty yawn. Scratching first her crotch, then her armpits, Sammie climbed out of the bed. She did not know how long her reprieve would be but she knew she was going to make the most of it.

After checking the driveway to make sure his car was gone, Sammie ran into the kitchen and pulled out the box of chocolate chip cookies she had hidden in the crock-pot. She glanced at the clock and realized that it was almost noon. It was unusual for Jessie to let her sleep this late on a weekday but she quickly dismissed her worries.

Gratefully, she bit down into the cookie and breathed in its sinful smell. With each bite, some of the tension that had been building in her neck and shoulders eased. Suddenly, she remembered the potato chips she'd hidden in the bathroom cabinet behind stacks of toilet paper. She quickly ran to the bathroom and retrieved her stash. She put the snacks on the table and grabbed a two-liter bottle of Dr. Pepper from under the sofa.

She could not eat these types of foods when Jessie was around so she decided to have a bonafide feast in his absence. From the linen closet, she retrieved some chocolate cupcakes and a bag of Doritos. She tore off the top of the Doritos and crammed a few in her mouth on her way back to the kitchen.

With her bounty laid out before her, she sat down to enjoy her feast. She briefly looked down at the frayed nightgown she wore and paused long enough to wipe her hands before tearing into the bags before her.

"I wonder who he's with this time?" she said out loud, but those thoughts did not slow down her fevered consumption. She alternately shoveled sugar and salt down her throat with pauses in between gulping her soda. She remembered the onion dip in the refrigerator and knocked over her chair in her haste to get it.

"Uh!" she said after letting out a loud satisfying belch. Crumbs spewed out her mouth and landed on the front of her nightgown but she didn't even notice. She also had a smudge of dip under her chin. She was so preoccupied with her meal, she did not hear Jessie's car when he pulled into the driveway. She also did not see the dark shadow that paused at the kitchen window momentarily blocking out the sun.

"What the fuck!" Jessie exclaimed when he saw Sammie hunched over the kitchen table and more importantly with all the junk food scattered all over the table. After watching her for a few minutes from the window, he approached the front door. He masked the anger he felt and noisily opened the door.

Sammie's head snapped up when she heard his keys jingling. She quickly threw all the evidence of her binge in the trash. She ran to the refrigerator and grabbed a carrot, which was an acceptable snack, according to Jessie. She bit into the carrot hoping it would hide the smell of chocolate on her breath. She did not expect Jessie to kiss her but you never knew with him.

"Hi," Sammie said brightly despite the brick of fear lodged in her chest.

"Um," he grunted in response. "What are you doing?" he asked angrily.

"Just having a snack," she replied, holding up the half-eaten carrot as evidence.

"I can see that; I ain't blind," he flipped back. "Is that all that you have eaten today?" he asked, going through the mail that was left on the table from the day before.

"Yeah, I'm still trying to watch my weight," she said, allowing her breathing to relax thinking she was in the clear.

"Where did you get that from?" he inquired, pointing to the carrot that she was holding.

"The refrigerator," she said, not understanding his line of questions nor where they were going.

"We had carrots just like that in the refrigerator?" he asked. "Are those the same ones I bought last week?"

"I am not sure when you bought them but I got them from the fridge. I sure didn't buy them 'cause I rarely have money for anything other than cigarettes." She really wanted Jessie to leave the room so she could take out the trash and destroy any evidence left of her binge. She was mad that she had to throw out her remaining goodies but wanted the opportunity to take them back out if they hadn't spilled onto the other garbage in the can.

"Those look like real special carrots to me," Jessie said, walking closer to Sammie. "And that's all you have had today?" he asked again. She turned the carrot over in her hand examining it. She didn't understand why he was making such a big deal of the carrot anyway but she continued to play along. She took another bite of the carrot before she responded.

"Yep, this is it," she said, wiping her sweaty palms down the sides of her tattered nightgown.

Jessie was fuming. Not only had he caught her eating forbidden items, but *she had the audacity to lie to his motherfucking face*, he thought. He was a mere two inches from her when he punched the shit out of her.

"My carrots don't leave crumbs, you dumb bitch!" His punch knocked Sammie clean off the chair and left her breathless. His fist hit her squarely in her face, busting her lip in two places and causing her nose to bleed profusely. Dazed, she did not know what he was talking about. She shook her head, trying to clear it, sending small drops of blood onto an already dirty white linoleum floor.

He stood over her, shaking with rage.

"Not only that, you would sit there and lie to my motherfucking face!" He drew back his leg and kicked her in the ribs. "I have been busting my ass for the last few years trying to make something of your sorry ass and all you do is lie to me!"

He bent down to get up close to her face. He had been drinking and she

19

chapter 6

Jessie impatiently waited for Sammie to emerge from the shower. The dope had him chilling but he was still pissed with Sammie for her defiance and he needed to teach her a lesson that she would not quickly forget.

"Hurry up," he barked through the closed door. His nose began to run. He was battling the sniffles and the constant nasal drip. *This was some good dope*, he thought. All he really wanted to do now was take a nap, but he knew that if he did not deal with Sammie right now, he would lose all control that he felt he finally had over her.

"It don't take that long to wash that fat ass of yours!" he yelled, opening the door and letting in a cool draft that enveloped Sammie's wet body. Sammie had been getting bold with her defiance and Jessie had had about as much as he could stand.

He slammed the door shut and stomped back into the bedroom. Moments later, Sammie emerged with her head hung down low. She was still dripping water and that enraged Jessie even more. Briefly he felt a familiar tingle in his loins that he used to feel when he saw her nude body but he quickly suppressed it. He could not get past her improper behavior and deception.

"Do you have any idea how much money I have invested in you?" Sammie did not know if he really expected an answer so she kept quiet. This only enraged Jessie further. He beat his hands on the dresser not wanting to hit her again since she would have to be leaving soon for the club.

Financially, they were on shaky ground. The money that Sammie made from her modeling gigs was long gone. Even the residuals were spent before he received them. He was supporting them solely on the money she made at the booty clubs and his day job doing hair. Unfortunately, his clientele at the shop was dropping because of his drug abuse so he needed her to be in top physical form for him to survive. The owner of Magic Weave told him that if he didn't come up with $700 for his booth rent that he could pack up his scissors. "Fuck him," he uttered out loud.

Facing her for the first time since she came out the bathroom, he saw the evidence of his anger. He momentarily felt a tinge of guilt but it quickly evaporated when he thought of all the things that were on the line if she failed. He needed money and he needed it now and Sammie was his only means to get it.

"No matter what I do for you, you continue to try to fuck it up!" he exclaimed. Jessie had worked his self up to a pretty good mad now and Sammie was afraid to even look at him let alone defend herself.

"We have been out here in this fucking hothouse for four years and don't have shit to show for it!"

Sammie went to the closet to pick out her outfit for that night. She thumbed through the thick closet looking for something that she could still fit into. All of her show clothes were too tight on her now pleasantly plump body. After several minutes of going from one end of the closet to the other, Jessie stomped over and pushed Sammie out the way. She stumbled but did not completely lose her footing.

"Here, wear this," he said, shoving a bright red dress into her chest while moving past her to select her shoes. This dress used to be her favorite but that was before she gained all that weight. It was a short spandex outfit that once accentuated her shapely hips and thighs but now did nothing but mock her former figure.

"Put it on," he spat when he noticed her hesitation. She wanted to protest but thought better of it since he was in such a sour mood.

Sammie struggled to get the dress over her head. It briefly locked up around her shoulders and she had to force it over her hips. It stuck to her like glue and folded around her growing stomach and ass. Jessie grunted in disgust as he watched her.

"That is what all those cookies and cakes have done to your body!" he snapped at her as if she didn't already know.

"I know. I will do better; you will see," she said although she had promised those words before in vain.

"Can I change into that black dress you bought last week?" she asked pleadingly.

It was a size bigger and was not quite as revealing as the one she was currently wearing.

"We don't have time for you to change now! Just hurry up," he exclaimed. Fearing another physical assault, Sammie swallowed her pride and went into the bathroom to put on her makeup. Ever watchful, Jessie followed her and grabbed her compact from her shaking hands.

"Sammie, I have had enough—you hear me? Sit down and let me finish this." His voice was loud but it was not the same angry, irate voice that she had heard earlier. She was hopeful that he had somehow regained his senses.

He artfully applied her eye shadow, mascara, and blush. He even penciled in a tiny mole on the right side of her face, which made her look more sexy and exotic. He then turned his attention to her hair and quickly swept her micro-braids into an uncomplicated French roll with tiny braids of hair hanging down framing her face.

Even though Sammie was still angry with Jessie she had to give it to him when it came down to makeup and hair. He was truly blessed and had the talent to make even the ugliest women look like beauty queens. Since she was already beautiful in her own right, he did nothing but enhance her outer beauty. Oddly, when he was working on her face or hair, she truly believed that he loved her.

They arrived at the same seedy club that they had been going to for over two years. Realizing that this was their destination for the night, Sammie sucked in her stomach and strolled into the club as if she owned it. This was a walk that Jessie had pounded into her head and it allowed her to alter her personality to be able to perform.

Instead of promoting and exploiting Sammie's body, Jessie should have concentrated on her acting abilities. Only an actress could have pulled off the charade that Sammie's life had become.

Jessie took a seat in the far right corner of the room. Sammie looked in his direction as he wandered off but knew that she was expected to take a seat up front and center of the stage. She was no longer ashamed to be in the front row with women prancing in her face. Her dance routine was to pretend that she was an audience member who got caught up in the moment and climbed onto the stage and stripped.

Jessie would pretend that he was a customer so enamored of her routine that he kept throwing money at her. He would hype up the audience of lustful men so that they, too, would dig deep into their pockets and throw money at the stage.

Her face still hurt as well as her ribs where Jessie had kicked her earlier. She tried not to think about those injuries as she waited for her introduction. Sammie scanned the crowd. She noticed Jessie was now talking with Kim in a corner booth and that her hands were all over him. He appeared to be oblivious to her even being in the room.

"Scotch on the rocks," she requested of a passing waitress. "Make it two doubles," she added. The waitress, Amber, arched her eyebrows and turned to look at Jessie and Kim. She patted Sammie's hand and headed straight to the bar. Tears pricked the back of Sammie's eyes, but she refused to turn and look back into that corner. Instead, she fought back the tears and stared straight ahead at the dancing women.

Sammie drank both drinks in quick succession. She tugged at the hemline of her dress and prayed that she would be able to get it off without getting stuck when it was her turn to dance.

From her seat, Sammie began taking her dress off from her shoulders, leaving her breasts uncovered. Normally she would have waited until she was actually on stage to undress but getting out of that dress was hard enough without trying to be sexy with it. She was lightheaded but she assumed it was 'cause of the drinks. Small beads of perspiration broke out on her forehead.

On cue, Sammie jumped up from the audience and yelled, "Hey, party over here!" while waving her arms above her head. Her large breasts were swinging back and forth as she swirled her hips to the beat of "Friday Night" by Earth, Wind and Fire. She bent over and continued to seductively slide the dress over her hips. Remarkably, it came down a lot easier than it had gone on. The men went wild. She stepped out of her dress and began making her way to the stage. The DJ slowed down the beat as Sammie approached the lip of the stage. Jessie and Kim came over to the table she'd just left and sat down.

Sammie kept her eyes focused on the other members of the audience until Jessie called her over. She stopped directly in front of him and squatted down with her legs wide open giving both Kim and Jessie a frontal view. She grabbed one of her boobs and put it in her mouth, gently sucking on it. She used her other hand to play with her clit.

Sammie was no longer lightheaded; she was down-right woozy. She did not realize that Kim had moved from her front-row seat to the lip of the stage stopping directly between Sammie's legs until she felt Kim's hands moving up her thighs. Kim was wearing a black g-string that contrasted with her bright yellow skin. She had removed her bra as well and the tips of her small breasts were erect. Kim's hands worked their way up Sammie's thighs until she reached Sammie's breasts. Kim grabbed them firmly and looked intensely in Sammie's eyes. Kim stood directly in front of Jessie, leaning on the stage with her ass jutted in Jessie's salivating face as he fingered Kim's round ass.

Sammie sought to see Jessie's face but could only see the top of his head as he bent to examine Kim's crack. He gave new meaning to the term, *head up her ass*, Sammie thought. She was confused about this turn of events and her limbs felt lethargic and heavy. Kim put Sammie's breast in her mouth while continuing to rub her hands on her thighs and in between her legs. Sammie struggled but did not have the energy to protest much.

Jessie peeked around Kim's ass and smiled at Sammie. This was the first real smile that she had received from him in months.

The predominantly male audience exploded to their feet trying to get closer to the stage. Kim pinched Sammie's already erect nipple sharply as she bent down and put her tongue onto Sammie's already enlarged clit.

"Mmm," Sammie moaned as she fought the emotions that shifted back and forth between pleasure and pain, passion and acute embarrassment. Kim released the pressure on Sammie's breast and nuzzled her face in Sammie's cunt. Instinctively, Sammie locked her knees around Kim's face. Money was raining down all over them but Sammie was oblivious. She forgot the audience, Jessie and even the fact that it was a woman who was making her feel so good. She gave herself up to the moment, offering her hips to get closer to the source of her pleasure.

Jessie was finger-fucking Kim and grabbing up the money being thrown at the same time. Although he had intended to use this night to teach Sammie a lesson, he found that he was enjoying the action as well.

Sammie screamed in climax as the song ended. Kim raised her head, and smiled. She blew a kiss at Sammie.

"Um," Kim said as she seductively licked her wet lips. She wiped her chin and licked her hands while devouring Sammie with a look of pure satisfaction on her face. Sammie, suddenly realizing the enormity of what had just occurred, suppressed the urge to gag. She stood up and dislodged the money that was stuck to her sweaty body and quickly ran from the stage.

"Oh God, what the hell have I done?" she uttered through her tears. When she reached the shabby dressing room, she threw on the robe that she kept in there and nauseously waited for Jessie to come. Sammie was deeply ashamed, and could not control the tremors that shook her body.

The owner of the club, Owen, stomped over to the table where Kim and Jessie were sitting. Jessie was pleased with the money he had made and was eagerly counting out Kim's share. Since Kim was bisexual, she only wanted $50 to perform oral sex on Sammie. She enjoyed it and would have done it for free but Jessie insisted that she take a share. He intended to put Kim in his stable and the $50 was an incentive of more to come.

"What the fuck did you two think you were doing?" Owen demanded. He was torn between greed, lust, desire and disgust. He had run this club for over twenty years and he had never had anyone openly have sex on his stage before—much less, two women.

"Chill out," Jessie said as he threw him his share of the take from the set.

Realizing how much his share actually was, Owen's anger quickly subsided. Carefully examining the hundred-dollar bill he held in his hand, he carefully turned it over in his hands to make sure it was real. He shoved the money into his pocket and continued to rave.

"You can't just have sex on stage, no matter what it pays. What if the law had been in here? They would have shut me down, man!" He huffed.

"But they didn't. I had my boys watching the doors. It's cool. Breathe, man, it's over!" Jessie said.

Owen shook his head not knowing whether to continue to protest or stay quiet.

"We need to discuss a business proposition," Jessie said.

"What would that be?" Owen asked as his curiosity piqued.

Owen took a seat and together he and Jessie decided to continue the show but on a more private scale. Owen agreed that he would present the freak fest to the high rollers that frequented the club. They'd have to pay $500 for a private set to see Kim and Sammie together. If they wanted to participate, naturally it would be extra. Everyone was happy with the business arrangement except Sammie. In fact, Sammie was the only person that was not consulted about the deal.

chapter 7

Jessie had unleashed a freak in Sammie that eventually destroyed whatever self-esteem she had left, and it only had taken him eighteen months to do it. After Sammie's debut in the lesbian love scene with Kim, she went home alone.

Jessie never showed up at her dressing room to bring her some clothes so she caught a cab home in the robe. She exited by the rear entrance so she would not have to face any of the patrons in the bar, and especially her so-called "manager."

"Alone at last," Sammie groaned out loud. Flopping onto the bed, she pounded her fists into the pillows in a fit of tears.

"What the hell is wrong with me?" she lamented. "I am not a lesbian, but I got off on Kim like she was strapping a big dick." She punched the pillows trying to understand what had been unleashed in her.

Amber, the bar maid, admitted to her that she had spiked her drink and tried to apologize for it as Sammie exited the club. Spiked drink or not, that still did not explain Sammie's reactions to Kim.

For the first time since leaving Atlanta, Sammie desperately wanted to go home. Living with Althea was bad but this took the case! She cried herself to sleep and did not hear Jessie when he entered the apartment sometime in the wee hours of the morning.

Jessie was buzzing from a fat blast of heroine and was turned on by the sight of Sammie's ass peeking out from under the robe she still wore. It had been a long time since he had had an erection from looking at Sammie, but that night he felt like he could fuck for hours until he pulled out his penis. He was horny as hell but his dick deflated. Briefly he considered his drug use as the problem but quickly shrugged that off and instead blamed his lack of libido on Sammie. Turning on his heels, Jessie left the room.

"Come out here, you freak bitch," he yelled to Sammie. Jessie was in the living room so Sammie did not hear him when he first yelled to her. When she did not respond to his call, he staggered into the bedroom and roughly began shaking her awake.

"I said get your freak ass out the bed!" he repeated, deliberately spitting on her in the process. Sammie's eyes snapped open as she tried to focus in the early-morning light that filtered through the torn mini blinds. Her head was still groggy from the drugs and alcohol she had consumed the night before. She was so disoriented that she did not have a chance to feel afraid.

"What?" she expelled in a rush of hot stale breath. Jessie slapped her in the face, thereby eliminating all remnants of sleep left in her brain. Her eyes refocused and she looked into Jessie's beady eyes.

"Get your fat, black, freaky ass out the bed. I wanna talk to ya," he demanded. He turned and walked out of the room again knowing full well she would follow him.

Sammie crawled out of bed, favoring her right side where he had kicked her the previous day. She shuffled down the hall, bumping into the wall occasionally but Jessie did not notice. His pants were unzipped when she arrived in the room.

"Suck on this, bitch," he said, pointing to his near flaccid dick. Sammie shuddered in revulsion. She had no idea where his dick had been over the past few months since he never touched her anymore. Hell, she wondered where it had been in the past few hours.

"I need to wash my face and brush my teeth," she said, trying to avoid looking at his limp dick.

"You don't need winter-fresh breath to suck on big daddy," he snarled, pulling it up to make it appear longer than it was. She stalled to think of another excuse as to why she couldn't put it in her mouth.

Realizing that she was stalling, he barked out his command, "On your knees, bitch," raising his right hand in a tight fist. Sammie dropped to her knees, landing on a pin. The pain from it caused her to jump right up. Jessie took her actions to be another act of defiance and slapped her in the back of her head. He grabbed her by the hair and forced her head into his crotch.

She clearly smelled the scent of another woman and she nearly threw up the remaining contents of her stomach. He held on tightly to her hair as he ground his dick into her mouth. Slowly his dick grew in measure and with it his cries of pleasure. Salty tears flowed in her mouth as she choked on his stank dick.

"Climb up on daddy," he demanded as he guided her by the roots onto his dick. Luckily for her, he exploded before she could lower herself completely onto him. The entire episode lasted two minutes but to Sammie, it seemed like two hours. He pushed her away in disgust and she went into the bathroom to sanitize her mouth and cried for what seemed like an eternity.

Jessie nodded off without bothering to re-zip his pants. His dreams were filled of erotic images of Sammie performing sex on other people while he watched. When he woke several hours later, he had jacked off again in his sleep as was evidenced by the dried semen on his hands.

This began a completely different dimension in Sammie's life as far as Jessie was concerned; he fully realized that he enjoyed watching Sammie have sex with other people and he spent a lot of time finding different mates for her. *Man or woman, it really doesn't matter,* Jessie thought.

For the next several weeks, Sammie made a lot of money but Jessie spent more. She became the freak of the week and actually started to enjoy performing on some primitive level. This was the only physical contact that she received and she learned to relish it. On occasion, Jessie would join in, while playing with his dick but mostly he just watched and collected the monies.

Afterwards, when they were alone, he would start an argument with her just to get out of the house which suited Sammie just fine. He would call her a whore and other degrading names. At the time, Sammie did not know he was using that as a ploy so he could leave to go and get high, but that information would come out soon enough.

Sammie would sit there with tears streaming down her face as she listened to him rant and rave, rarely bothering to defend herself.

"Look at you. You miserable fat fuck! Wipe your damn nose. I don't want to have to look at that nasty shit," Jessie would yell.

Sammie used the hem of her shirt to wipe her face. She did not want to make Jessie mad by leaving the room. She just never knew what particular action would cause him to strike out at her.

"Goddamn, you're so disgusting! Get off your fat ass and go wash your face," he demanded while pulling back his leg as if he might kick her.

Quickly, she stumbled down the corridor, blinded by a fresh wave of tears. Deep down she believed the things Jessie said about her to be true. When she reached the bathroom, she ran water in the sink trying to control the racking of her shoulders as she gave in to her emotions. She used the balled-up washcloth to smother the sound of her crying. Jessie didn't much care that she cried; in fact, he liked it. He just didn't want to have to hear it. He knew that as long as she cried, she was afraid and he wanted to keep her that way.

After a few moments, she walked back into the room, sat on the edge of the bed and watched while he got dressed. He was such a particular dresser who fussed about every wrinkle and crease. When he bothered to take her out, he took more time to get dressed than she did. He would never allow her to iron his clothes preferring to have them drycleaned and laundered, regardless of the cost.

"Why in the hell are you staring at me like that?" he snarled. The very sound of his voice snapped her out of her reflections and back into the present. She turned her gaze to look at him through the mirror on the dresser. She wanted to keep an eye on him in case he planned on sneaking in a punch.

"Nothing," she said, uttering the first thing that came to her mind. Unfortunately, it was the wrong thing to say. Jessie quickly crossed the room and kicked her in the knee. Sammie was too stunned and afraid to cry out.

"So, Bitch, I'm nothing now? I wasn't nothing when I took your ass in, you pathetic piece of shit! You aren't even a mother to your own fucking children!" he snapped back at her.

Sammie's head rocked back as she raised her eyes from the floor to look him in the face. This was the first time he had acknowledged that he knew that she had children. All this time, she thought she had succeeded in deceiving him. She had not wanted to lie about being a mother, but her own mother convinced her that if she told Jessie the truth about her having kids, he would not want her. The intense shame she felt started another wave of emotions inside of her. This time she was not crying from her physical pain. Now she was crying for her motherless children.

"Bitch, don't look so surprised! I'll bet your dumb ass thought I was stupid enough to believe those kids belong to your ignorant ass mother!" He spat those words directly in Sammie's face, spraying her with spittle as he emphasized each word by poking his finger in her face. Fresh mucus ran from her nose and landed on Jessie's fingers. He promptly punched her in the eye, causing her to fall off the bed and land on the floor.

Jessie thought this was funny and burst into laughter. His reaction seemed to have ended a tense situation for Sammie. Normally, when she landed on the floor, Jessie would either stick his dick in her mouth or kick her. She was not in the mood to bear either that night. Now, instead of wanting him to stay with her, she could not wait for him to leave.

He paused at the door and threw his final dagger for the night. "And, if I didn't know those crumb snatchers were yours, your mother made sure that I knew before I married your sorry ass! She didn't want you to come back to her when I kicked your fat ass out! She said you fucked up your life and she would be damned if she let you fuck up theirs, too." He shut the door before Sammie could react to his remarks. Not that she would have done anything. It was Jessie's way of saying, "Take that, bitch" and Sammie understood that all too well.

Sammie crawled over to the bed and pulled herself up. She was sobbing so hard she could barely lift herself up. She tried to think back to the times when she was happy with Jessie, but those memories refused to surface. She finally realized that he was only nice to her before they got married. She also acknowledged that after she said, "I do," he started treating her like shit.

"Lord, it's me again. Please don't place me on ignore. I am drowning here and am in need of some help. God, I know I have made some mistakes but I don't think I deserve all this!" she said, pounding on the mattress and adding more streaks of blood to the tousled bed. "Please God, help me! Tell me what to do 'cause I'm lost."

She collapsed on the bed in a fit of tears, further soaking the ruined sheets. God did not answer her that night. She'd never felt so completely alone in her life.

It was the ultimate betrayal. She now knew beyond a shadow of a doubt that her mother truly despised her. Why else would she have told Jessie the truth about a lie she conjured up. The only problem was that she didn't know why. Sammie wanted to go claim her children since she was beyond legal age, but she knew that Jessie would never agree to that. Feeling hopeless, she drifted off to sleep.

Sammie awoke to the ringing of the phone. She groped for it without opening her eyes. Since she did not hear Jessie come back home, she assumed he was still out and grabbed the phone.

"Hello," she mumbled into the handset and immediately thrust the phone away from her ear. Her mother Althea's scaly voice was screeching on the other end.

She belched. "Sammie needs to come home."

"For what?" Jessie cut in, ignoring the fact that Sammie was also on the line.

Sammie sucked in her breath. *Damn, he's back*, she thought, shaking in fear. She wanted to tell her momma that she needed to come home, too, but was scared of what Jessie would do. She wanted to talk to her daddy who she knew would protect her.

"Her father died. She has to be here for the reading of the will next week," Althea declared.

"When did Daddy die?" Sammie uttered, shocking both Jessie and Althea since they both assumed she had hung up.

Sammie would not dare answer the phone if Jessie was home, and he was pissed that she did so now.

"That old buzzard has been dead about six months. Get your lazy ass down here so we can finalize this shit," Althea exclaimed, speaking directly to Sammie.

However, Sammie had dropped the phone. Her father, the only person that ever loved her, was dead and she hadn't even known it. Hot tears flowed freely down her cheeks. She didn't even know that Althea had their phone number and now, after all this time, she was calling to tell her that her daddy was dead. Sammie cursed both Jessie and Althea under her breath. She even cursed her dad for leaving her. Her heart and head felt like they were about to burst.

Dismayed, Sammie thought, *There is no one left on the face of the earth that cares whether I live or die!*

Sammie knew that Jessie would not let her go home and this really hurt her heart. She needed to say goodbye to the only man that had ever loved her.

Sammie went back to sleep. The pain of Jessie pinching her breast awakened her. "Pack, bitch, we're leaving." She eased up off the bed, allowing him to maneuver her body in the direction he was pulling her nipples. She looked around to see what needed to be done. Since they did not own any of the furniture they only had to pack their clothes.

Sammie did not ask Jessie any questions. She went to the closet and removed their suitcases. This was their third move since arriving in California and she just assumed they were moving again to avoid paying rent. She had completely forgotten the earlier phone conversation she had overheard with her mother.

She didn't realize that they were headed to Atlanta until they hit the highway. "Oh shit," she exclaimed both excited and scared.

chapter 8

I t was August of 1995 when the kids and I moved to Atlanta. I was thirty years old with two small children; Keira was six and Kevin was four. We arrived around lunchtime with little fanfare after the untimely death of my father and the recent separation from my husband of eight years. Although Momma appeared to be happy to see me, our relationship was strained. In my heart, I didn't feel like she fully supported me in my decision to divorce my husband Keith.

I arrived in a U-Haul truck loaded with a bunch of junk I hastily threw together to make the thirteen-hour trip from Baltimore. I immediately placed my belongings into storage and moved in with Momma. I wanted to move closer to her after Dad had suffered a fatal heart attack. It was so sudden and we were both so grief stricken that neither of us wanted to be alone.

"Hey, sugar," Mom said when she answered the door. Loaded down with suitcases and children, I felt like a young kid again instead of a grown woman coming to live with her. In addition to "moving back home" syndrome, I was bringing home two small children.

"Grandma!" Keira and Keith yelled in unison, throwing themselves against her legs. She bent and hugged them both, smothering their faces with kisses. I kissed her on the cheek and squeezed past her to put down my bags. I didn't realize that I would feel like such a failure crawling home to Mom but I could not deny the heavy knot I felt in my chest. Although my life would not be classified as a dismal failure, there was something very demeaning about moving home even if it was with the best intentions.

This was only my third visit to Atlanta since Mom and Dad moved from Baltimore three years earlier. Dad only had two more years to work before he could retire and they wanted to move to Atlanta for the warmer climate. Mom had already retired on a medical disability and Dad died one month before his retirement party. We still had the unsent invitations.

When I made the trip for his funeral, I could still feel and smell his presence in the house. I kept looking for him to be seated at his computer, which was his favorite spot. As I looked around my "temporary home," it was missing Dad's familiar scent of peppermint. Fresh tears welled in my eyes and I tried to conceal them from my mother.

"It's okay, baby," she said as her own tears slid down her full cheeks. "It will take some getting used to but we will be okay," she assured me.

I wanted to bury my face in her chest and demand answers to all of life's questions, which had plagued me since Daddy died. I quickly brushed away my tears, hoping to change the mood.

For the first time since I walked through her door, I really looked at her face. It was pinched and I could tell that she had been crying a lot longer than the few seconds I had just witnessed. I understood why but that didn't make it any easier to swallow. My dad was very special to me and to her. He was the only man that my mother had ever known in the physical sense, and she was having a tough time adjusting to life on her own.

"Momma, you've been crying a lot; it is written all over your face," I said, fighting back my own tears again. She hung her head but did not acknowledge my comment.

"How are we going to be any use to each other when we can't stop crying?" I asked, feeling like my heart would break. I just hated to see my mother cry.

"I don't have any answer for that," she said. That scared me even more because Luetta had an answer for every damn thing whether you liked it or not. And for the ninety-nine-thousandth time, I thought I had made a mistake by moving in with her.

I don't know what delusion I had fed myself to make me think things would be easier for her if I came, but in retrospect, I gave myself too much credit. I was not the balm Momma needed to heal her aching heart. Time and only time would heal her, not me. Shit, how was I going to be a pillar of strength for her when I could not hold my own shit together! Although my heart was pure at the time it was suggested, I could not help but think that together we would feed on each other's grief.

"Mom, was this a good idea?" I finally asked the question, and was afraid of the answer. It wasn't as if I would turn around and move back home if she said no but I had to voice my concern.

"It's all good," she said and smiled as she wiped the tear smudges from her face. "You and I will still have our moments but these two will bring us through," she said, pointing to Keira and Kevin. They squealed with joy and flung themselves at Momma's knees again.

"All good? You trying to get hip on me, Momma?" I asked, smiling. I chuckled and walked into the dining room.

Mom was right. Children do tend to take your mind away from everyday problems, especially when they are as young as Keira and Kevin. It was when they got older that they became another source of emotions. Keira and Kevin really didn't get to know Dad all that well. Sure, they visited at least twice a day but they left Baltimore when they were so young! That's one thing about children; they forget very quickly.

My heart was still heavy about Dad since we had just recently mended our broken fences and I felt cheated that he died so soon afterwards. I don't think he ever forgave me for marrying Keith. He wanted so much more for his only daughter and he knew that our marriage wouldn't last. I could not even comprehend my mother's misery. Dad was the only man that she was ever with.

In a way, my separation from Keith happened at the best possible time. I was able to sever my ties in Baltimore and move to Atlanta to be closer to Mom just in case she needed me. On the flip side, she would be able to help me if and when I succumbed to the deep depression I felt when I acknowledged my failed marriage and the fact that I was now a single mom.

I carried my bags to the guest room that I had occupied just a few short weeks ago for my Dad's funeral and returned to the kitchen. The children were having cookies and milk and Luetta was enjoying the moment.

"This is good!" I said, gently massaging Mom's shoulders. She reached up and put her hand over mine.

"Yes, it is." I kissed her again on the cheek as I grabbed my own cookie.

"How was the drive?" she asked. "And where is your friend?"

"His name is Dennis, Mom, and he went to get a hotel room," I said, not wanting to answer too many questions about how I knew Dennis.

"I thought he was going to stay here?" Mom replied, her tone revealing her relief and regret that he was not.

"He wanted to get some rest and he knew he would not be able to with these energized bunnies," I said, looking at my kids lovingly. "Mom, you should have seen them. They bounced around that truck all down the highway, and didn't take a nap until we turned off on your exit ramp. I thought they would talk us into a coma. And if that wasn't enough, they got into this 'stop touching me' argument that lasted for at least 250 miles," I said, laughing as I remembered the expression on Dennis' face after the first two hours.

"So, where did you meet this Dennis?" Mom asked slyly while playing with a lone cookie crumb left on the table.

Here we go, I thought. *Damn, I knew it wouldn't be long before she started to dip into my business.*

"Before you go into Inspector Gadget mode, Dennis and I are just good friends," I responded.

"Some friend." She huffed. "I don't know too many men who would drive a truck for thirteen hours and fly back home at their own expense without expecting some sort of payback," she stated flatly.

"You don't know Dennis," I said, refusing to disclose any more details of our relationship than I had to. Dennis was another reason I had left Baltimore. I fell in love with him and for a while, I thought he loved me, too. But when he found out that I was not going to have any more children, our relationship cooled off quickly. I thought my heart would break when he told me that we should see other people. Secretly I had hoped that he would come to his senses and turn the truck around, but he didn't.

"Will I get to meet him?" she inquired.

"Sure," I said. "He's staying the weekend so you will get to meet him tonight. We want to go out. Would you mind watching the kids for me? I promised him I would show him the nightlife."

Mom didn't answer so I continued to babble. "Dennis wants to move here, too, but is afraid to leave his own mother alone."

"He's close to his mother?" she asked.

"They are real close. Ms. Malcolm is a very sweet woman. You would like her," I said.

"You must be good friends. You know his mother, too?"

"Enough questions, Mother! What are we going to do about dinner? I need to unpack a few things and wash off some of this road dirt," I said, rising from the table. I knew as long as I sat there, she would pump me for information.

Changing channels, Mom said, "What does Keith say about your traveling across country with his children and another man?"

"Keith has no say," I responded. "What I do is none of Keith's business!" I snapped.

"He's still your husband!" she said adamantly but not angry about my response.

I breathed deeply and responded. "On paper only. As soon as he signs those divorce papers, that will be the end of it." Talking about Keith always put me in a bad mood and I quickly left the room before I lashed out at my mother.

"I gave Dennis the phone number. If he calls while I'm in the shower, get a number from him, please." I kissed the children and quickly went off in search of a hot shower and some clean clothes. I dropped off the children's suitcases in the other guest rooms and took several minutes to unpack them.

"Take a bath in my bathroom," Momma yelled.

"Yes!" I exclaimed and leaped into the air. I was dying to get in that Jacuzzi, but was afraid to ask. That was just the type of relaxation I needed. I ran in hurriedly, turned on the water and positioned the jets as the hot water poured out of them. I liberally poured bubble bath and bath beads into the swirling water, turning the water blue. Locking the door, I quickly got undressed. I grabbed a scarf from my mother's dresser and quickly wrapped my hair. Since I had forgotten my robe, I looked into her closet to borrow one of hers. I knew she wouldn't mind.

When I opened the walk-in closet, I noticed Mom still had Dad's clothes hanging there as if he would be coming in at any moment to change. Tears began to flow again as if for the first time. I closed the closet and returned to the bathroom. Suddenly very observant, I noticed that Dad's cologne bottles still lined the bathroom sink and his toothbrush still occupied its normal spot.

The waiting Jacuzzi suddenly lost most of its appeal. I was depressed and I sorely missed my dad's booming voice. I soaked for a while but didn't nap as I had previously intended to do.

I changed into a pair of shorts and a halter-top. Atlanta was hotter than Baltimore and Mom kept her house fairly warm. Although Mom was not yet sixty, her prior health problems were aggravated by cool temperatures.

I was sweating again by the time I finished my bath. I used the ceiling fan to cool myself off as I dressed. It was 3:30 and I expected to hear from Dennis at any moment. I didn't know where we were going, but I suspected we would find something to do downtown.

"Where are the kids?" I asked when I got back to the kitchen.

"Sleeping. They claimed they wanted peanut butter sandwiches, but fell asleep before I could put it on the table. I wrapped the sandwiches up and put them in the refrigerator," she said, chuckling.

"It figures. They were wired the whole trip!" I said.

"Your friend called. Said he would be by at 7:30."

"Oh, okay." I was sorry that I didn't get a chance to speak with him. I wanted to warn him not to say too much about us but I knew that he would play along with whatever I said.

Dennis is such a joker. We met at a Halloween party. I was dressed as Tina Turner coming out of a club that he and his friend were going into. His friend talked me into coming back inside. He turned out to be a jerk but Dennis and I had been friends ever since. The memory brought a smile to my face.

"Where did you say you met him?" Mom inquired again as if she had ESP.

"Okay, Mother, I will explain this to you one time but I will not be interrogated about him. Agreed?"

"Agreed," she said, eagerly pulling out a chair for me to sit on. Even though it was just 5:00, she had already prepared hamburgers and mashed potatoes with gravy so we both decided to eat and get it out the way. The children could eat when they got up from their nap.

After pouring us both some fresh lemonade, I began telling her our story.

"I met Dennis at a Halloween party. He asked me to lunch the next day and I went. That's it. We are friends, okay."

"Must have been some lunch," she said with a grunt.

"Actually, he played a joke on me," I said, laughing.

"A joke," she said, frowning. Mom had zero tolerance when it came to jokes. I inherited my sense of humor from my dad. Ignoring her sarcasm, I continued with the story.

"We were going to have lunch the next day, and I got this call from the FBI..."

"The FBI!" she exclaimed.

"Calm down, Mother. Don't get your panties in a knot," I jokingly said. "The caller said they were from the FBI and that I was seen in the company of a suspected rapist."

"Oh my Lord!"

"Mom, it was a joke. The caller asked if I would be seeing the guy again and I told him that I was having lunch with him that day. They told me they did not want me to alert the guy that they were on to him. They had been following him for some time and wanted to monitor our next meeting."

"Marie, this is not funny. You could have been raped!"

"I know. I flipped out and kept telling the agent that I didn't want any part of the date. The agent, I forget his name, kept saying that I had a civic duty to see the guy again. He reminded me of all the people that I might save if I played along and assured me that if he tried anything, they would be right there. I hemmed and hawed and was almost in tears before Dennis told me that it was him."

"That's some joke," she snapped, wanting to get mad.

"Mom, it was perfect. I remained friends with him 'cause I want to get him back but I've never been able to really catch him off guard like he did to me."

Shit, if she is flipping out like this, I ain't even telling her about David, I thought.

chapter 9

After my initial separation from Keith, I went buck wild. I ain't ashamed to say it 'cause I had a hell of a lot of fun. The only problem was, I was not used to casual relationships.

My first affair started right under Keith's nose. We were attending the same cookout although we took great pains to avoid each other. My girlfriend and neighbor invited me and her husband invited Keith. When I found out that Keith was coming I almost stayed home but the music was sounding too good! The noise coming from their backyard beckoned me, and it appeared like they were having a lot of fun.

Sherry and Howard usually gave good parties, which lasted well into the night. Eventually the party would turn into several cutthroat card games and I loved to play cards. Keith liked card games as well and we used to be a pretty good team but that night, I was not feeling that. Instead of going to the card tables I wandered off by myself to just enjoy the music and sip on my beer.

Much to my surprise, a guy I had grown up with stopped by the party to grab a plate. I didn't know that he was a friend of Sherry since she was much older than he and me. I had not seen him since I had worn pigtails.

"Marie?" he asked obviously shocked to see me as well.

"I don't even believe this," I said, jumping to my feet to embrace him. "David, oh my goodness, I haven't seen you since we were kids!" I exclaimed excitedly. He looked me up and down and even swirled me around and as he did, my face grew plum red from the animal lust I saw in his eyes.

"Damn girl, what ya been doing? The last time I saw you, you were... How should I say this…thick?" he stammered.

"I was more than thick; I was down-right fat!" I exclaimed, punching him in the arm. I had slimmed down and was showing curves that I never knew existed. For this cookout, I wore a black bodysuit without a bra that left nothing to the imagination. I was enjoying his attention and started to warm up to his mild flirtation.

"Well, let me say, you got it going on now!" he yelled and dropped his voice for a deep bark. I felt my nipples stand up and he noticed it immediately.

"I didn't know that you knew Sherry," I said, trying to change the subject.

"Girl, my mom used to live across the alley at the corner house, so I'm over here a lot. My brothers and I have the house now since Mom died, but I ain't never seen you here," he said. "I heard you got married and shit," he said as he realized for the first time that we weren't alone.

As a child I never found him to be attractive since he was a year younger than me and always full of games but as a man, the brother was cut! I fought to keep from looking at his broad shoulders and his muscular arms.

"Let's catch up," he said as he steered me back down to the bench I had been sitting on. I looked around to see if we were being watched. Even though Keith and I were officially separated I did not want to flaunt a man in front of his face. After a few too many beers, he had a tendency to get belligerent.

"I ain't gonna bite ya," he said, patting the seat beside him.

"I know." I sat down and tried to appear as nonchalant as he was but I was failing in my attempt.

"So, fill me in on the gaps. I know that you got married and moved away. Did you have any children?" he asked.

"Two, they are around here somewhere," I said, again scanning the crowd.

"There, see that little one with all the curls on top of her head. That's Keira." He turned his head and body to look in the direction of my pointed finger.

"Hell, if I would have looked around, I would have been able to pick her out of a lineup. She looks just like you!" he said.

"And, that's Kevin holding onto Sherry's leg. He is already a ladies man and he is just turning three!" I said, laughing.

"He looks just like you, too! There is no way that you would ever be able to deny either of those two. What about your husband, where is he?" I shifted in my seat and took a big swallow of my beer. I crossed my legs and then quickly uncrossed them. He placed his hand over mine and looked deep into my eyes. "I wasn't trying to pry. It's just that I haven't seen you in so long," he assured me.

"It's okay, really, it's fine. We are separated but he is here tonight. He and Howard are friends," I said, referring to Sherry's husband. He pulled back his hand and looked around at the crowd. I felt him pull away from me and I did not like it. I could hear Keith talking shit as usual at a card game.

"That's him, with the big mouth," I said when he glanced back at me.

"He's willing to let all this go?" He eyed me up and down again. Another smile tugged at my lips.

"When did you grow up to be such a flirt?" I said. "Back in the day, all you wanted to do was throw snowballs and pull my hair. You gave me such a hard time I almost developed a complex." His smile was too sexy. He had the whitest teeth and two perfect dimples. Funny, I just didn't remember him that way. I related more to his serious brother than I did to him as we were growing up. Not that we didn't speak, we just didn't talk.

"Dance with me," he said, pulling me onto my feet and into his arms. He wrapped his arms around my waist and gently pulled me to him until I was flush against his chest. My head automatically tilted and was laying on his shoulder. Damn, it felt good! His breath was warm against my neck as he sung softly into my ear. I felt his nature rising and could not resist grinding against it. Johnny Gill was crooning about a red dress and high heels as we danced under the stars.

"I've loved you since I was ten," he said, kissing me softly on the neck. I pulled back from him to look into his eyes. Surely I was imagining things.

"Get the hell out of here. You treated me like crap!" I said ready to disengage from his arms but lacking the willpower to do so.

"I didn't know how to tell you," he said, kissing me again on the neck. His dick pulsed and so did my clit.

"Well, you sure had a messed-up way of letting me know," I said, playfully punching him in the chest. "You told me that all girls were stupid and I was the leader of the pack! I used to go home crying every day," I said as the bittersweet memories came back to me. All the boys used to tease me then. My body developed early and it drew unwanted attention. As a defense mechanism, I ate. I grew round all over and that just caused the neighborhood boys to pick on me more, but David was the worst.

Under the stars and in the presence of my soon to be ex-husband, my neighbors and God, he kissed me. *Good Golly Miss Molly*. All the years of sexual repression and frustration melted into a hot ball of lust. It was not a meek kiss either. He put it on me! We acted as if we were alone and naked on a beach some damn where. Moisture seeped through my underwear and my nipples strained against my bodysuit. I wanted to step away but was afraid that the moisture would show in the crotch on my outfit. Abruptly, he pulled away. Although he still held me in his arms, our lips were no longer locked.

"I'm sleepy, Momma," Kevin said, locking his arms around our legs. I looked down into my little man's eyes. He really did look like me and my heart swelled with pride.

"Kevin, this is David. We grew up together," I said. David released his grip on me and went down on one knee to talk to Kevin.

"What's up?" he said, holding out his hand for Kevin to give him five. Kevin played along while suppressing a yawn.

"I gotta go," I said, searching the other partygoers looking for Keira. She was at the table near her father fast asleep. I glanced at my watch and noticed that I had been talking with David for almost two hours and could not remember anything except the feel of his dick on my leg and the touch of his tender lips.

"You're living in your mother's house now, aren't you?" he said. I looked up at those words.

"Damn, you have been keeping an ear out, haven't you? Mom and Dad moved to Atlanta and I got the house. I'm looking to buy it but they are not cooperating," I said, clearly pleased that he was keeping tabs on me.

"What do you mean, not cooperating?" he asked.

"They don't want to sell it to just me. They only want to sell it to me and my ex and that ain't gonna happen," I said.

I gathered the kids' things and started to head toward home. "Sherry, I will be back for Keira in a minute. Just let me carry this stuff home," I said.

"No problem. I'm glad you could make it," she said, winking at me. *So much for David and I being discreet*, I thought.

"I'll carry her," David said, swooping her up in his arms and following me down the alley to my house.

"Get your hands off my daughter!" Keith said, jumping up from the table and knocking over his drink. He was drunk and stumbling as he lunged for Keira. I stepped between them and grabbed Keira. "Go away, Keith. I got this," I said. Confused, Kevin dropped my hand and grabbed David's. David looked down at him and smiled.

Keith noticed this but was slow on the uptake. He turned around totally disoriented. "Come here," he said to Kevin in a fierce tone. Kevin started crying, tightening his grip on David's hand.

"Look, Keith, it's late; we are all tired. They will see you later but right now, we are going home," I announced. Kevin did not respond well to yelling and I could understand his tears when his father started acting the ass again. I was fighting to keep my voice low but my tolerance level for Keith was non-existent. I spun around and started for the house with David following close behind me. At that moment I knew there would not be another chance for me to be alone with David but I was grateful for the time we had. It had been so long since I had felt desired by anyone of the male species or since I had desired a man, for that matter. David had done wonders for my self-esteem in the short time we were together. Surprisingly, Keith did not follow in protest.

David paused at the back gate not sure how to proceed. I switched hips since Keira was entirely too heavy to carry. I looked into David's deep brown eyes.

"I want to see you again," he said softly so that the children could not hear.

"Me, too," I said and opened the gate to our yard. Keith was still standing in the alley glaring at us. I told David goodnight and went into the house. I undressed the kids and put them down to bed. I, on the other hand, was too restless to sleep. I drew a hot bath to soak. I could still hear the music from the party and could even imagine hearing David's sexy voice. I climbed out of the tub all shriveled and cold. The cool water helped to soothe my hot flesh but did nothing for my heightened libido.

Switching on the ceiling fan, I pulled on a plain Jane nightgown and turned back the covers on my bed. As I was climbing into the bed, I heard a knock on the door. It wasn't the nigger knock of the police; rather it was the knock of someone that did not want to draw attention to themselves.

I thought it was Keith as I hurried down the steps to stop him from waking the kids. In his drunken state, I was not up for a confrontation with him.

"Who is it?" I demanded, still trying to keep quiet but maintain some authority in my voice. My agenda for the night was to climb into the bed and dream about David, and the visitor was an unwanted distraction.

"It's me. Could you please open the door?" I peeped through the curtain and saw David's broad frame on the porch. It was then that I realized that the music from the party had stopped. I had been playing the same song in my head since our dance and did not recognize that the party was over. I unlocked the door and cracked it open.

"What's wrong?" I said, checking his body for blood. I thought he might have gotten into a fight with Keith and was here to tell me that he had whipped his ass.

"I need to talk you. Can I come in?" he asked. I looked down at the nightgown that I was wearing and started to protest wishing for something more provocative. My mind said *no* but my body was saying *yes, sir!* I opened the door and quickly let him in. I was naked before the door was bolted shut and I don't remember taking off a thing. His hands were kneading my body as if it were dough. Slowly he took off his clothes. My breath caught in my throat when I saw his dick. It was huge. Although Keith was not short by a long shot, he was thin. David's dick was long and big! I have never had any thing that big pointed at me before. I backed away from him and he understood right away. "I'll be gentle," he said. My mind screamed, *bitch, is you crazy;* and my pussy answered, *hell fucking yeah!*

David made love to me like I had never been made love to before. It wasn't just his size that overwhelmed me. It was the total package. I felt like he made love to my mouth with each searching kiss; my pussy when he stuck his exquisite dick in it; my head as he whispered words of love into my ears; and my heart when he washed my clit with his mouth. Exhausted, we collapsed on the floor. I had major rug burns; I'm sure he had them as well, but I was not complaining. After we caught our breath, we went upstairs to my bedroom for another session of hot steamy passion. When sanity returned, I worried about the consequences of allowing him to stay the night but to be honest, it felt too good to deny.

"Damn, baby, you were so tight! I could hardly control myself," he said, snuggling my neck and caressing my breasts. I sank into his arms and we fell deeply asleep.

He woke me two hours later by sucking on my breasts and made love to me again. To my surprise, the third time was the charm. We got to know each other's bodies intimately. I was whipped and I knew it.

The sun was shining in my eyes and Keira was kissing my face when I finally opened my eyes. I looked over to the other side of the bed and thankfully it was empty.

"I'm hungry!" she said. I pulled the covers to my neck and told her to go wash her face. My head dropped back to the pillow when she left the room. *Damn, what have I done? Not only did I screw this man that I hadn't seen since grade school; I didn't even bother to think of protection!* I gathered myself out of bed and grimaced in pain. My pussy was sore and my back was hurting. I also had small carpet burns on my elbows and knees. But truth be told, the shit was worth it.

chapter 10

The phone rang before I could get out of bed good. I really wasn't in the mood to talk to anyone since I had a lot of things on my mind.

"Hello?" I growled into the receiver.

"Girl, I just wanted to give you the heads-up," Sherry whispered. "Your husband saw David leaving your house and he is fit to be tied. He spent the night on the damn porch and that old fool Howard is feeding him a bunch of shit."

"What are you talking about?" I asked as I started feeling the effects of a slight headache in the center of my forehead.

"Look, I don't care who you sleep with. It ain't none of my business but that old buzzard Howard done told your husband some shit to get his dandruff up!" she warned.

"Look, Sherry, I don't mean no harm but your husband needs to mind his own fucking business. And, as far as I'm concerned, Keith is my ex-husband. I can see who I want when I want!" I declared, stomping my foot in defiance.

"Shit, girl, I ain't mad at ya. If I were twenty years younger, I would drag his ass between the sheets, too! But you know how it is when two fools get together. I heard him tell Keith that he didn't stand a chance in hell of getting back with you now that you had sampled some of David's stuff! Got him all fired up. Keith done started drinking already this morning acting like he got a damn bee under his shorts," she said.

"Well, he better stay his silly ass over there. I am not going to take his shit today or any other day for that matter. I told Howard it's over between Keith and me; why is he still trying to fix this shit that needs to stay broke?"

"'Cause he's an old meddling fool that don't know how to mind his own business," she exclaimed. "One of these days he is going to stir up the wrong pot and it's gonna burn his old ass."

"Thanks for the warning," I said, trying to end the conversation at this point.

"How was it?" she excitedly asked before I had the chance to put the phone back on its base.

"Ha ha ha. Your husband ain't the only one in your family tryin' to get in my business," I said, laughing. Even though Sherry was old enough to be my mother, I considered her a good friend. She was young in mind and spirit.

"None of your damned business! Hell, if I told ya, I might have to fight ya," I exclaimed with a smile and hung up the phone. Although I wanted to talk to someone about last night, I knew better than to speak to Sherry. She just might get drunk her own damn self and start blabbing my business to Tom, Dick, Harry or worst still, Howard or Keith.

It pissed me off that Keith was still in the neighborhood but hey, it's a free country. When he first moved out of the house, he would find all kinds of reasons to come back. The only problem was that once he was there, I had hell to pay in order to get him to leave again.

He came over a couple of weeks ago claiming he wanted to stain the deck. I didn't ask him to do it and had every intention of doing the job myself. I'd bought all of the supplies and had just changed into some old jeans when his ass showed up. He kept criticizing the way that I was doing it until I finally let him have the brush. It took him all weekend to complete the job! Every time I went to the back door to check on his progress, he would be lying in the lawn chair sleeping.

The same thing happened the week before when he stopped over while I was cutting the grass. He kept at me until I let him do it. He stretched that job out until way after the sun had gone down. I was not buying the "just happened to be in the neighborhood" since he was staying all the way across town.

After hanging up the phone with Sherry, I realized that I had missed the perfect opportunity to pump her for information about David. We had done so little talking the night before that I had more questions than I had answers about his background. I knew that I couldn't call her back so I went to the kitchen to start breakfast.

I decided on making pancakes and bacon, as they are a big hit with the kids for the sugar, I guess. Besides, I was in the mood for them as well. I wore a smile that stretched from one ear to the next while I mixed the batter and lightly hummed a sweet melody.

Kevin and Keira were watching television and surprisingly, weren't fighting about which cartoon to watch. That was temporary and I knew it so I enjoyed the blessed silence. I was just about finished with cooking breakfast and putting it on the table when the phone rang again. "Damn," I said out loud.

"Hello," I demanded and whoever was on the other end of the line hung up as soon as I picked up the receiver. I had hoped that it might be David calling until I realized that he didn't even have the number. At that point, instead of being relieved that he had left in the early morning hours for the sake of the kids, I felt apprehensive about whether or not I would ever hear from him again.

My mind played tapes where he would be laughing it up with his boys telling them how he boned me on the first date. Hell, it suddenly occurred to me that he might even talk about it to Howard.

I shook those unpleasant thoughts away from my mind and finished setting the table. Smelling the aroma from the food, Kevin ran into the kitchen and took a seat. He pulled his plate in front of him and eyed the huge stack of pancakes.

"Did you wash your hands?" I asked. He slid off the chair and went to wash them without any further instructions from me. I could hear the water running but I doubted that he would put his hands under it. Kevin, like all little boys, had this aversion to water. I had to constantly keep behind him 'cause his little narrow ass would never get wet unless he got in a pool!

I snuck up behind him and sure enough the water was running, but he was playing with one of his toy soldiers.

"Boy!" I exclaimed loudly and it scared the shit out of him. He jumped, dropping his soldier in the sink. He looked at me with those guilty eyes and my heart melted. I knew from that moment that he was going to be some looker when he grew up.

"Sorry, Mom," he said and began washing his hands in earnest. I turned my back to keep him from seeing the smile on my face. He should have known I was going to check up on him but little boys are like men; they never learn the easy lessons.

"Keira, come wash your hands," I shouted before returning to the kitchen to get out cups for their milk and juice. I didn't have the same hygiene problems with Keira. If I let her, she would take a bath ten times a day. She was so prim and proper. She never wanted to leave the house until every strand of hair on her head was in its proper place.

My biggest problem concerning her was with her clothing. I always laid out her clothes the night before and she invariably wanted to wear something else. We fought a few minutes, depending on how much time we had, and she ended up wearing what I originally had picked out. The thing that pissed me off was that I always asked her first before I ironed her clothes what she would like to wear. So it was not so much me being the boss as it was her being pigheaded.

We ate breakfast in silence and they went back to the living room to finish watching cartoons as soon as their plates were empty. I quickly cleaned up the dishes and scanned the freezer for what I was going to make for dinner.

I always cooked my biggest meal of the week on Sundays so that I usually had enough to stretch that meal for two to three days afterwards. For the remainder of the week, I'd make simple dishes that could quickly be prepared in minutes. The phone rang again as I was leaving the kitchen. My heart began racing even though I knew that it would not be David.

"Good morning," I answered sweetly. Again, there was silence on the other end of the phone. I purposely held onto the phone waiting for a response.

"Hello," I said again with a touch of irritation.

"Bitch," a male voice said and then the line went dead. The voice did not sound like Keith's or anybody else's that I recognized. As far as I knew, Keith was the only person that hated me enough to call me a bitch, especially after what he had seen this morning.

I looked at the receiver in disbelief before hanging it up. Briefly I toyed with the idea of changing the number but it had been my parents' phone number ever since we moved into the house when I was in fourth grade. All of their old friends had this number, it was engraved in their hearts and I did not want to part with it. I still received calls from people looking for them and I would give them the number. No, changing the number was not an option.

It was already hot outside. I decided to go upstairs and take a shower. I laid out some shorts for me and quickly made my bed. I wanted to get in some yard work early before the temperature was hot enough to fry eggs on the concrete. Although I hated to admit it, I was beginning to like playing in the dirt. When Keith and I were together, I left all of the yard work to him. In fact, I rarely came out the house unless I was going somewhere. For some reason, since Keith had been gone, I liked to sit out on the deck in the back yard reading a book. With the children playing, I read and listened to their playful chatter. Since Keith was out of my life, I was finding a lot of stuff enjoyable that I used to detest!

Although I liked to cook, I hated cooking for him. I hated coming home, lying in the same bed with him, and I detested the thought of sex with him. He had me convinced that I was the problem. Every time we had sex, I felt like he was peeing on me. I had really forgotten what it was like to be dicked down proper and that feeling was "all good."

It's amazing what a good dick can do, I thought, absently turning pages but digesting nothing of my book. I laid the book down in my lap and began to seriously think about my sexual nature. Truth be told, I never had an active libido. Sex for me was never something that I craved! It was more like something that I had to endure in order to get to the next level. My intense observations were so profound I had to share them.

I went into the kitchen and grabbed the cordless phone. I dialed Angie's number and waited patiently for her to answer.

"Gurl!" I said when she breathlessly picked up.

"Oh shit," she replied, laughing.

"I'm gonna say something to you that I will deny if it ever gets repeated back to me," I said, still chuckling. I felt like I had a supreme revelation.

"OK, you got me going. What is it?" she asked.

"Do you know that I never had a real orgasm until last night! I'm tripping so bad that I wasted all these years only to find out what all the whoopla was about!" I said, practically yelling in her ear.

"Gurl, you are lying to me! I ain't even believing you stayed with Keith all them years and he wasn't ringing your bell!" she shouted.

"It's true, girl, and the bitch of it all is, I'm just finding it out. I just thought sex was overrated and forgot about it. I mean, don't get me wrong, I had moments with Keith where I actually enjoyed it but..." I just shook my head unable to continue. I walked into the kitchen for a little more privacy.

"Oh, I get it, you tried you some new dick!" she said, laughing loudly. "And he turned you out!!" she howled and I began to regret even telling her that shit.

"OK, you can laugh at me now, but I know now and this shit is on! No more will I settle for the mediocre shit!" We laughed together for a few more minutes and I ended the call. I hated that my best friend lived out of town but I was glad that we still kept in contact.

chapter 11

I was outside watering the flowers I had just planted when I saw David walking up the alley. He wore an all-white outfit and, upon closer inspection, it appeared to be some sort of uniform. He carried a medium-sized white paper bag in the crook of his arm. Flustered, I did not know what to do so I tried to ignore him hoping to appear nonchalant. I continued watering the flowers as if I didn't see him. In my mind, I decided that if he kept on walking, that would be that.

He stopped at my gate and opened it as if it and all that lay beyond belonged to him. I looked into his eyes and jolts of pleasure electrified my entire body. Even in his uniform, David was sexy.

"What's up with you? Aren't you gonna speak to a brother?" he said with a smile on his face. I was tempted to spray him full force with the hose for making me doubt what had transpired the night before, but the reality was I needed to spray my own hot ass!

"Hi," I said, blushing as brilliant flashes from the night before flooded my senses. He handed me the bag that he was carrying and I peeked inside. It was full of little ice cream cups. I was surprised and didn't move from the spot I had planted myself in.

"You should put them in the freezer before they melt," he said, still grinning. My feet did not move from the carpet of grass. I felt that if I took my eyes off of him, he would disappear. Unglued, I dropped the hose and turned to take the treats into the kitchen.

"Wait," he said and I paused as he walked closer to me. I turned around and our eyes locked, burning a deep hole into my heart. I was thinking about the night before and I imagined that he was thinking the same. I thought he was going to kiss me right there, in the middle of my back yard for all of Garrison Avenue to see but he didn't. Instead, he reached into the bag and grabbed three of the cups and some spoons, which were also in the bag. Deflated and a little dejected, I turned around again and went into the house. I looked back to see if he was still standing there and he was in the same spot grinning at me and shaking his head.

"Whew," I said, putting up the frozen treats and fanning my hot face. The door slammed behind me as I came back out onto the porch. I had been meaning to get that fixed but tended to forget about it until it slammed, scaring the shit out of me. I looked back at the door and silently cursed it. He was sitting at the picnic table with Keira and Kevin eating their ice cream. Kevin had a spot of it on his nose. He had the bad habit of smelling everything before he ate it. I chuckled and returned to the kitchen for napkins.

"Where did you get those?" I asked David, referring to the ice cream.

"At the hospital," he said. "I work in the cafeteria."

That explained the white uniform and why he was walking up the alley. The hospital was a few blocks away from my street.

"You had to work today?" I asked.

"Yeah. You don't think I got up that early for fun, do ya?" he replied with a wink.

The kids were oblivious to our conversation and finished their ice cream within minutes. I had to remind them to say thank you and to wash their hands. They bolted inside, allowing the door to slam behind them.

"And I thought you were being polite leaving before they woke up," I answered sheepishly.

"Girl, if it wasn't for work, wild horses would not have driven me from that bed! I was so worn out and I had to drag my butt home for a hot shower. You put it on me, that's for darn sure!" he exclaimed. He was cleaning up his language for the sake of the kids and that made me happy. My mouth was foul enough so I appreciated the gesture.

I was simply euphoric. *He felt it, too,* I thought. To think that he enjoyed me as much as I did him almost made we wet myself. My hot ass started to wiggle on that bench like I was riding on his dick again! He chuckled like he could read my thoughts. I quickly got up from the bench and went back to watering my flowers. He laughed out loud but did not bother to follow me. He sprawled out on the bench and put his hands behind his head.

I could see the rise of his dick through the fabric of his pants. If I were an artist, I would have drawn that picture of male perfection. His arms simply bulged out of his short-sleeved shirt. The top two buttons were undone and I could see the tiny hairs of his chest peaking out. His bald head was glistening in the afternoon sun. I gazed at him until it physically hurt my eyes. I would have never believed it, if I hadn't seen it for myself. To think that skinny little David would evolve into such a fyne specimen—it was just unheard of!

"Sweet Jesus," I said to myself as I cupped some of the water from the hose and pressed it to my face.

Keira and Kevin raced out the house slamming the door again. If I didn't fix it soon, it would break the glass for sure. Since it was late spring, it was time to take the glass out anyway. I didn't know how to do it but was sure I could figure it out once I found out where Keith had put the screens from last year.

Energized with sugar, Kevin chased Keira in circles in the yard. They were having a ball. I shot the water into the air and they ran under its spray. They squealed with joy. It looked refreshing to me since it was already eighty degrees outside. Briefly I glanced over at David and he appeared to be asleep. Sighing, I continued to alternate between watering the flowers and the kids. I would have to get some towels before they went in the house for their afternoon nap 'cause they were dripping wet.

Momentarily possessed, I turned the hose on David full force, drenching him from head to toe. He leaped up in shock.

"Oh shit," I said to myself as I dropped the hose and took off running. I couldn't make it to the house but I could exit the fence and flee up the street. I slipped and crashed down on one knee. David cleared the deck and ran after me flinging drops of water as he approached. I tried to get back up but I could not stop laughing. Always the joker, Kevin picked up the hose and sprayed us both!

The water was very cold. Keira was cackling as we scrambled to get out of range of the water. Kevin had a maniacal look in his eyes.

"Stop it!" I sternly shouted. I wasn't mad at him but he was having way too much fun. He continued spraying water in our direction for a few more seconds before dropping the hose. My hair was completely soaked and my tee shirt clung to my breasts. David looked at my hair and burst out laughing. He looked down at my chest and his dick stood up. "Sweet mother of God," I exclaimed through clenched lips. I ran towards the house shouting over my shoulder for them to stay outside. I ran upstairs, dripping water all over the floor and carpet to grab some towels. I stepped into the tub and quickly took off my wet garments. I wrapped a towel around my head and dried off the rest of my body. I looked at myself in the mirror and saw the carnival lust in my eyes.

"Nap time!" I said out loud, giving high-fives to my mirrored image as I grabbed the extra towels. I changed into another pair of shorts and a dry tee shirt. I added a dab of my favorite perfume and went back outside.

David was lying back down on the bench when I opened the door. His clothes were already beginning to dry. He didn't even open his eyes as I approached but he was smiling. I dropped a towel over his smiling face.

"Okay, you both had your fun. It's nap time," I said to Kevin and Keira.

"Aw man," they exclaimed in unison. I dried each of them off and led them upstairs for their naps. I took their damp clothes and turned on the washing machine throwing them all in together with the ones that I had taken off as well. I drew the blinds in their rooms to darken it and advised them against any further playing.

"The sooner you get your nap, the sooner you can get up," I promised. I expected more of a protest but they closed their eyes as I drew the door shut on their respective bedrooms. I leaned against the door, trying to slow down my rapid breathing.

Outside again, I wound up the hose and hung it back on the rack. I put away my planting tools and locked the garage. The yard was really looking good. David was still lying on his back and I took every opportunity to openly stare at him.

"How long before they fall asleep?" he asked, startling me out of my reflections.

"I thought you were sleeping," I responded, avoiding his real question. I wanted to drag his ass upstairs but I didn't want to appear too eager.

"How the hell can I sleep with you looking at me like that?"

"I wasn't looking at you," I lied, turning my head away from his prone body. It was all I could do not to reach out and touch him. I went over to the chaise lounge and opened up my book that was laying in the chair. Surprisingly, it escaped the water. I looked over at both my neighbors' yards to see if anyone was watching us. Normally, when one person started piddling in the yard, everyone came out the house to work. Nine times out of ten, they were at their windows with their ears pinned to the screen trying to hear our conversation.

I pretended to read for the next fifteen minutes or so but could not remember for the life of me what I had just read. Silently I held a debate in my head. Did I brazenly invite this man into my home in broad daylight? Or, did I try to wait until after dark when the kids went to sleep? Decisions. Decisions.

Fuck it, I'm an adult and it ain't nobody's business but mine who the hell I sleep with, I said to myself, slamming the book down on the deck and stomping to the door. Without turning, I said to him, "You coming?"

He sprung up from the bench and followed me inside. I shut and locked the door. Keith crossed my mind for about two hot seconds before I locked lips and limbs with David.

The day before I allowed David to fuck me, and he opened doors that I never knew existed, made me feel emotions that I had only read about. That afternoon I intended to make love to him 'cause nothing that sweet should be considered a fuck!

I led him to my room. I slowly undressed him savoring each eye-full that I exposed. I pushed him up against the bed and told him to lie back. I eased his zipper down and he assisted me by lifting his hips up so I could take his pants down. Next I removed his shoes and socks. After I had his shoes off, I pulled the rest of his clothes off leaving him clad only in his white BVDs.

"I'll be right back," I told him as I quietly left the room and went into the bathroom. I tiptoed past the kids' rooms and ran some warm water in a tub I generally used to soak my feet. I filled the tub with scented water and mild soap. I carefully carried the tub back into my room and set it on my nightstand.

"What's this?" he asked with this deep sexy voice.

"Shush," I said. "Close your eyes, relax and enjoy." I tenderly washed him from head to toe. He moaned with pleasure when I licked his nipples and practically sat up when I touched his dick.

"Wait your turn," I told it and I swear it winked at me. I removed the wash-basin and put it on the floor.

"I'll be right back," I said as I left again. Hiding the oil that I had in my hands, I went downstairs and put it in the microwave for fifty seconds.

"Perfect," I declared as I climbed the steps. The anticipation was making me weak. I pushed open the door and checked to make sure his eyes were still closed.

"No peeking," I admonished him when I saw him crack open an eye. Quietly I undressed. I started rubbing the warm oil over his feet and legs, gently working it into his skin and in between his toes.

"Goddamn, Girl!" he exclaimed.

"Be quiet," I instructed. When I was finished with his lower legs, I moved on up to his powerful thighs. I wanted to get to his dick while the oil was still warm. Not that I was going to put the oil on his dick, I wanted him to feel the heat on his balls. Naked, I sat on his thighs. He tried to move but I clamped down with my thighs holding him prisoner. I poured a generous amount of oil in between his legs and let it drip down onto his balls. Squeezing them, I massaged the oil into his sack. A pinprick of moisture appeared at the top of his massive dick. I licked that with the tip of my tongue and moved up higher to work on his chest. I was sitting so close to his dick I could have ridden it, but I was not finished yet.

I really wanted to run back downstairs so I could heat the oil again but I was too impatient for that. I smeared enough oil on his chest to cover it and then massaged it in with my fingers and my breasts when I laid down on him. I worked the oil down over his arms and ran the tip of my clit over his dick. I wanted to ease the fire burning in me that he had created but it was much too soon.

"Turn over," I huskily demanded. I sat on his back with my head facing his feet. I leaned over and gently massaged oil into the soles of his feet and the back of his ankles. I worked my way up and was turning around to work on his back and arms when he said, "I can't do this anymore." He flipped me over on my back and plunged his dick into my vagina. I gasped with shock and pleasure. He didn't have to work as hard to get in the house this time. Collectively we moaned in ecstasy. I was so wet I was dripping. I clutched his back and wrapped my legs around his thighs locking myself to his body. United we rode the tremendous waves of passion and exploded into each other. He rained kisses on my face and neck as sexual aftermath rocked our bodies.

After we caught our breath, he rolled off of me. I turned over and we spooned our bodies together. In my ear he whispered, "You are full of surprises, aren't you?" He kissed my earlobe while fondling my breasts. "I always knew that you would be the full package but I never dreamed it would be like this. You trying to hook a brother or what?" he asked before he drifted off to sleep.

I didn't respond to his questions 'cause I didn't know the answers. All I knew was he made me feel good and that was good enough for me. I dozed for a few minutes and then got up and took a shower. I let him sleep for about a half-hour before I woke him so that he could get dressed before the children woke up. Seeing him naked made me want to strip off my clothes and have him again but I didn't want us to get caught with our britches down.

chapter 12

After dinner when the children were bedded down for the night, David and I finally talked.

"You're so good with children," I said, setting him up for an inquisition. Before their bedtime, he rolled around on the floor with them as if he were their ages. He didn't respond so I turned it up a notch.

"Do you have any?" I asked, waiting for his answer with baited breath. We were seated on the sofa supposedly watching television.

"Yeah," he said not volunteering anything other than that.

"Really," I said, trying to hide my disappointment. A man this well endowed had to have children so I could not understand why I was trying to get upset. He changed the subject on me but since it was something I felt I should know, I decided to talk about it.

"Tell me about your marriage," he said. It was like he had thrown cold water over me and for a moment my heart hardened.

"Not a whole lot to tell, really. I was young and dumb. He filled my head with a bunch of nonsense and I fell for it. By the time I realized what was really going on, I had already had Keira, and Kevin was on the way. Keith had me so brainwashed, I was scared to leave him," I said, hanging my head. David lifted my head and looked deep into my eyes.

"Brainwashed? What do you mean?"

"He told me that I would never find anybody else that would love me and my children. He also said that if I left him I would be alone for the rest of my life. At the time, I was so scared to be alone that I put up with his shit until I got sick and tired of being sick and tired! When I reached that point, I didn't care if my shit shriveled up and weathered away. I was just that tired."

"So, you are ready to move on with no regrets?" he asked.

"You damn Skippy, I'm ready to move on, but I still have regrets; the biggest one is that it took me so long to wake up. I woke up one day and decided I'd rather be by myself than put up with that shit any longer."

"And he just decided to move, just like that?"

"Hell no! It was rough. We were living in the same house but would not even speak to each other. He stayed in my room and I slept in the basement. Every few weeks he would demand sex and when I would not comply, he raped me to get it."

"That little piece of shit," he growled.

"Tell me about it. I tried to kick his ass but he always got the upper hand," I said, remembering some of the more brutal fights. "When he started acting a fool, I usually tried to leave our apartment and come over here but he got hip to that and started fucking with my car. He would take it apart so it wouldn't start."

"Where was Keira and Kevin while all this was going on?" he asked.

"Oh, they were there but it didn't stop him once he got going. They lived through that shit with me and that's another one of my regrets. If it wasn't for them, I would have stabbed his ass while he was sleeping and went to jail for the rest of my life. Hell, I might have got him while he was raping me; that way I could have caught him coming and going," I said with a smile. I could laugh about it now but when I was in the mix, I found few things to smile about.

David leaned forward and kissed me on the forehead. I closed my eyes and savored his warmth and closeness.

"Do you know what he told me?" I whispered softly.

"No baby, what?" he asked.

"He told me I was a cold, frigid bitch. He said having sex with me was like humping a piece of wood," I said as fresh tears pooled in my eyes. "He had me believing that shit until you came along."

"Was he your first?" he asked gently.

"He might as well have been. I had done it once before but I didn't see what all the hype was about," I stated.

"Damn," he swore under his breath. He pulled me to my feet and led me upstairs where he made passionate love to me. When it was over, I cried. I was stretched and sore beyond belief but for the first time in my life, I was satisfied.

The phone rang just as we closed our eyes. I groped for it, knocking down several items from my nightstand including the oil, which spilled all over the dresser and floor. "Shit!" I exclaimed, snatching up the phone.

"Hello," I snapped while looking around in vain for something to wipe up the mess. David propped himself up on his elbows curious at my reaction.

"Just because you're fucking that steroid-taking motherfucker, don't think our shit is over. You're still my wife and I won't allow you to flaunt your niggers in front of my children!"

I slammed down the phone shaking with fury.

"Keith?" he asked and I quickly nodded.

"What did he say?"

"That he was not going to allow me to flaunt my steroid-taking niggers in his children's faces."

"He's just talking, Marie, 'cause he still loves you," he explained.

"He doesn't love me. He just needs me. I wasn't a wife to him; I was his fucking mother! He wanted someone to provide for him and take care of him. Hell, I got two kids, and I don't need no more." I got up from the bed to get a washcloth to clean up my mess. I was fuming mad now and knew it would be a long time before I would be able to sleep.

David sat up as I came back into the room. "Marie, calm down!" he said, sitting upright in the bed and exposing his beautiful chest. Not wanting to be distracted I looked away.

"You know what makes me so mad? My family thinks I'm wrong to divorce him. His family calls and cusses me out on a regular basis for kicking him out. My neighbors think I'm wrong but none of them had to live through what I went through. That's what pisses me off the most. If they knew he raped me, would they be so forgiving? If they knew that he lived rent-free, would they be as understanding? If they knew that he lost the only good job he ever had 'cause of some stupid ass drugs, what the hell would they say then? That car he drives, I bought that. Those clothes he wears, I bought them. Hell, I didn't tell anyone all the shit that has been going on. I keep that shit bottled up in here," I said, pounding my heart.

"I don't want my children to know that their father was a dumb ass fry jock until I arranged to get him a job with the post office," I continued. I didn't want them to find out that he allowed himself to get fired over some bullshit. But he calls me a damn bitch!"

I sunk onto the bed and cried big crocodile tears. David held me while I cried but his touch was different. When I awoke, he was gone.

I did not see or hear from David for three days. I was frantic but I tried to keep it together for the sake of the children. I could not understand why something so right could go so wrong in such a short period of time.

On the third day after I came home from work, I called Sherry. Short of going to David's mother's house, she was the only link I had to him. I asked her to come over when she got a chance. Mentally and physically I was a wreck. I had dark circles under my eyes from crying and lack of sleep. I was irritable and as much as I hated to admit it, horny as hell.

I started on Sherry as soon as she walked in the door. I knew her well enough that she wouldn't tell me what I needed to know until I satisfied her curiosity.

"Okay, I fucked him. Satisfied?" I snapped, not wanting to be mad at her but feeling angry nevertheless.

"Was it good?" she asked, ignoring my attitude as she pulled deeply on her cigarette. I didn't smoke but I took one of her cigarettes and lit it. I coughed for a full five minutes before I could talk. The smoke felt like it went all the way down to my toes and my body was trying to expel it as quickly as I was trying to inhale it.

Humbled I said, "Yes. It was good. Un-fucking believable as a matter of fact, but I haven't heard from him in three days. What the hell is up?" I asked in between puffs.

"He came over yesterday," Sherry said.

"Did he mention me?" I asked, barely able to contain myself.

"Yeah. He's hurting, too," she said. I was treading on dangerous ground. Sherry, even though I considered her my friend, was the biggest gossip in Baltimore. If I wasn't so desperate, I would have never come to her for answers. I knew she would spread my business, out of love, all over town but I was beyond caring.

"Hurting, why is that? He's the one that dropped off the fucking planet."

"How much do you know about David, other than his dick size?" she smugly asked.

"We grew up together, for Christ's sake!"

"You tromped on his toes and you didn't even know it."

"How?"

"You did not hear this from me, okay? Do you know where he works?" she asked.

"Yeah, at Sinai Hospital."

"Doing what?" I knew it was in the cafeteria but I didn't know what he did for them.

"Try fry jock," she stated. Flickers of conversation from my rampage started to come back to me. I had no idea that I had hurt his feelings.

"He was a master baker. Making $50,000+ a year. He quit the job 'cause the white man disrespected him. His girlfriend and the mother of one of his children left him. He is very bitter about that," she finished.

I heard everything she said but one thing stood out more the most. "One of his children?" I asked.

"That boy got four other children but he don't claim them like he does Jamal. And that's a spoiled ass little boy if I do say so myself. David thinks the sun rises and sets in that child's eyes, but he is caught in between that bitch baby momma drama and the love of his son. Hell, that baby doesn't look nothing like him, and that bitch that had the child is working the fuck out of him! Every few weeks, she decides not to let David see him and that is tearing him up."

To say that I was shaken to the core was an understatement. He admitted to me that he was a father, but a father of five? That was a little too much. Then, Sherry said he only recognized one; what the hell did that mean? I had no problem believing that he fathered five children given his aversion to condoms but I could not understand his denying paternity. If he slept with the women, there would be no doubt in my mind that he left a baby. The only reason I wasn't jumping off a fucking bridge was because I had my tubes tied, burnt and buried in the backyard.

"Where does he live?" I asked, afraid of the answer but needing to hear it anyway.

"He is staying at his mother's house but you know she just died. His brothers don't want to have too much to do with him, but the baby's momma put him out so he's kind of stuck between a rock and a hard place."

Suddenly a light flashed in my head. The same things that I had said about

Keith applied to David. The only difference was that I fell in love with David. "Damn, Sherry, I can see why he is avoiding me. But I fell in love with him," I said. "I can't help the similarities between the two but I also can't control my heart."

Inwardly I cringed. Getting with David was like signing up for another no-account man. What was it about me? Did I have a sign on my fucking forehead that said "now hiring no-account losers?"

Sherry understood my dilemma but she was as powerless to change it as I was.

chapter 13

t had been three months since I had seen or heard from David. Although it still hurt, I figured that all things happened for a reason. I was still getting harassing calls from Keith's family but I was coping with that as well.

David had left a uniform at my house and I washed and ironed it hoping he would come back for it. My body did not care what he did for a living or how many children he had. All I really cared about was how he made me feel.

I packed up his things along with a pair of shoes he had also left behind with a handwritten plea that he reconsider what he was doing. I took those items to his mother's old house and waited to hear from him.

Every time the phone rang, my heart skipped double time in anticipation. Meanwhile, life went on even though I hardly participated in it.

"Hello," I said when I snatched up the phone.

"We need to talk," Keith barked at me.

I was hardly in the mood to deal with his silly ass but had no plausible excuse to dish out at the moment.

"Hold on," I said as I went back to the car and carried in the rest of my groceries. It had been a long day and I just wanted to fix something quick for the kids and turn in.

"I'm back," I said. I had not seen or heard from Keith since his last call that threw my happy existence into turmoil.

"I wanna see my kids," he snapped angrily at me.

"And your point is," I fired back.

"I can't make it all the way over there. Why can't you bring them to me?" he asked. True he was living on the other side of Baltimore but it was only twenty minutes by car so I didn't understand the problem.

"No, why should I?" I declared. I had stopped allowing him to come visit the kids at my house since he had a tendency to stay all day. Once I hooked up with David, the mere idea of him lurking in the area turned my stomach. So, if he wanted to see his kids, I felt it only fair that he come pick them up and take them elsewhere for the visit. I suggested that he pick them up from Sherry's house since he was such "good friends" with Howard and he had not bothered to see them since.

"I don't have transportation at the moment," he mumbled. That statement just did not compute with me. Last I knew he was driving the 1979 Toyota Celica that I had purchased and there was nothing wrong with the car. Out of the goodness of my heart, I let him have that car when I packed his shit up in it.

"What the hell happened to the car I let you have?" I asked, fearing the worst. *Thank God, I didn't carry insurance on the car,* I thought.

"I had an accident. The steering wheel fell off when I was going around a corner. I ran into a tree."

"How the hell does the steering wheel just fall off? You know what, that doesn't even matter to me. I guess God was just paying you back for the parking tickets you got on my car!" I stated. He didn't have any response.

After I had put Keith out, I found out that he had over $400 in parking tickets on my car. Although the original ticket was only for $50, interest and late charges added up. When I went to get my new tags, I had to pay for his ticket and the fines.

"I still want to see my kids!" he exclaimed, ignoring the rest of my comments.

"I'm not bringing them all the way over there unless they can stay the weekend."

"Marie, I don't have space for overnight visitors. I'm renting one room!"

"And, is that my fault?" I asked, tired of being sympathetic to his plight. All of his troubles he had brought down on himself. I was tired of trying to fix his shit. "Let me know what you work out," I said and hung up. Throughout our marriage, I had been bending over backwards to help Keith. Thankfully, I was finally at a point where I really didn't give a shit what he did to make things right for him. My sole focus was my children and for once, myself.

The phone rang again and I assumed it was Keith calling back. I snatched it up without bothering to say hello.

"We need to talk," David said. My breath caught in my mouth and my chest started to ache.

"Hi," I said.

"I don't appreciate your dropping off my stuff like that," he angrily spat.

"Wait, hold up. What was I supposed to do with it," I responded, getting angry myself.

"I could have come and got it myself!" he stated. "You slung my shit on the porch like you were putting me out and I don't appreciate it."

"First of all, I didn't sling anything. I took them to the only address that I knew of. You cut us off at the knees, not me, and you didn't have the balls to tell me why!" I shouted. I didn't want to let him know about my conversation with Sherry.

"You made it quite clear how you feel about no-account niggers!" he said.

"And you took a conversation I had with you in my moment of pain regarding my stupid ass ex-husband out of context and used it against me. Yes, I'm bitter about that relationship but that was between him and me. I didn't bring him into our relationship; you did," I yelled back at the phone.

"I was just saving myself some trouble," he fired back. The conversation was not going anything like I had intended. I didn't want to argue with him; I wanted to wrap my arms and legs around him and lose myself in his warmth. But I was not going to beg. I had already done my share of begging with him. My letter to him was from the heart. I asked for a second chance to make things right even though I didn't do anything wrong to him.

"I'll talk to you later," he said. He hung up before I could interject anything else. Hot tears streamed down my face as my chest heaved. I thought I was past the hurt with him but I guess I wasn't. I sank down at the kitchen table and had a good old-fashioned bawl. I forgot about supper until Kevin came into the kitchen to find out what was for dinner.

I leaped up and began hurriedly putting up the groceries. I didn't feel like cooking so I called Pizza Hut and ordered a pizza for delivery. Kevin was so excited, he ran from the kitchen to let his sister know we were having weekend comfort food on a weekday.

Had I known that Kevin and Keira would get so excited by pizza in the middle of the week, I would have forgone the "pleasure/pain" of cooking every day and opted for a more regimented diet of pizza. The phone rang as I was dishing out slices. It was Keith. All the warm and fuzzy feelings I had disappeared.

Keith begrudgingly agreed to keep the children for the weekend. I told him that I would drop them off on my way home from work. After getting directions from him, I gave thought to what I was going to do with a free weekend.

Since it was Halloween, I went to a party shop to choose an outfit. I wished that my girlfriend Angie was home to party with me but I was determined to make the most of it. I had been in a rut over David and could think of no better way to forget a man than to replace him with another.

Before Angie moved to North Carolina, we always dressed up on Halloween and hit the clubs. One year we dressed up and she was wearing this beautiful cat suit with a long tail and furry sleeves, and her face was made up complete with moveable whiskers. I went as a she-devil, wearing a red body suit with plastic horns, a pitched fork and long red tail.

It was Angie's turn to drive and we were riding down the highway. She was smoking a joint and I had just said to her, "Gurl, if you drop that shit, you will go up in flames." Damn if she didn't drop the joint right between her legs! She jerked the steering wheel to the left and I tried to grab it back to the center of our lane. We were weaving back and forth from lane to lane until she could get it.

I didn't want to reach between her legs to grab it. She was dancing around so much I might have burned my damn self. Plus, I was laughing too hard. She didn't want to get a burn mark in her rented costume. She preferred to wreck the car and it was my car. Luckily, she found the joint before she took out a car or two. *Those were the days*, I thought.

I didn't find anything that I liked in the costume shops. My boss, Donna, had a most excellent suggestion. She suggested that I dress up as Tina Turner since I had the legs. Persuaded, I shopped for the shortest dress I could find that wasn't a tee shirt and a wig styled in the same fashion as Tina Turner. I found the dress in the last shop I went into and I was ready. I had fake nails and eyelashes and a pair of four-inch fuck-me heels. The dress was gold lame cut low in the front exposing my boobies, and it clung to my body like body paint.

Since I was going solo, I didn't want to go too far from home. I stopped by the neighborhood club but I was the only one dressed up and I doubted if anyone knew why I was dressed the way I was. I wanted to scream at them that it was Halloween for crying out loud. "Ignorant asses," I muttered to myself as I walked around the club. Frustrated, I was headed out the door when I met two guys coming into the club.

"Oh please, say it ain't so. Tell me you aren't leaving," the bold one said.

"It's dead in there," I replied. He turned to his friend, pointing at him for emphasis, and said, "Could we try to entertain you for a while? Maybe for a drink?" His friend shook his head in agreement and not having anything better to do, I agreed.

"My name is Malcolm and this is Dennis," said the bolder of the two as we grabbed the first available table.

"I didn't catch your name?" Malcolm said. Surprisingly, I detected a bit of attitude and raised my perfectly arched brows. He smiled so I dismissed the notion. After all, he was the one who had asked me to come back inside, not the other way around.

"It's Marie," I said. Malcolm began looking around the club as if already bored with my company.

"Tina Marie Turner?" Dennis said, smiling.

"You noticed," I responded with a grin of my own.

"I'd have to be blind and stupid not to," he said with a chuckle. "And I must say, you are wearing it well, Ms. Turner. At least I hope you are a Ms.," he said, looking at my hands for a ring. Malcolm bolted from the table as if his ass was on fire. Perplexed, I looked at Dennis for insight.

"You have to excuse my friend. He gets this way sometimes after a few drinks," he explained.

"Did I do something wrong? He did ask me to come back in, didn't he?" I said, totally confused.

"It's not you, trust me. What are you drinking?" he asked.

"Sex On The Beach," I boldly answered. His head jerked in surprise as he got up to go to the bar.

"Don't you go and disappear on me," he said before he turned away. He had a nice round ass and I could not help but admire it. Of the two men, Dennis was definitely better-looking. He was about 6'2", cocoa brown with nice broad shoulders. He also had these big suck-able lips and intense dark brown eyes. Although I had no intentions of walking on the kinky side with him that night, he still was a nice piece of eye candy.

He came back shortly with my drink, a glass of wine for himself and a beer. I raised my eyebrows at the third drink since I assumed Malcolm had left for greener pastures.

"He will be back," Dennis acknowledged when he saw the look on my face. I shrugged my shoulders and took a sip of my drink. I purposely let some of it slide along my lips and used my tongue to lick it up. I was flirting with this guy and he loved it. He knocked over his drink to prove it. I could not hold back the laughter.

"I'm sorry; it's the costume. I'm normally not this kind of woman," I said, holding back the snickers.

"Hey, I ain't mad," he said, mopping up the table and his pants at the same time. "People are going to think I came in my pants."

"You wasted your drink. Let me get you another." I got up from the table allowing him to get a good look at my phat behind. I didn't look back as I walked to the bar. I ordered him a glass of white Zinfandel and headed back to the table. He had removed the empty glass from the table and thanked me for the drink. I looked around the club; nobody was dancing and I really wanted to dance. I glanced at my watch trying to figure out just how much time I had left. I had spent a lot of money for my outfit and I wanted to be seen. Although I could wear the dress again, the wig was a one-night deal.

"You were right. It is dead in here," he said. "How about us going downtown and checking out a few of the clubs on the strip?"

"I would like to but I really don't want to be drinking and driving that far. I don't live far from here; that's why I chose this place," I told him.

"I'll drive. You can park your car and ride with me. I promise not to do anything to you that you don't want done," he said.

"Is that supposed to be reassuring?" I asked.

"Yeah. You are looking so fine and there is no one here to appreciate it. I promise you, scout's honor. If you agree to ride with me, I will bring you back in one piece. I further promise to step to the side if you find someone that you want to spend time with and still take you back to your car." He raised his fingers to his head and placed his right hand over his heart. I didn't know whether that was the scouts' pledge or not but he sounded so sincere that I agreed.

"What about your friend?" I asked.

"He'll be all right. I'll tell him where we are going. If he wants to go then he can come; if not, oh well. We didn't ride together or nothing like that," he said as he got up to search for his friend. He grabbed the beer as a peace offering I imagined.

My mother would knock the hell out of me if she saw me right now, I thought. It was so out of character for me and I blamed it on the season. Halloween always brought out the devil in me! I shook my head to get rid of the unpleasant thoughts that followed. Dennis came back before I could completely talk myself out of going. I really wanted to go out and dance and this place just was not happening.

He followed me out to my car and said he would follow me to my house. I drove there and parked right in front and got into his car. He had a sporty Toyota of some sort but since I was not all that up on cars, the make and model escaped me. He shook his head as I climbed in.

"What?" I said, prepared to get back out again.

"Nothing. I just can't believe that you were right around the corner and I didn't know it."

"What are you talking about?" I asked.

"I'll show you." He drove around the corner to the next block. He lived on the very next street with the same house address as mine. "Fate," he said while shaking his head. I did not know what to make of the information. He lived on the same street as David on different blocks. I doubted they were friends 'cause Dennis was at least five years his senior.

During the drive, Dennis told me that he was studying to be a psychoanalyst. He was most interested in phobias. He worked as an intake intern at Rosewood Mental Hospital and would complete school in the fall. I was impressed but didn't quite believe his story. I was from the old "show me" school plus, I was not interested in him 'cause of his "profession." I liked him 'cause he looked nice and knew how to treat a lady. He opened all the doors and grabbed my chair when I was sitting down. Those were the types of things that got my attention on the upsweep.

He told me that he was rebounding from a seven-year relationship with a woman with two kids. He admitted that he still loved her but that it was over. I confided in him about my marriage and the break-up. I did not tell him about my own case of rebounding from David. That was too much information.

Our first stop was Odell's. It had a long line out front but Dennis knew the bouncer. We walked to the front of the line and went inside. The place was jumping. I used to have the hook-up with the old bouncer at that club but that was before I had gotten married. Everywhere I looked, there were people in costume. I felt more relaxed with the other partygoers.

My mother always frowned on celebrating Halloween. She said it was the devil's night to play. She might have been right 'cause I sure felt devilish. I immediately pulled Dennis onto the dance floor. I thought I was going to show him some of my moves but he was time enough for me. We made a good couple dancing to the popular beats.

After a few records of non-stop dancing, the DJ slowed down the pace. I wanted to leave the floor for a cool drink but Dennis had other plans. He snatched me into his arms and molded his body against mine. I could feel his nature rising. I instantly tensed up but his body was feeling so good, I began to relax. His body felt good but different. Although David and I had not been together long, I knew every nuance of his body and this one was different. It was not unpleasant, just different. When the record ended, I quickly stepped back. I realized the last time I had slow danced with a man, I wound up in bed with him and it did not turn out so well. I didn't want to make the same mistake with Dennis.

We agreed to leave Odell's and go down the street to Gatsby, another club where he also had a hook-up. It catered to a more mature and sophisticated crowd. They had more places you could go where you could actually talk to your date without screaming at them. It also served alcohol and we both ordered a drink. I ordered a rum and Coke and Dennis stuck with the wine. I was glad since he was driving.

As we sat at the table, Dennis grabbed my right hand. "This mole, have you always had it?" he asked, referring to a one-eighth inch mole on my right hand. It was a flat mole and I didn't pay much attention to it. It was just something that I'd always had.

"Ever since I can remember," I said, examining my hand.

"Hmmm," he said with no further explanation. Intrigued, I asked him why.

"Oh nothing." He glanced at his watch and we both realized that we had been out for quite a while. It was approaching 3:00 a.m.

"What time do you turn into a pumpkin?" he asked with a smile.

I glanced at my watch as well and told him that I should be heading home. He paid our tab and we left. Our conversation on the way home was about the other people that were in the club and the costumes they wore. He made me laugh and I liked it. All too soon, we pulled in front of my house.

"See, I promised to get you back home safely," he claimed.

"Thank you," I said. "I really had a nice time." I turned to get out of the car. He didn't ask for my number and I damn sure was not going to throw it at him.

"Okay, can I make another promise?" he asked.

"Uh, what is it?" I said, suddenly feeling nervous after all the shit I had willingly done.

"Can I come in for a while? You're not sleepy, are you?"

I thought about it for a moment and had to admit to myself that I wasn't sleepy nor did I relish the thought of going into an empty home. It had been a long time since any house I was living in was empty for more than two seconds.

"Scouts' honor?" I asked.

"Scouts' honor," he replied with the salute again. I opened the door and turned on the lights in the living room. I turned on the jazz station and fixed him another glass of wine. I also poured a glass for myself.

Once again, he grabbed my hand and studied my mole. At this point, I was scared. He was so intent in his scrutiny that I felt there was something wrong with me. I had heard about moles being cancerous.

"What?" I cried, drawing back my hand. "Why do you keep looking at my mole?" He offered his own right hand and he had a perfectly shaped mole in the exact same place as mine. We held up our hands to see if they were the same size and it appeared they were replicas.

Any ideas that I had about not having sex with him went straight out the window. We tore off each other's clothes and headed upstairs to the bedroom. He was not as physically endowed as David but he was more than adequate and still put poor Keith to shame. Where he was lacking in David's girth, he more than made up for it in initiative. We fucked like rabbits.

Exhausted, we lay in each other's arms basking in the warm afterglow of sex. He again raised my hand to his face. At the time I thought he was going to kiss my mole. Instead, he turned his head, raised his own hand and licked off the drawing he'd made on his hand.

Son of a fucking bitch, I thought. This nigga just played me! I wanted to get mad and all indignant but I had to look at myself. Mole or not, in my mind I had already made up my mind to screw him that night. I had been working my way up to it all night and if he used the subterfuge of a mole as an excuse to get it, I only had played myself.

So after I calmed down the question was, what now? Did he toss me aside like a used rag? Did I pretend to be tricked and wounded? Or, did we step off from there and see what happened?

"So what happened to your promise?" I asked.

"Uh, I kept my promise. I didn't do anything to you that you didn't want me to," he replied. He had me there. Caught up in the moment, I wanted each and every inch of it. Afterward, I was feeling pangs of regret but I refused to beat up on myself. Sure I was on the wild side since Keith and I had broken up, but I was finding out what sex was all about. No longer was it a burden or curse; the shit was fun. For the moment, David was pushed out of my brain and I only concentrated on Dennis as we started round two.

chapter 14

I arrived at work breathless and in the nick of time. That's what I got for staying up half the night fucking. But it was well worth it. It was just what I needed to get out of the blue funk I was in over David. Around 10:00, I got word from the receptionist that there was a delivery for me. I strolled to the front lobby and picked up a beautiful bouquet of yellow roses.

"Damn girl," Carla said. "You did somebody right."

"Yeah, I guess I did," I answered, taking my bouquet and hurrying back to my office to read the card. I could tell Carla was pissed that I didn't offer to share the card but she was the biggest gossip in the office. Nine times out of ten, she had already read the card anyway. I didn't want my business spreading through the building like that.

The card said, "You can dance on my face anytime you want!" It was unsigned but I was sure it was from Dennis. We were supposed to go to lunch that day. I was interrupted from my reenactment by the shrill ring of the phone.

"Marie Morgan, may I help you?" I answered in my most professional tone of voice.

"May I speak with Marie Morgan," an authoritative voice replied. *Duh, did they not just hear me introduce myself,* I thought.

"You are speaking with her," I responded, still trying to be a professional.

"This is Lieutenant Jones from the Federal Bureau of Investigation. May I speak with you about a matter of utmost secrecy?"

"Yes, hold on for a minute." I got up from my desk and went to close my door.

My heart was beating a mile a minute. I had no idea why someone from the FBI would be calling me.

"I'm back," I said.

"Ms. Morgan, you were seen in the company of a suspected rapist yesterday evening."

"Excuse me?" Surely I did not hear him correctly.

"Yes, Ms. Morgan. You were seen with Dennis Edwards at Club Gatsby last night and he is the number one suspect we have in several rape cases in the Baltimore, Washington, D.C. area."

I was truly outdone. I could've understood it if they were talking about Dennis' friend whose name I had forgotten, but Dennis, no fucking way! Hell, I gave my shit to him on a silver platter.

"Ms. Morgan, we need your cooperation. Are you planning to see him again?"

"We were supposed to go to lunch but I'm not going now!" I stuttered.

"NO!" He shouted back at me. "The suspect must not know that we are on to him. You need to keep your date."

"You want me to become a target or potential victim?" I inquired, still stunned and pretending to myself that I hadn't already slept with him. Hell, for all I knew, the FBI had followed us home last night and knew that he had spent the night.

"You will be closely guarded. Just act natural," he said as if his request was the most normal thing in the world.

"Act normal!" I screeched as if he were talking in a foreign fucking language. "I'm not the type. I'll panic and he will know the gig is up. Hell, I'm so nervous now I can barely hold the phone." I needed a cigarette so badly I was shaking, but I worked in a smoke-free environment. "Look, I'm not the one to help you Mr. Whatever the fuck your name is."

"Marie, it's me," Dennis said, trying to hold back his laughter.

"Look, Mr. FBI man, I got kids. I can't be putting my life in danger…"

"Calm down, baby. It's me!" Dennis said again. I rambled for a full two minutes more before I realized what he was saying. He got me again. Luckily, I like practical jokers. That appealed to me and I was already trying to figure out how I was going to get him back.

"Did you get the roses?" he asked sweetly as if he did not just catch me in the biggest joke ever.

"You motherfucker!" I exclaimed. I was upset but I could not really get mad at a brother who fucked me like he did last night. Shit, I wasn't stupid.

That was the start of many star-filled days and nights. I thought I had died and gone to heaven. I had never had a man treat me like Dennis. He took me to movies, plays, romantic walks along the Inner Harbor, concerts at the pier, bicycle rides through the park. He valued my opinion about everything regarding his career choices and his life. He was the first man to actually listen to everything that I had to say and pay attention. I thought it was a match made in heaven. I totally understood when he had to study and was ready to play when he was available. Life was good.

Although I still had flashbacks of the hot sex I used to have with David, I was content with my lot in life. Dennis did not play with the children like David but they didn't seem to mind his presence. In hindsight, we mostly got together when I had a baby-sitter. Despite this fact, I fell in love. I loved the romantic dinners and weekend getaways. We even went roller-skating and I busted my ass enough to prove it. We were sitting in the bathtub one night when he told me he loved me. I had been fighting those words for months. They scared me 'cause they put a label on our bliss.

"I can see us together, as family," he said while nibbling on my toes. "Our children will be so beautiful; I want at least two."

A brisk breeze blew my way like someone had turned on the cold water in our tepid bath. Was he thinking about more kids? I don't think so! Snatching my toe from his mouth, I drew my knees up to my chest. "I can't have any more kids and furthermore, I don't want any more." He did not respond immediately. In fact he was pretty much silent for the rest of the night. Normally, we would have left the tub and made passionate love for the rest of the night. I was concerned but I thought he would get over it.

He didn't. He called me the next day and told me our relationship held too many paradoxes for him. His past relationship was with a woman who didn't want any more kids; she had two (boy and girl) and he wanted to take a break from us. What was I to say? He had made his decision. Once again, a man put me on the back burner. Hell, I was used to that.

Because our relationship was so special, I didn't believe him when he told me that we should start dating other people. In fact, I didn't even react to the women that he told me he was meeting while we were on break. I just sat back and took it until he told me about the Amazon Queen. She was about 6'2", 185 pounds and was very straightforward. She had no kids and was ready to make Dennis her man. Then, I got pissed. I began to say yes to some of the men who approached me. One guy in particular set my shoes on fire. He was from Jamaica and he was fucking gorgeous. Jamal was lightskinned with dreads; he had light brown eyes and a body that would stop a clock.

I agreed to meet him one night at Fargo's. Dennis called as I was getting dressed.

"Hey, what's going on?" he said.

"I am getting ready for a date," I replied. This was the first date that I had been on since Dennis had called it quits.

"Oh yeah, where are you going?"

"Fargo's," I said with a tightening in my chest. I felt like I was betraying him even though he had been actively dating for the last couple of months.

"No kidding. I'm going there tonight as well. You want to ride with me or is your date picking you up?"

"I'm meeting him there. Are you sure you want to do this? Are you meeting the Amazon Queen?" I asked, not really wanting to know the answer.

"Nope. I'm hanging solo tonight but I could use the company on the drive." I thought about it for a minute and agreed. Since I hated to drive, it would be perfect. If Jamal didn't work out, Dennis could bring me back home. Secretly I hoped that Dennis would come back to his senses once he saw me with someone else.

We arrived at the club and I walked around trying to spot Jamal. When I didn't see him, I danced a few records with Dennis. He was feeling confident that my date had stood me up. But his elation stopped when I leaned into him and said, "It's him. Jamal is here."

"Where?" he said, looking around the club. I pointed Jamal out as he walked over towards us.

"Jamal, Dennis. Dennis, Jamal."

"Hey, man, what's up," Dennis said. Jamal kissed me on the cheek and asked me to dance. I smiled at Dennis and moved out on the dance floor with my new beau. Dennis didn't think I had a date. On the inside I smiled. Every time I looked over at Dennis I could tell that he didn't like this new turn of events, but he had made the decision, not me. I was just playing by his rules.

When we made our way back to the table, Dennis said, "Is he going to take you home 'cause I need to leave." We had only been there an hour so I did not see the urgency I heard in his voice.

"Jamal, I came with Dennis. Will you take me home or do I need to leave now?"

"I'll take you home, beautiful; no worries, mon." I turned to Dennis and shrugged my shoulders.

"I guess I'm riding with him," I said.

"Oh, okay, I'll see you later. Nice meeting you, man," he said and left the club. He looked back once and I could see the pain on his face but what was I supposed to do? The whole thing was his idea. Our relationship was truly over at that point. Before, even though we were not sleeping together, he called at least three times a week. After that night, I heard nothing from him unless I called him. Go figure.

Jamal distracted me for a minute but he was only looking for a fuck buddy. I was after the long haul and he did not fit the bill. I never told Dennis since it was really none of his business. I let him think that we were an item and he treated me with kid gloves after meeting Jamal. Dennis' whole attitude changed towards me. He stopped making his weekly calls and we never just hung out anymore. I was so absorbed in concentration that I almost missed the phone ringing.

"Marie, it's Mom. You need to come right away."

"Mom, what's wrong? You are scaring me! What's wrong?" I screamed into the phone.

"It's your father. He is in the hospital. Hurry!" She hung up the phone.

I grabbed the Yellow Pages and immediately started dialing the airport. The first flight that I could get was at 8:00 in the morning. I packed enough clothes for us for a week and made our flight.

Dad was dead by the time I got to the hospital. They had just announced his death to my mother as we were running down the hall. I could hear my mother's wail long before we approached the family waiting room.

"Sweet Jesus no!" I screamed as I rounded the corner. Surely my father could not have been that seriously ill—the man had never been really sick in his life. Mom had collapsed on the floor. The doctor attempted to collect her and I yelled out, "Don't touch her!" I dropped to my knees and cradled my mother in my arms. I wanted to tell her everything would be okay but that lie would not escape my lips.

"Mom, I'm here now," I said as the children crowded around us on the floor.

"He's gone, baby," she said. I looked around the room wondering what mom was talking about. Surely she could not be talking about my dad. Not him—he was too ornery to die. I looked her straight in the eye and I knew beyond a shadow of a doubt that Daddy was dead. I was devastated.

We stumbled through the funeral in a daze of hurt and pain. I think I helped my mother but I could not be sure. My children were the most affected because I was emotionally unavailable to them. My mother's friend approached me about a job and I agreed to interview for it before I left. I did it to go through the motions, not 'cause I seriously considered the job. I did it 'cause I thought it was the right thing to do. I thought I did it to please my mother but had no intentions of actually taking it, especially when they told me they could not meet my salary requirements.

I was shocked when I got home and heard the message on my answering machine that they wanted me to come back for the job. So, there it was; my big decision was on the table. I had to weigh what I had in Baltimore, what I stood to lose and what I stood to gain. After looking around, I realized that there was really nothing in Baltimore to hold me. Mom needed me and to be honest, I needed her. I was Atlanta bound. I accepted the job offer and told them I would be there in two weeks.

I went back to work and gave my notice. I had been with the same law firm for over ten years and my notice came with mixed reactions. My immediate boss, Paula, got pissed and would not talk to me. I tried to explain why I was leaving but she was not hearing me. I finally said, "Damn, Donna, I'm leaving the fucking state, not you!" She relented.

I had a lot to do to sever my ties with Baltimore. I started packing and making moving arrangements. I could not fly back to Atlanta with all my stuff and I had no intentions of leaving them behind. My stuff may not have been quality but it was still mine. I started looking into renting a truck. I got prices on different truck lines and found Ryder to be the cheapest, but the only problem was I could not drive a damn truck.

David learned of my Dad's death from Sherry and we had been speaking on a fairly regular basis since I had gotten back. Although we had not resumed a physical relationship, he was supportive. He called me the night I finally made my decision.

"The kids and I are moving to Atlanta," I said during the lull in conversation. He didn't say anything and I peeped at the phone to make sure we were still connected. Part of me wanted him to cry out, "Baby, don't go," but the other part of me knew that was not going to happen.

"Oh yeah, when?" he asked.

"I was offered a job and since there is nothing physically holding me here, I accepted. I start in two weeks." I did not mean that as a personal dig at him; I was just being honest.

"Dag, girl, you fly down there and come back and now you're moving. You sure do keep a brother hoping," he said.

"Hoping," I asked, not understanding where he was coming from. I started to get mad but quickly realized there was no point. "Yeah, I'm going to get rid of the stuff I don't want to take and rent a truck to carry the rest." He did not bite. He knew good and well that I couldn't drive a truck. This would have been his opportunity to step forward and volunteer to help me. I thought that if he had cared about me as much as I cared about him, he would have done just that. Instead, he just let the conversation die.

"Look, I have a gazillion things that I need to do. I will talk with you later," I said, 'cause staying on the phone was just too painful.

"Oh, okay then; I'll catch you later."

I hung up the phone with tears streaming down my face. He had hurt me much more than he had loved me. Although I was still traumatized by the loss of my dad, my tearful episode had David's name written all over it. I wiped my tears and began the long task of separating the junk from the treasure.

I was given a reprieve when the phone rang again about an half-hour later.

"Hello," I said, still hoping that David was coming around.

"Hey, baby girl," Dennis quietly said into the phone. I had left a message on his service that I was back in town but had not spoken with him yet. I started to cry again at the sentiment in his voice. Dennis had also lost his father so he knew what I was going through. I loudly broke down into the phone and he said, "I'm on my way!" He was there before I could wash my face and pull back my wayward hair.

When I opened the door, he just rushed me with this massive hug. I clung to his large frame and cried all the tears of anguish that I thought I had left in Atlanta.

"I didn't get to say goodbye," I wailed. "Momma said he just fell over to his side and she called 9-1-1. She never got to say I love you or nothing."

"Hush, baby girl. I know you are hurting. Just let it out," he said.

It felt good to be in Dennis' arms. He rubbed my face and hair at the same time while wiping away the tears that still flowed from my eyes. He kissed each eyelid and the tears stopped for the moment.

"What were you doing, boo?" he gently asked me.

"Packing," I said between sniffles. I was reluctant to step away from him but he pushed me.

"Packing, for what?" he inquired.

"I'm moving to Atlanta to be near my mother," I said. I did not need to say any more to him about that since he had done the same when his own father passed.

"When are you leaving and when were you going to tell me?"

"I just decided tonight. Dennis, she needs me and to be honest, I need her," I said with more tears flowing. He followed me upstairs to my bedroom where I began my packing.

"How are you getting there?" he asked when he looked around my room. "By hurricane?"

"You still got jokes," I said, attempting to smile. "There is a method to this madness. This pile is trash, this pile is possible and this pile is going with me," I said, pointing to the largest pile of them all.

"How are you getting there?" he asked again.

"I need to rent a truck but I don't know how to drive one," I answered, not expecting him to say anything else about the matter.

"When are you leaving?"

"I got a job there. Did I tell you that? I start in two weeks so I have got to get going."

"Damn, baby girl, you are moving fast! Are you sure about this?"

I didn't want to go into the "there is no one to keep me in Baltimore speech" so I simply said, "Yeah."

"I have some vacation time coming. I could drive the truck for you and fly back," he said.

"You would do that for me?" I asked stunned.

I dropped to my knees in the pile of clothes. His offer was so unexpected that I didn't know what to say. Instead of giving way to tears, I said, "You trying to get rid of me?" I chuckled uneasily.

"You need to go, right?"

"Yes, I do," I replied.

"I want to see Atlanta anyway. Once you get settled, can I count on you for a place to crash?"

"And you know this!" I cried. *God has a way of working things out when you don't know what to do.* I stopped packing and Dennis and I worked out the plans. Forever the gentlemen, he wanted to split the cost of gas for the truck. I volunteered to pay for his plane ticket back to Baltimore, but he said I should consider it his going-away present.

For the next week I worked, took care of the kids and packed. I had no time to dwell on the bad things or unfinished things that I had in Baltimore. I spent countless hours on the phone with my mother encouraging her to go on day by day. Dennis and I had planned to leave Thursday night, arriving in Atlanta by Friday and spending the rest of the weekend partying. He would fly back to Baltimore on Monday afternoon.

David came by on the last Monday night that I would spend in Baltimore. He came walking up the alley like there was nothing wrong. I was in the kitchen cooking dinner when I heard the kids in the back yard screaming and laughing it up. I glanced out the window and saw David playing with the kids. It was a touching scene. They had missed him almost as much as I had. I moved away from the window and allowed them to have their time.

I had mixed emotions about his dropping by. On one hand, I felt I needed to see him before I left, but on the other hand, I was pissed as shit that he had wasted the precious time we had left. He came to the back door about twenty minutes later. He knocked and I called out to him from the dining room that it was okay to come in. I had already turned the stove off and was in the dining room putting the finishing touches on the last few boxes in that room.

"Damn, I guess you are really doing this," he softly said.

"Hello, stranger," I said over my shoulder, barely looking at his face as I spoke. He grunted and looked around, I guess for a place to sit. Finding no available chair, he said, "Do you need any help?"

"No, not really, the hardest part is done. I'm just doing a little bit before I call them in for supper. Do you want to have dinner with us?"

"Uh, no, I just stopped by to see how you were doing?" I put down the tablecloth that I was folding and walked past him to go back to the kitchen. I felt myself get mad and I wanted to put some distance between us.

"What? You can't stop a minute to talk to a brother," he said after a few minutes of silence. I turned and glared at him.

"Hell, I ain't the one that has been a stranger, my brother!" I snapped.

"I deserved that," he said. He started walking towards me and I froze. I longed for him to touch me but then again I didn't want it. It took me a long time to get the yearning for him out of my system. It was too late in the game to rehash that shit.

"Please don't," I said, raising my arms to ward him off. Instantly, he was angry as if he had earned the right to be mad.

"Oh, it's like that. Your ass is going to leave a brother, and now you don't want to be touched?" His voice was rising as he spoke.

"Don't you even think about getting no attitude with me. You are the one that quit on us! I'm not some fucking puzzle that you can pick up any time you feel like it and expect all the pieces to still fit. Shit, I was there while you were playing dead." His head snapped back with each accusation as I put my hands on my hips and flipped my neck.

"And then, when you had a fucking chance to spend some time with me before I left, your ass goes AWOL again! So please, 'my brother,' spare me this bull-shit!" He raised his arms in defeat and backed up a few feet.

"Can we just sit down and talk like two grown-ups?" he asked, looking for a clear place to park his rump.

"Who are you going to get to stand in for you?" I asked.

"Marie, damn it, I said I deserved all this and more but I need to talk to you now. Can you please give me a moment with no more of your sarcasm?"

I was so mad I could fire-spit! I realized that arguing would not change a damn thing that had transpired between us. I went into the living room and moved a few boxes to the floor. I sat down and he sat next to me. Close but not close enough to rub legs or anything.

"I've been an ass," he said.

"That's the understatement of the year," I quipped.

"Are you going to let me finish or what?" he said. He took my silence to mean yes and continued.

"There are a few things that I need to explain to you about me. Number one is my past relationship with my son's mother. It was the most important relationship in my life. We had it all for a minute. I had a great job and I took pride in the fact that I was the breadwinner. When she got pregnant, she quit work. I held on to everything and I even liked having her home but the pressure got to me. After the baby was born, I took my frustration out on my boss and got fired! I thought she loved me enough to stand by me while I got things together but she didn't. She left me so quick and cut off all ties I had with my son. She called me a failure." He looked into my eyes to see if I was still paying attention. I didn't comment so he continued.

"I vowed to never let my feelings get so involved that I would put myself in that position to feel so much about anyone other than my son and myself again. Then you come along. All of a sudden I want to do for you and your kids and I got lost all over again. When you were speaking about your ex, it brought back all my old pain. I realized that I would never make as much money as you do at my present job and that I would always be lacking in that department unless I got my job back. I could not stand to see the same disappointment on your face so I ran. Can you understand that?" he asked.

"We have been through some of this before, and at that time, I forced myself to understand where you were coming from. I thought we were past that until now. But since you want to talk about old feelings and hurt, it's my fucking turn. I fell in love with you and you dumped me. Not because of anything that I did to you. You dumped me 'cause of an argument I had with my ex-husband. You did not give me a chance to explain the hell I went through. You tried and convicted me based on your past! Let me tell you something; I never asked you for a thing. Hell, I never asked my husband for a thing but in the end I got fucked!" David grabbed me and kissed me, killing all further arguments. I felt like I had just come home after a long absence.

"May I come back after the kids have gone to sleep?" David asked when we stopped to catch our breath. I had bittersweet tears on my face as I nodded yes. We had four days left. I wanted to make the best of them. I hated that I gave in so easily but I needed that man.

chapter 15

David came back that night around 9:00 p.m. I was anxious and didn't know what to expect of the encounter. Part of me wanted to throw on a sexy nightgown but I didn't want to be rejected again. He swooped me in his arms as soon as the door closed and carried me up the stairs.

Damn, I should have put on the sexy underwear instead of the comfortable ones that I wore to work, I thought. I had already cleared the bed and we fell into it making such hot love that we both were left panting for more. When we were spent, we started talking again.

"Are you still driving to Atlanta?" he asked. Apprehension knotted my stomach.

"Yeah, we leave on Thursday." I didn't know where this conversation was going so I started applying small kisses to his upper body. I didn't want to talk about my imminent departure. I just wanted to get my fill of him. His dick responded by getting rock hard again.

"Can I drive you to Atlanta?" he asked quietly. I stiffened in his arms. He blind-sided me since I didn't expect to go back there with him. Too many plans had been made to back out now. Dennis already had his return ticket. I would not do that to him. I pushed away from David's luscious chest so I could look him in the eye.

"I have already asked someone else to drive down with me. They are going to drive me down and fly back," I said.

"That the same nigger you been hanging out with in the clubs and shit?" David said with a snarl.

"He is a friend of mine, plain and simple."

David huffed and acted like he was getting ready to get upset but he deflated himself. "If he was more than a friend, I would only have myself to blame, right?" he admitted.

"Yeah. Hell, I would have never met him if you hadn't dumped me!" I cried.

He pulled me back to him and rested my head on his shoulders.

"Can I visit you in Atlanta?" he whispered and my heart soared. I wanted to say, *pack your bags and ride in my suitcase.* The only thing that stopped me was the fact that I would be living with my mother until I got myself established.

"Anytime you want once I get set up. I will be staying with my mother until I get up enough money to make my move, but housing is cheaper there so it won't be long," I said.

"Two more questions before we go to sleep. Do you love me? Do you love him?"

I could answer the first question without hesitation.

"Yes, I love you and I probably always will." I did not immediately answer the second question so he nudged me.

"I love him, too, but it's in a different way that I can easily describe. You excite my mind, body and soul. You make me feel young. I love looking at you and running my hands along your body like this," I said as I trailed my fingers along his neck, down his legs to his groin. I wanted to change the subject but he pushed my hand away from his balls.

"And him? What is his name again?"

"Dennis. He made me feel attractive and viable after the dismal failure of my marriage and the failure of our short relationship. He came at a time when I needed him and he raised my self-esteem and made me laugh."

"And?"

"It didn't work, he wanted kids and I was through in that department, so we just agreed to be friends." I really did not want to discuss yet another painful episode of my life that night. David sensed that and allowed the conversation to lapse. We held each other for most of the night or until our limbs grew numb. I didn't ask him anything else about us and he didn't offer.

Sherry threw a going-away cookout for us that Wednesday. Before the party, David and his three brothers helped Dennis load the truck that was parked in front of my house.

I invited Dennis to come to the cookout and he accepted. Luckily, Howard did not invite Keith. I had not seen Keith since we got back from Atlanta. The last time I spoke with him, we fought about my taking the children out of state. David and Dennis greeted each other with handshakes and soft pats on the back. I was a little uncomfortable with the fact that David had to touch me every time he passed me, and I think it bothered Dennis, too, but he didn't comment. He left after an hour but that could have been attributed to the fact that he didn't know anyone at the party but the kids and me.

The whole neighborhood turned out and we partied until 2:00 a.m. We had steamed crabs, shrimp, crab cakes, ribs, hamburgers, steak and hot dogs. I was so nervous, I could not eat but that didn't stop the other partygoers! There was a card game going at every table and the alcohol was flowing. Sherry got drunk and made a farewell speech to me. She started crying and some of the other people that I knew well also emptied their eyes. We all cried for the loss of my father and my mother's grief. I left the party in an emotional state.

David asked if he could spend the night and I was so glad that he did. Ever since his visit on Monday, we had been spending every possible moment together with the exception of each of us working. We fell in bed after making love in every conceivable position known to man. At 6:00 a.m. the alarm rang and marked the end of our blissfulness. Dennis would be there at 7:00 so I got up and showered. I woke the kids to get them dressed as well. I waited until 6:30 to wake David up. He quickly took a shower and got dressed. We took apart my bed and stacked the mattresses against the wall. We also took apart the children's beds. I could not look David in the face as I opened the door for Dennis. They loaded our love nest into the back of the truck with the rest of our belongings. I made a final walk-through of the house and was ready to leave.

I cried as I hugged David.

"I'll call you when we get there. You will write, won't you?" I asked, steadily wiping away my tears.

"I'm not much of a writer but I will keep in contact," he promised.

Dennis was quiet the whole time we said our goodbyes.

"Nice meeting you, man. Ya'll drive carefully," David said as Dennis got into the truck. "Hit me up when you get back!"

"Thanks for your help," Dennis said as he buckled up his seatbelt. As we drove off the street that I had lived on since I was in the fourth grade, my floodgates opened. I didn't know I had any tears left, but you could not tell it by the amount of tissues I went through.

I cried for everything I knew, didn't know and couldn't have known. Dennis let me cry until we got to West Virginia, which was more than an hour.

"You are going to have to shut the hell up with all that damn crying. When we stop at the next rest area, they might haul my ass off to jail for physical abuse! Look in the mirror!" he shouted to me over the road noises that vibrated through the truck.

Dennis was right—I looked like hell. I scared my own self when I looked in the mirror over the visor. I used some wet wipes to clean my face and applied a little makeup to my face. It did not disguise the fact that I had been crying but I did not look quite as scary.

Outwardly, I tried to pull myself together. The kids woke up from a power nap that did not really count as a real nap, complaining of hunger. My heart, however, was still sick. I didn't want to piss off Dennis with any further tears and since I had no clue how to drive a truck I suffered in silence.

"Thank you," I whispered loud enough for him to hear. "I know that whole scene was hard for you to witness and I appreciate all that you are doing for me. I know, if it were me, I would not have been able to handle seeing you with another woman." He chuckled and it broke the ice that had formed in the cab of the truck.

"You ain't lying. You would have freaked the hell out. Remember that night we were in the club and this woman asked me to dance? You pulled a Sybil on my ass and I thought I was going to have to dial 9-1-1," he said, cracking up with laughter. I remembered that night and he was right.

"She was lucky that you had sense enough to say no," I declared. "Plus, it was not that serious," I said, trying to save face but that was all a front. I was pissed that night 'cause this heifer came up to Dennis and asked him to dance even though we were standing together.

"Oh it was serious all right," he said. "She looked over at you and asked if you minded and you just about came unglued. I was waiting for you to snatch off your earrings and take off your heels," he said, laughing.

"I only did that 'cause I didn't like her looks," I stated. "She looked like she was about to eat you for supper!"

"And...I like to be eaten!" he promptly responded.

"That bitch would have chewed and swallowed!"

Dennis sat up straight in his bucket seat and grimaced. "You did not even have to say that part," he said, laughing to ease the tension. He glanced over at me and said "Girl, you still look like hell. You need to do something with your face before we make a pit stop. Put some ice on your eyes to make the swelling go down. I sure don't want any trouble from these country bumpkins thinking I'm responsible for your tore-up face!"

My eyes were bright red and closed to mere slitters. My hair was all over my head and I had crust coming from both my eyes, nose and around my lips. Even though I had just wiped my face, it was still nasty.

"Give me a kiss," I said, attempting to move closer to plant a wet one on him. He swerved the truck trying to avoid my lips.

"Girl, stop playing! I almost killed us all." I grabbed another Wet One from the bag in the back seat and carefully cleaned my face and reapplied my makeup. I combed my hair in some semblance of order and instantly felt better.

"Now, you almost look like the woman I know and love," he said when he again glanced my way. I was still incredibly sad but I refused to think about that for the moment.

When we crossed the North Carolina state line we stopped for breakfast. I called my mother and told her where we were. I also slipped in a call to David but he was not at home. I let David keep the keys to my house but the phone had been turned off this morning. He was going to clean it up so that my neighbor could list it for sale. I left behind a lot of trash, and he agreed to haul it away.

On the back end, David was going to be a big help. He agreed to paint the inside of the house. Mom said she would pay him for his services but our plan was that he would use that IOU to get round-trip tickets to Atlanta for him. His goal was to move to Atlanta as soon as possible. Although he never made it clear whether he was coming 'cause of me or not, I was just glad that he was coming.

The rest of the trip was uneventful but long and we arrived in Atlanta about dinnertime. I tried to be good company and keep Dennis alert but my eyes were burning so badly, I could not keep them open. When I awoke, we were crossing the Georgia state line. Immediately, I felt bad about not helping but I could not do anything about it at that moment.

"Sorry," I said as I stretched and yawned. I looked in the back of the truck and the children were all sprawled out in various stages of sleep.

"Did they sleep like I did?" I asked.

"Hardly. They just fell out about ten minutes ago. I didn't realize that Keira could talk that much. That child liked to have talked me into a coma. I kept hoping you would wake up to give me a reprieve. She talked to me until she became delirious. You didn't feel her crawl all up in your arms?" he asked.

"She was up here?" I asked, totally confused.

"Yeah, pulling your hair, picking your nose and everything. You were out like a light!" he said, laughing.

"Damn, I don't remember anything past breakfast. See that exit sign coming up; that is the one we should be taking."

"Marie, I got this. Just let me handle it." He moved onto the exit ramp and I sat up taller in my seat. I was nervous again. We stopped at the storage unit, unloaded the truck, disconnected my car and drove to Mom's.

We piled out of the car grabbing suitcases and Dennis sped out of the subdivision in search of a motel. He didn't want to stay at my mom's house and I honestly didn't want him to. Mom would've killed him with questions and innuendos! I didn't want to explain my relationships with either Dennis or David so I thought that was the best way out of it.

Dennis came back at 10:30 and we drove downtown to find the nightlife.

"You rushed me in and out so fast, I didn't even get a chance to talk to your mother," Dennis complained.

"She's been wearing her Inspector Gadget hat all day. If we didn't make a break for it, she would have been drilling you for the next few hours about your intentions," I said with a smile.

"I liked her; she seems sweet," he said.

"She is until you cross her and then she becomes a mad pit bull! Do you know where we are going?" I asked.

"I figured if we head downtown, we could look for crowds of black people and follow them."

I tried to pay attention to my new environment but I was still having trouble concentrating. Although I was not exactly lonely with Dennis beside me, I could not help but speculate on how I would feel on Monday when I started my new job.

We stopped the first black couple we met when we got downtown.

"Excuse me, where do black people go to have fun?" Dennis asked.

"Church," said the lady dressed in a stiff blue dress.

"Oh okay, thanks," Dennis said.

"Let me pick the next person," I said. "That woman was a prude. I could tell that by her tight ass shoes."

"You could tell all that by her shoes?" Dennis asked in disbelief.

"Sure, no woman that wore shoes like that could possibly know anything about getting down! Her feet would hurt too much to let it all hang out."

We drove for a few more blocks before we came upon three guys walking in suits. Dennis pulled over close to the curb and I let down my window. In my best come-get-me voice, I said, "Hi, we're new to Atlanta and wanted to know where the hot spots are."

"Church," was the joint response of all three of the guys nodding their heads in unison. They pointed to a building on the corner and asked us to come.

Dennis took one look at me as we pulled away from the curb and said, "You are going to die down here!" He was joking when he said it but I realized there were some major elements of truth in it. Although I believed in God, I was not a devoted Christian. I could not remember the last time that I got up in time to go to church or the last time that I considered church fun.

There was a time when I was a teenager when all we did was hang out at the church but those days were long gone. I had found myself stuck in a heavy Bible-toting Belt unsure of my future. It was going to take some major adjusting to.

Eventually, we found a club and had a good time. The music was more old school than hip-hop and the crowd seemed to prefer more line dancing than doing their own thing but I felt I could adjust in time.

Unfortunately for me, I drank too much and Dennis had to help me inside the house. Luckily, Mom was not waiting up. For better or worse, for sickness and in health, I had become a Georgia Peach.

sammie and marie

chapter 16

I had been working at my new job at White, Miller & Stevens for three months. It was not the job that I had accepted when I had agreed to move to Atlanta but so far, I was digging it. I had my own office, a secretary and so far the people were cool. They had me in orientation, which I thought was unusual since I had been working there for the past three months. However, this was the South and they tend to do things differently.

During orientation, I got to go around to meet the partners and learn a little bit about each of their practices. I had already done some minor projects for most of them. The firm was mostly white with a few black people splattered over the four floors. Usually, I stayed to myself and kept a low profile. I did not try to get to know most of the black faces any better. The only one that looked like she might be cool was Leah. She was Mr. Miller's secretary but time would tell on that end. The rest of the black folks had their noses so far up the white man's ass I had absolutely no time for them.

I just wanted to do a good job and go home without any unnecessary drama. I did not intend to exert too much energy in work relationships and since I was new at the firm and trying to prove myself, I really didn't have the time for it.

The job I originally had accepted when I decided to move to Atlanta did not pan out. It was at a small black-owned law firm and those Negroes were tripping all the time, especially on payday. One of the partners would come around about noon and hand out checks. When it came time to give me mine, they practically threw it on my desk. I had a real problem with that! I saw them hand our checks to everyone else in the office but mine was delivered with attitude! I took it for about two weeks and told them I had to go. I called an old boss in Baltimore and asked for her help. She called an old friend of hers and I started work the next week with this new firm.

The money was good by Atlanta's standards and the work was interesting. I began to make plans to move into my own house. I found one not too far from Mom's that was for sale on a lease-to-own basis. Momma was not happy about me moving but since I was still going to be close she couldn't complain too much. She was still going to watch the kids for me in the morning and pick them up after school, which was a big help.

I was on the phone trying to arrange for a mover when Leah stuck her head in my office.

"Ms. Morgan, I have some papers for you from Mr. Miller. He wanted me to bring them to you right away," she said.

"You can dispense with that Ms. Morgan crap. I'm Marie; come on in," I said. I took the papers from her and began to review them. It was a request to do some research on a wrongful death case he was working on. When I first had arrived, the most that they would allow me to do was real estate matters such as property and lien record searches. This was the first beefy assignment that I had gotten and I felt like I was moving up. Putting down the papers, I wanted to celebrate. Looking up at Leah, I said, "Do you want to have lunch sometime?"

"Uh, sure. Just let me know when," she replied.

"Did I say something wrong. Why the hesitation?" I asked.

"Most of the paraprofessionals here don't mix with the secretaries. I was just surprised, that's all."

"I'm not like them. How about today; do you have any plans?"

"Today is good but I have to go at 1:00."

"That's cool; I hate going early. It makes the day go by longer. Meet you at the elevator at 1:00. You pick the spot, okay? I'm still new here and I don't know the good places to eat yet."

"Ok, see you at 1:00. Oh, do you have a message for Mr. Miller?" she said, all business again.

"Just tell him that I will jump right on it. He should have my research by the end of the week barring any unforeseen circumstances."

Leah left and I resumed making calls for a mover. I wanted to move over the weekend. The phone rang before I could complete my dial. Miffed, I answered with attitude.

"Marie Morgan, can I help you?"

"It's me, baby," David said. His voice sent tingles down my spine to every part of my body. I snapped my knees shut to keep in the heat. Immediately my tone softened and my body relaxed.

"Hey, sunshine," I said 'cause he was truly a ray of light in my life. We had been talking almost daily since my move. I missed him with ever fiber of my being and I was horny as hell.

"I just called to hear your voice," he said.

"Guess what?" Before I could allow him the opportunity to offer a guess, I rambled, "I got my own place. I am moving this weekend." I was excited beyond words.

"That's great, baby; any room for me?" I thought he was joking so I quickly replied, "Anywhere I am you're welcome to come!"

"I'm serious, all jokes aside," he said.

"I never joke about your moving to Atlanta," I said, suddenly very serious.

"I want to come but we have to lay out a few ground rules. This is not a commitment. I just need somewhere to stay while I find me a job. I don't want there to be any misunderstandings."

Whoa, I thought. I had to think about what he was really saying. He wanted to come to Atlanta and live off me since I knew he didn't have any money. Next, until he found a job, this arrangement could be indefinite and once he did, he might just go off with someone else. I don't fucking think so. By agreeing to this arrangement, I would get the short end of the stick. Plus, if his search took too long, I would be supporting a grown man. I loved him but I was not a fucking fool.

"I really can't talk to you about this now. I will call you when I get home," I said, stalling.

"I need an answer now," he demanded.

I spoke from my head and not my heated pussy. "Well then, I cannot agree to your terms. I have to think about my mother and my children. I can't allow a man to move into my house unless he is committed to us," I whispered.

"Thanks anyway," he said and hung up the phone. My heart froze. I wanted to take back the words just to hear his voice on the phone again. I was so tired of the sorrow that hung over every day at my mother's house and in my own heart when I thought about the people I left behind and the uncertainty of the future.

Over lunch, I broke my own cardinal rule and discussed this with Leah. I have always made it a rule to never ever air my personal business with my coworkers but that day I made an exception.

I met Leah at the elevator and we walked to Mick's Bar & Grill. It was a mid-sized restaurant that I had passed several times before, not bothering to go in. Most of the time, I worked through lunch anyway. We got a seat and looked at the menu.

"How long have you been working for the firm?" I asked, trying to break the ice.

"Too damn long, if you know what I mean," she said with a smile. "I have been going to school on the side and I almost had your position before you slipped in."

"Oh, I'm sorry. I didn't mean to block nobody, especially a sister!" I was upset about that and figured she had every right to be mad at me.

"Don't worry about it; it's cool. When I saw the assignments that they were giving you, I realized I was not ready anyway. I will get my chance so don't sweat it."

"Are you sure?" I asked. Not that I was going to quit or anything, I just wanted to know if I had the enemy in my camp or not.

"I'm positive. I'm glad that they gave it to someone with a good head on her shoulders instead of the other assholes that they have been hiring since I've been there. This will make my fifth year. The only black people they hire are Uncle Toms. You can't even talk to them; they are so full of themselves and can't be trusted," she exclaimed.

I could not help but laugh 'cause I felt the same vibe from them. I could not relate to any of the other black people that I had met since I had joined the firm other than Leah.

"Are you married?" I asked once lunch was served. The inquiry slipped from my lips before I considered that the question might have been too personal. "Hey, I'm sorry, I wasn't trying to dip in your business, I just feel like I have known you for a minute and it would be okay," I said feeling embarrassed.

"Don't sweat it. I feel like I have known you, too. And to answer your question, not yet but I'm hopeful. I am dating this wonderful guy that my girlfriend hooked me up with," she gushed, glowing with excitement.

"Congratulations," I said.

"What about you?"

"Separated, two kids and waiting on those blessed papers of freedom. Do you have kids?"

"Not yet. I plan on it if this relationship works out."

We ate our meal and talked about trivial matters until it was almost time to go. I needed a second opinion real bad to my nagging problems and I just belted out my dilemma before I chickened out.

"Leah, can I talk to you in confidence?"

"Sure, Marie," she responded.

"I've got a situation going on in my life and I want an unbiased opinion to make sure that I am handling it correctly."

"Shoot."

"Okay, I left a man in Baltimore that I care about. He wants to move to Atlanta to see if he can make it here. He wants to live with me but on a no-strings-attached basis. He just needs a place to stay until he establishes himself. Would you go for that?" When I said it out loud it sounded totally ridiculous and I wished that I could've taken back my dilemma but it was too late.

"Oh hell no. So you will have to foot the bills while he 'finds himself'? I hope you told that man to forget it!" she shouted.

"I did. But I thought about how much I missed him and I started second-guessing myself. Thank you!" I said as I paid the check and we prepared to leave.

"You are welcome and if you ever have any doubts again, think of it this way. You already have three dependents; do you really need a fourth?"

"Three?" I asked confused.

"Yeah, you got to depend on you, don't ya?" she answered with a smile.

"I knew I liked you when I first met you but now I know why," I told Leah, shaking my head. We walked back to the building chatting away like old friends. Talking with Leah, I knew I had done the right thing but I still wanted to run it past Sammie. Leah was nice and all that, but she was younger than I was. On the other hand, even though I didn't know Sammie that well, she was older than me and was a lot more experienced. I wanted to hear her input.

Back at my desk, I searched through my bags for the phone number that she had given me when we went out to Fat Tuesday's. It was her home number so I called to leave a message. In my heart, I was comfortable with my decision, but I was having a hard time convincing my heart about David. But I wanted all the support that I could garner on that end. Getting neither answering machine nor Sammie's voice, I hung up the phone.

Sammie called before I could hang up the phone good. "Hey, girl," she said.

"Damn. I thought I was leaving a message on your home phone. Are you off today?" I asked.

"I have my home phone transferred to my cell phone and I constantly check my messages," she replied.

"Are you that important?" I asked, laughing.

"Only in my own eyes," she said, sharing the laughter. "So what have you been up to? I haven't heard from you in a minute."

"Girl, the same old, same old. I am in the process of moving. I need to give you my new number."

"All right then. Where are you moving? Don't tell me I won't be able to catch the train with you anymore. That would truly upset my day!" she said.

"No, I will still be catching the same train 'cause I still have to drop the kids off at Mom's. Look, I am having man troubles and I wanted to bounce it off you. Are you available for drinks one night this week?"

"I will have to get back to you. I'm on lockdown right now. But I will get back with you."

"Surely you jest," I said, getting mad at the thought of a man placing a woman on lockdown.

"I can't go into any details at the moment but things are tight around my home front. My husband ain't dealing too tough with my mother and she is taking her frustration out on me. Jessie and I need to be finding our own place to live with a quickness!"

"Will you be able to talk at home or should I try to catch you on the train?"

"Catch me on the train. I get off at 5:00," she said and hung up the phone. Since I started the new job, I had been working overtime and getting off closer to 6:00 instead of 5:00, so I rarely got the chance to ride home with Sammie. Although we still caught the train together in the morning, our conversations were limited because of the early morning crowd.

I piddled through the rest of my work that was on my desk and even started to work on the project that Mr. Miller had sent me. That was the type of work I liked, something with meat to it. The client's husband was employed at a local landfill. He was making repairs on a tree grinder and signaled to his coworker to turn the machine off as he climbed in to make repairs. The coworker, who had a history of showing up on the job drunk, turned the machine on instead and it killed our client's husband. She was suing the county and stood to make a killing. The county was trying to say that he was negligent by climbing into the grinder but my research was proving there was no other way to make the repairs once the problem was isolated.

I glanced at my watch and realized that I would have to hurry if I wanted to catch Sammie at the train. I turned off my computer and closed up my files, checking to make sure that everything was put back in place before I turned off the lights and left. I hated coming into a messy office and made a point to clear off my desk every night in order to start fresh in the morning.

Sammie was already on the platform when I got there. We walked to the very end of the station hoping to get a semi-empty train car so that we could talk in private.

As usual, she was looking great. She had on a slamming red dress with matching heels. Her hair was done in an upsweep with red pieces hanging down.

"Where did you say your husband's shop was? He sure does know how to hook a head up! Hell, I might want to get him to do a little something with this mess," I told Sammie, tossing my own locks around.

"Girl, he can do some hair when he wants to but he has gotten so lazy since we moved here it don't make no sense. He only does my hair to keep my mother out my shit. I don't think he has done anybody else since we came back."

"So, you are the sole breadwinner in a house full of grown-ups? That is too much drama. Why don't you move out if things are so bad?"

"We are trying but my credit is shot and I don't think his is any better. Even with the $20,000 my dad left me, most people don't want to take a risk on you. Momma don't help none either 'cause she is charging us $100 a week just to stay with her. Girl, I'm getting it at both ends. Jessie hates Althea, and Althea hates us both."

"Hell with $20,000 why don't you buy a house?" I asked clearly confused.

"Credit issues; weren't you listening?" she demanded. She busted my chops. Even though I was listening I just assumed that she could put $10,000 down and most lenders would be agreeable to take a chance.

I felt sorry for Sammie but I didn't know what I could do to help her. I had my own troubles.

"I am so blessed; my mother ain't charging me anything. I would have never been able to save for this house if I had to pay rent and child care," I said. In hindsight, that probably wasn't the best thing to say at the moment but it was all I had come up with.

"Girl, the more I stay in that house with Althea, the more I learn about her. All this time, I didn't know that my mother cheated on Daddy. She was about to leave him when she found out she was pregnant with me. That's why she has always hated me!"

Wow, that was some deep shit, I thought.

The train came and we were able to get a seat together so we could continue our conversation.

"She just came out and told you that? She is a hateful bitch, ain't she?"

"Girl, that's putting it mildly. She got mad when she found out Daddy left me some money. We got into an argument right there in the lawyer's office. She said, 'I'll bet that son of a bitch would just roll over if he knew he just gave $20,000 to a bastard that wasn't even his!'" Rocked, I placed my hand over hers and tried to keep from crying for her.

"What did your husband say?" I whispered totally dumbstruck.

"He just laughed! I bolted from the room and Momma and Jessie stayed to finish the paperwork. I never knew that Daddy was not my father, but he treated me more like his own than my own mother. All Jessie and Althea wanted from me was a signature on the paperwork. Jesus himself could not have persuaded me to go back in that office to face them," she moaned in the thick of pain again.

I was overwhelmed with emotion.

"Did she tell you who your real father was?" I asked, still fighting back the tears for her.

"As far as I'm concerned, that was my real dad. I don't want to know who the sperm donor was. He didn't stick around long enough to see about me, so fuck him! Daddy was the only person that ever cared about me."

She had a point. We rode in silence for a few minutes.

"Why don't you leave them both? You got money. I'm sure you could talk someone into renting you a small apartment. Hell, you could just charm your way in!" I said, trying to bring a smile to her face.

"What money? Jessie got the money. Plus, he said he would kill me if I left him."

"He's joking, right?"

"Hey, sorry, but I don't want to talk about this anymore, okay? What's up with you? Where you been hiding?" Sammie asked.

"Like I said, girl, I've been working my ass off trying to make a good impression. Between work, spending time with the kids and my mother, I have a full plate. Now, with this move, it's really been crazy. And to top that off, I have man problems."

"What man? I thought you were too busy to be out shopping for men?" she said.

"I have. It's one I left behind. He wants to come and stay with me while he finds a job."

"Girl, don't do it. The last thing that you need is another dependent! I don't care how good the shit is!"

Laughing, I said, "And it was good, too, gurl! That man was slinging dick at me and I was lapping it up! But you are right. I have my hands full trying to take care of myself, not to mention the kids!"

"I know that's right. Where are all the real men?" I gave her a high-five and we got off the train laughing.

"Hey," I said before I got into my car. "When you get some time, I want you to meet my coworker. She seems real nice and I think you will like her."

"Sure, but it will probably have to be for lunch since I don't get out much when I get home."

"Okay then. But on the real tip, you have got to do something about your situation. You should not have to spend the rest of your life like this."

"I know, girl. I know. Hopefully, I will see you tomorrow and if I get the chance, I will call you tonight."

"See ya," I said and drove home. My heart was heavy. Alone again, I thought about David and my decision not to let him come to stay. There was so much to do if I wanted to be ready for my move so I shook off the bad thoughts and prepared for greeting Keira and Kevin.

Atlanta was agreeing with them or should I say, my mother was agreeing with them. She spoiled them rotten.

I opened the door to Mom's house and interrupted a game of Chutes and Ladders. Keira squealed and raced to the door with Kevin flat on her heels. They wrapped their arms around my knees squeezing me so tightly that you would have thought I had been gone twenty years instead of ten hours. I bent and kissed each of them on the mouth.

"Hey, Momma," I said as I walked up to her and gave her a special peck on the check. I also licked her face, which she absolutely detested but it always brought about peals of laughter and threats of a beat-down.

"Oh, you," she said, wiping off the spit with the back of her hand. The kitchen smelled of fried chicken. I followed my nose. Once again, Mom showed out in the kitchen. She had cooked fried chicken, potato salad and corn on the cob. I licked my lips in anticipation. It was going to be tough to leave all that good cooking behind when I moved. I was getting used to having supper on the stove when I got in from work.

"Have you all eaten yet?" I asked, grabbing a plate from the cabinet.

"You know those two could not wait. They were practically grabbing legs out the pan as soon as they were done. I hope you don't mind that we didn't wait for you," Luetta said.

"No, there is no need to wait on me 'cause you never know when I'm going to get out of that office."

"So things are still going well?" she inquired.

"Yeah, things are definitely looking up. I'm getting more and more work from the senior partners and that's unheard of for someone as new as I am. Some of the other paralegals are not happy about it but what can I say. I'm good," I said, patting my own self on the back.

"Have you finalized the move yet? I sure wish you would reconsider. I like having you around," Mom said with a grave tone.

"Mom, I will still be around. Hell, I'm right around the corner and you will still have the kids with you most of the time. But I need my space and so do you. I'll still come to stay some nights and hey, if you want to continue cooking us dinner, I'll come by every night!"

We both laughed at that. Mom was doing well even though I knew she still was lonely. I talked her into taking piano lessons, something that she had always wanted to do but never pursued, and she was becoming more and more active in the church. She joined the choir and a group I dubbed the Loyal Order of Water Buffalos. It was a secret organization whose purpose I had not figured out yet, but they did good things in the community like offer college scholarships for the church youth. It kept her busy so it was all good!

I ate my dinner and it was delicious. Satisfied, I cleaned up the kitchen and went into my room to pack. I thought about calling David but quickly dismissed the idea. Dennis was the one on my mind so I gave him a call. I glanced at my watch and assumed he would be getting ready to go to work.

"Hello," he answered, picking up after the first ring.

"Hey," I replied, knowing he would know who it was.

"They ain't killed you down there yet?" he said with a loud laugh.

"I'm still hanging in here but it's such an adjustment. Did you know you can't even buy booze here on Sunday? I made a fool of myself last week 'cause I wanted a wine cooler. First of all, they call liquor stores 'package stores.' I didn't know that shit so I never stopped at them. I was getting gas and saw some wine coolers and I picked up a four-pack. I took it to the counter and the woman said, 'I can't sell you that.' My dumb ass pulled out my ID, feeling flattered that she thought I was underage. Wrong. She said, 'Honey, we can't sell that on Sunday.' I took it back and got a six-pack of beer and she said the same thing. It was like she had to hit my ass over the head with a two-by-four before I understood that no alcohol was sold on Sunday."

"I told you that you were going to die down there. When are you coming back home?"

"Dennis, I'm going to try to make this move work if it kills me! I could not come back to Baltimore even if I wanted to now. Mom has already signed a contract on my old house. It is supposed to go to settlement at the end of the month. So I would not even have a place to live."

"I know she did; I bought it," he said.

"You are shitting me! Why didn't you tell me?" I was stunned.

"I wanted to surprise you. That way, if you ever feel the need to visit, you will be able to. I could not help it; the price was right and your parents made a lot of improvements to the house. It's the best value on the block. And I will still be close to my mother."

"I'm happy for you, Dennis. So, how's your love life?" I asked. "Found the woman of your dreams yet?"

"Not quite but I'm working on it. What about you?"

"Nope, haven't ventured out since you were here. Just taking it slow. I'm moving this weekend so let me give you my new number. It's 404-555-5175."

"Good. Look, I got to run. Stay sweet and keep in contact. Did you get my letter?"

"No, not yet. I will let you know. Tell your mom I said hi," I said before hanging up. Shit, he was moving on, too. I really needed to do something to get out of my rut. When I got settled, I was going to have to do something about my social life.

chapter 17

"Where the hell have you been?" I demanded when Sammie picked up the phone. I had been calling her all fucking weekend and only had gotten her answering machine. Although I never left a message, I knew she was aware I was trying to reach her. Ever since Sammie had moved from Althea's house, the violence between Sammie and Jessie had escalated and it kept me feeling frantic.

"Shopping," she said with little enthusiasm.

"Oh shit," I replied with a sinking feeling in my stomach. "Since you don't appear to be happy about this particular shopping trip, I can only conclude that you were fighting with Jessie again."

"Yep, we went guilt shopping again," she said with a heavy sigh.

"Well, how much did the bruises to your self-esteem and body cost you this time?" I asked sarcastically. I truly could not understand why she put up with this shit. There was no amount of money in the world that would make me put up with the verbal and physical abuse he dished out.

"We did not buy anything today; we visited the things that he is going to get me when he gets the money."

"You have got to be kidding me. Visit; what the hell does that mean?"

"We go to all the stores where he would buy me something from if he could afford it. He points it out, I try it on and pretend that I like it and either hang it back up or give it back to the clerk depending on where we are."

"What a waste of time and energy," I replied.

"Yeah, but I'll bet you won't say that to Jessie's face."

"That nigger may have you scared but he don't scare me. I would pop a cap in his ass for real! So what sparked the shopping trip this time, did he have a hangnail?" My blood pressure started to boil. I hated it when men tried to use their physical strength to dominate a woman. Even though I was not much of a fighter, I was ready to pounce on Jessie.

I recalled my own earlier attempts of violence but it did not defuse the anger I felt. Fighting was never one of my fortes! One time, in my younger days, I decided I was going to whip my boyfriend's ass. I picked up a brand-new knife and decided I was gonna cut his ass. I lunged at him and did a roundhouse curve that should have cut off his head but he ducked. I wound up cutting out a slice of my own shoulder. Next, I picked up a brand-new frying pan, cast iron and swung in the same fashion. When I woke up, he was stomping me into the kitchen floor. I guess he ducked and I struck my own self in the forehead. Those were dismal thoughts but I flicked them away in my rage. It just confirmed what I was previously thinking. I may not have won the battle but at least I had the courage to fight back.

I was in a kick-ass mode and it didn't matter that I was ill-equipped to carry it out.

"He lost his job yesterday and took it out on me," Sammie said so quietly I had to strain to hear her.

"Is he there?" I whispered back before realizing that I had no reason to whisper.

"No, he's out somewhere," she replied.

"Then why are you whispering?" I asked tired of trying to drag information out of her.

"Throat hurts."

"He didn't!"

"Yeah, he did and almost succeeded. Lucky for me I passed out and he got scared."

"I'm coming over there."

"No! I don't know when he will be back and you know he can't stand your ass."

"I still don't understand why he is hating on me. I only met the trifling mother-fucker once!"

"He doesn't want me to have no friends! I just don't know how much more of this I can take. He won't let me leave but when I stay he beats my ass up. Part of me wishes he had killed me last night. I made the mistake of asking him if my kids could come and live with us and he became uncorked!" She started crying and I joined her.

"I told him that I wanted a baby," she said quietly.

"You did what?" I screamed at her. "Why would you want to bring an innocent child into this sick shit you call your life?"

She still was talking so low that I had to strain to hear over the loud beating of my heart.

"Marie, I need someone to love me for me," she said.

"Sammie, I love you for you! You can't even think about bringing a child into the relationship you are in. What you need to be doing is trying to find a way to get the fuck out of that sick shit!"

"I thought he might change with a baby; it just might be what we need to make this marriage work."

"You don't honestly believe that, do you? The man is abusive and controlling. Do you want that for your child?"

"I don't know what I want, Marie. Anyway it doesn't make a difference what I want. He told me that if I tried to trap him with a kid that he would kill us both."

"Look, if I can't come over there, could you at least come over here. I want to take a look at your neck and we have to talk seriously face-to-face."

"I won't promise but I will try to be over there real soon."

Damn, if it wasn't one thing, it was another. I had been riding this emotional roller coaster with Sammie since the first day we met. I loved this girl but I was tired of the dumb shit.

She finally broke down and told me about the bizarre shit she had done in California. I didn't judge her. I just listened and the more I heard, the more I wanted her to get out before he killed her. I begged her to come live with me but she wouldn't do it.

When I thought about it, all my friends were bugging. Leah and I had been spending more time together. She had her nose wide open by this guy her girl-friend had introduced her to. I tried to open her mind but she wasn't hearing me. The ringing of the phone interrupted my thoughts. The kids were taking a nap so I snatched it up quickly.

"Hello," I said.

"Girl, guess what?" It was Leah. I must have thought her up.

"I was just thinking about you. This is too funny. I'm not going to guess so you might as well tell me."

"Kentée proposed!" she gushed. I was speechless. I had only met the man once and was not impressed. They had only been dating for about three months and something didn't feel right.

"Well, aren't you going to say something?" she said.

"Congratulations, I guess. Did you give him an answer?"

"YES! Of course I did. He is a good man." Again, I didn't respond. All kinds of thoughts flooded through my head. I wanted to speak but was afraid to hurt her feelings. I also didn't want her to think I was "hating" on her.

"I'm going to say what is in my heart and hope that it does not destroy our friendship. I am saying this out of love and I hope you hear it as such. Will you try to keep an open mind and listen?" I asked before going any further.

"Sure, I'll listen," she responded with a hitch in her voice.

"Stop me if I get something wrong. You met this man who was living with his wife. Supposedly, they were living separate and apart with him living in the basement. Now I can accept that 'cause Keith and I were doing that," I said, pausing to regroup my thoughts. Leah did not say a word.

"He is paying all the bills and is the perfect husband but his wife uses him. He was content to live that life until he met you. Am I getting this right so far?" I asked to see where her mind was.

"So far, that's right," she said with a heavy voice. I could tell she was about to freak on me but I continued anyway.

"The question I have in my mind is, if he is such a 'good' man, why is she willing to throw him away?"

"Oh, well, he said she is crazy," she responded.

"That's just it, 'he said.' Before you agree to marry him, why don't you talk to her? It couldn't hurt could it?" I asked in all sincerity.

"Marie, I respect your feelings but I know this man and you don't. I don't want to upset the apple cart by bringing her into our relationship."

"Leah, she has been in your relationship all along since he is still living with her. Don't you want to know if they still have a physical relationship? Don't you want to know if he is really paying the bills or is it the other way around?" I asked, getting an attitude.

"No, I don't! He makes me happy and I make him happy. That's all that really matters. I would hope that as my friend, you would be happy for me!" she said, suddenly angry with me.

"See, that's why I wasn't going to say anything! Regardless of how this relationship pans out, I'm here for you! Let me make myself clear. I am happy for you if, and I stress the word *if*, he is right for you and his motives are pure. Please believe me, I only want to see you happy, girl. Yes, there are a lot of haters out there that want everyone to be miserable just like they are but I ain't the one. I've been around the block for a minute and I am skeptical; that's all I am saying. There ain't no hate in my game, I promise you, and that's the God's honest truth. I said what I have out of love for you and if you are happy, then I'm happy for you."

Leah backed off a notch and started going on about the wedding plans. I wanted to ask her if she knew if he was already divorced but I figured I had pissed her off enough as it was.

"How about I cook dinner for you two?" I asked, throwing her a bone.

"That would be nice. Let me get with Kentée and find out what his schedule looks like. We are busy looking for an apartment and are making plans for a small courthouse wedding. I'll get back to you and I am sorry for flying off the handle at you. I have had enough flack from my own family and that shit is getting old real quick," she said.

"Cool, just give me enough time to plan the menu," I responded. We hung up and all I could do was shake my head. I could not shake the feeling that Leah was making a big mistake. It was just not logical to me that a woman was throwing away a good man, especially since they were so hard to come by!

Her reaction also made me take a look at myself. I was lonely but I still didn't think my life had turned out too badly since I moved to Atlanta. I had no further contact with David, but Dennis and I kept in contact by mail and an occasional phone call.

The only real sore spot in my life was Keith. He was calling on a regular basis asking to see the children. Although I had nothing against him seeing them, I was not ready for the drama that went with it.

Although Kevin never asked about his dad, Keira continued to make nightly prayers to see her father. It was touching to hear but I could only do so much.

I got busy cleaning up the house. It was coming along well and I was quite proud of it. After I finished, I had time on my hands and thought about going over to get Mom to take her out for a change. She still made our meals during the week and I wanted to show her how much I appreciated it. The doorbell stopped me from picking up the phone. Sammie was on the front porch.

"This is a surprise," I announced as I opened the door and practically dragged her in. I looked around, a recent habit I had developed, checking to make sure she was not being followed. My earlier conversation with Sammie had me feeling paranoid even though I refused to admit it. I didn't want Jessie coming to my house acting a fool.

"Hey, girl," she whispered. I took a good look at her face and neck and cringed.

"I ought to whip your ass," I said mad as hell that Sammie continued to allow Jessie to put his hands on her. I got even madder when I thought about the fact that she could have whipped his ass with both hands tied behind her back.

Sammie had been gaining weight. Although she never would have been labeled *petite* because of her height, she always had a nice waistline and fat butt. The more weight she gained, the more disproportioned she became. Her face was huge and her stomach and butt were massive.

Although I didn't want to say anything that might hurt her feelings, I worried about her rapid weight gain.

"I don't have much time but I needed to tell you a few things just in case something happened to me," Sammie whispered.

Fear pricked my heart and ran up my spine. Sammie was so serious that I didn't know what to say. I led her to the sofa and we sat down. Luckily, Keira and Kevin were still upstairs.

"What are you talking about?" I said, fearing the worst. I noticed for the first time the skimpy attire Sammie was wearing. It was different from the vibrant business attire that I was used to seeing her in. She was dressed like a cheap whore.

"Just in case something happens to me, I need someone to know the truth," she continued and I waited for her to go on.

"Jessie has been pimping me again. Ever since we moved from Althea's, I've been walking the streets." Sammie hung her head in shame. I could not think of anything to say to her so I just nodded my head for her to continue.

"Also, Jessie is hooked on heroin. I didn't want to face it before but it is true. I caught him shooting up and now all the pieces of the puzzle are beginning to fit.

He spent all the money my daddy left me and we can't make it on what I was making at the temp service. I haven't worked there in over a month. I had been doing this part time for about three or four months but for the last month, I have been at it full time."

"Girl, this is crazy! You don't have to do this. I told you that I got your back. Move in with me; we can get through it," I pleaded with her with tears of outrage running down my face.

"Yeah, then what? Do you want him to stalk you and me and possibly kill both of us in our sleep? I don't think so! I told you, you just don't understand. Jessie's new love, heroin, does not care whether it's right or wrong. The only thing he cares about is being able to score more drugs and I am the means that he is using to continue to get it and that's the bottom line. He would kill me if he knew that I told you. I'm only telling you now 'cause he don't watch my back like he used to."

"Girl, I don't understand this; he has been using for some time. Weren't there signs?

"Now that I think about it yes but, back then, I did not pay attention."

"But going from snorting heroin to shooting up, that's a big step. It should have been written all over him!" Sammie just shrugged her shoulders and shook her head.

"Hey, wait, back up. What do you mean, watch your back? This is getting too confusing. Are you trying to tell me that he watches you have sex with other men?" I asked.

Sammie nodded her head. "He used to. He would drive me down to Boulevard and Moreland and make me stand on the corner for hours until I made enough money. We would do it in the back of the car," she whispered.

I was appalled at her acceptance of the situation. You could not get me to go on Boulevard in the daytime let alone at night. Of course, selling my body would have never been an option either, unless you had a gun to my head and even then I think I would have opted for the bullet, but that's just me.

Once again, I urged Sammie to get out but I guess I really didn't comprehend how profound Jessie's control over Sammie was.

"Sammie, I can't say this to you enough. I got your back, girl, and one of these days you are going to hear me. If you need a place to stay, come with it. You only have to say the word and we will handle the other bullshit as it comes."

Sammie shook her head. "It sounds worse than it really is." We both knew that wasn't true. I played along not knowing what else to do. I had never felt so helpless in my entire life.

"I'm fine, at least I was," she said. "Jessie would conduct the actual money transfers and stand guard while I do the do in the back of the car. Jessie said that's where most whores make their mistake by getting hotel rooms or doing it in gas stations."

She told me that she was doing at least three to four guys a night. I felt sick to my stomach and my agony left me at a loss for words.

"How much money are you making?" I asked her. Sammie was the only person I knew that was prostituting and I was always curious.

"I don't even know. I never get to see any of it anyway."

"Un-fucking believable! You are doing all the work and you don't get a dime? I'm sorry, girl; all I can say is it wouldn't be me. If I were going to be a trick, then I damn sure would be getting a treat. You know what I'm saying."

"I don't have a choice. Aren't you listening? He will kill me if I don't. You don't understand, Marie. He's not just doing drugs now; drugs are doing him. He will do anything, and I mean anything to get them," she shouted, straining her already abused vocal cords. "My number one problem right now is that he does not play lookout anymore. I'm on my own. I just wanted someone to know if I turned up missing."

Comprehension was slow to evolve but I finally understood; short of leaving the state, Sammie was stuck with him until the shit played itself out. And that is exactly what happened.

No longer content with the money that he was getting from Sammie's whoring, Jessie started pimping himself. In the beginning he would only offer himself to women but later he really didn't care. Sammie was not exactly sure how much money he was spending daily on drugs but she assumed it was quite a lot 'cause they no longer had any electronics in the house. Hell, he even sold the damn cordless phone.

He sold the TV, radios, DVD player and most of the CDs and DVDs that they had been collecting. He stopped doing hair all together. He spent his days copping and the rest of the night trying to finance the next day's activities.

After a while Sammie and I stopped talking about her marriage and Jessie's exploitation of her 'cause she felt hopeless and I felt helpless. Not knowing any better, we just ignored it. That didn't mean that I wasn't scared for her, but what was I to do if she couldn't help herself? Her situation continued to get worse. She called me one night in tears.

"I'm scared, Marie," she said.

"What now?" I asked, not meaning to sound so cold but she didn't give me any other options. I couldn't do anything but listen.

"Jessie is really nutting up. I am not bringing home the money I used to because he won't watch anymore. It's scary out there. Half the time, I don't know who to trust and the men aren't offering me much money. I told him it was different than when he was there but he wouldn't hear it. He said, 'Ain't no nigger dumb enough to fuck with your fat ass! Shit, I make more money in one hour than you make all night.'"

"Then tell him to step it up a notch and sit your happy ass on the sofa and count the money he brings in!" I said. "Why do you continue to do this to yourself? I don't understand Sammie. Just stop doing it. If he's making all this money, you don't need to subject yourself to that shit!" I angrily declared.

"How many times do I have to tell you this, Marie. He will kill me, plain and simple. I'm not ready to die yet."

"Are you going out tonight?" I needed to know but I did not want to know. It was so much easier to plead ignorance.

"Yeah, I'm leaving now. I just wanted someone to know where I am, just in case..." She deliberately did not finish that statement.

"Shit, Sammie, what am I supposed to say or do when you talk like that? Do you want me to go with you?"

"Don't be ridiculous. You would get both of us locked up and with Jessie out there doing God knows what, who would bail us out?"

She had a point there. At least with me on the outside, if she got in any trouble with the law, I could always go get her out of jail.

"Call me, girl, if you need me—do you hear me?" I demanded.

"I hear you." She hung up the phone before I could say anything else to her. "Be careful," I whispered into the dead line.

chapter 18

hung up the phone with Sammie feeling emotionally drained. Sammie had a way of doing that, sucking me into her drama and draining my energy. I needed an instant pick-me-up, so I called my mother. Our conversation was short but that was par for the course. The mother/daughter relationship had been strained ever since I made the decision to make my divorce final and that just didn't sit right with me. Although Mom seemingly accepted my decision to separate from Keith, I knew that it was still a sore spot with her. Unfortunately, she did not understand that some marriages fail. She was lucky enough to find a man that was as committed to her as she was to him. Every time I tried to speak to her about my marriage we ended up fighting. She was totally against my convictions to make the separation from Keith final. As long as were separated, she felt there was still hope of us getting back together.

Mom was from the old school and she believed that no matter what, marriages were made to last. Only death should break apart two people who were joined by God. Up until my last trip home to Baltimore, I believed that as well. I decided to spend some time with her when I picked up the kids later that evening.

"Hello," I yelled when I walked in the door of Mom's house.

"I am downstairs," Mom yelled from the basement. "I'm just putting their clothes up. I will be right there."

I realized that it had been a while since I had actually come in the house and sat for a spell. She had redecorated the living room. There was new furniture and she had painted the walls a soft shade of cream. It looked really good. Mom always had a way with decorating. I tried to get her into interior designing after Dad passed away but she said she could not do it for money. She wasn't hurting financially so I didn't press the issue. I just thought it would be a way for her to meet more people and keep herself busy.

Mom finally came up the stairs with the childrens' clothes in her hands. They had stayed with her over the weekend so she washed everything that I had packed for them. Mom was incredible; she even washed the clothes that they didn't wear.

"Mom, why did you do their laundry again?" I asked. "I asked you not to do that!" I wanted to get angry with her for not listening to me, but that was the way she had always been. Even when I was little, she used to wash my clothes every night and put them back in my dresser. It got me so confused that one week I wore the same thing for three days in a row before some of my classmates started teasing me about it.

"Nonsense," she said with a wave of her hand. I wanted to argue with her but realized that it was pointless.

"Where are they anyway?" I inquired about Keira and Kevin.

"They are down the street at Pat's house. Her number is by the refrigerator on that little pad," she said.

"Oh, well, I'm not in any rush; they can stay down there while you and I visit." She raised her eyebrows at me but did not say anything as she put their clothes back in the suitcase. I went into the kitchen and turned on the instant pot. I grabbed two cups, the coffee and some sugar. Mom came into the kitchen as the water began to boil. She pulled out a chair and folded her arms defensively across her chest. I did not say anything until I was done preparing the coffee.

I went up to my mother dropping to my knees and hugged her around the waist. I shocked her as well as myself since I had not given into this luxury in quite a long while. I looked into my mother's eyes and tears began to form in the corners. We stayed that way for about ten minutes and it felt good.

"What was all that about?" she said when I finally took my seat.

"I just wanted to hug you. Dang, can't a girl hug her own mother?" I said, trying to appear nonchalant about it.

"Sure you can, honey. You just caught me off guard, that's all."

"Mom, I owe you an apology. I came over to tell you I'm sorry for the way I have been behaving over the last six months."

Mom didn't say anything. She knew what I was talking about and also knew that if she interrupted me before I finished talking there was a good chance that I would clam up and go home.

"I was angry with you for not supporting my decision to divorce Keith and I just wanted to say I'm sorry. You are entitled to your opinion and I need to respect that."

"Honey, I have always supported you," she interrupted. "I will say that I was disappointed that things didn't work out for you two, but I have always been in your corner."

"Mom, you told me that we should plant a garden together and our love would grow!" I said, starting to get agitated again but quickly lowered my tone. I didn't want to fight with her; I wanted her to understand where I was coming from.

"I only wanted you to take your time before you rushed into a decision. It's hard being a single parent in this day and age. I wanted you to be sure that this was what you wanted to do."

"Mom, that's the point. I am sure. We have been in Atlanta for two years now. Keith has been here once to see the kids and we saw him when I went home. There is nothing left for us. I was unhappy with Keith for eight years. I told myself that I would hang in there until Keira and Kevin were older, but when I got home from Baltimore I realized that I might not have the luxury of waiting."

Mom didn't interrupt so I continued. "I tried to look at Keith in a different light when he came to visit but the feelings were just not there. Remember the first summer we were here when Keira got sick with pneumonia?"

"How could I forget?" Mom said, shaking her head and holding herself.

"I considered taking Keith back then. I was tired of carrying the responsibility for the children by myself. It opened a dialogue between Keith and me, and we started talking again. But it wasn't enough! Forcing it would have been a bigger mistake than marrying him in the first place."

"We went through the motions but it just didn't work, and there is no fault to be placed here. I should have listened to Dad in the first place and never married him."

We both sat quietly for a few minutes while our coffee grew cold in their cups.

"Marie, baby, regardless of what you think, I never judged you. I may not have understood what you were going through but I still supported you. I wanted you to remember you have a responsibility to those children first and foremost," she said.

"I know that and I live up to that responsibility each and every day of their lives. They come first but don't I deserve some happiness, too? Everyone can't have the kind of marriage you shared with Dad. Sometimes, for whatever reasons, people make mistakes and I'm woman enough to say, I made a mistake marrying Keith."

"That man loves you, Marie," she said.

"No he doesn't—not in the true sense of the words. Not like Dad loved you. Keith loves what I brought to the table. He loved the fact that I would provide for him when he fell short. He loved having me around to sleep with, but that's it. I'm a possession to him—not a wife or friend. I need more than that and the kids deserve more, too."

I paused for a cleansing breath and continued. "If we stayed together, I would have resigned myself and them to a life of fighting. Keith and I fought about everything. We could not have a simple conversation about anything without it ending up in a battle. I was sick of arguing."

"You could have gone to counseling," she said under her breath.

"Keith would never agree to that and you know it. He said he didn't need anybody, including you, sticking their noses in our business!"

"You never told me this before," she said. "You just came back from your vacation, marched in here and said, 'Mom, I'm getting a divorce' and walked out. What did you expect me to say?"

"I am sorry I did not break it down for you, but I didn't really know what to say to you. I didn't want to disappoint you, but I also did not want to continue along the same path that I was walking either. Do you remember Cheryl from my high school?" I asked.

"Sure, the little girl that used to live around the corner from us in Baltimore?"

"Yeah, she died. She had just gotten married and had another child. It was a boy. I saw her when I went home. I cussed her out for not returning any of my letters since I moved to Atlanta. We made arrangements to go to lunch and catch up and when I called her all that night and the next morning trying to confirm our lunch, she didn't answer. So I cussed her out again on her answering machine. Her mother called me back and left a message on my voice mail that Cheryl had passed," I said in a whisper as new tears dropped from my eyes.

For a few minutes, I could not continue as my body shook with fresh sobs and bitter pain. My mother came over to me and put her arms around me. I grabbed her and we cried together. When I calmed down, I continued.

"That day when I saw her, she had been complaining of a headache all day long and her husband wound up taking her to Johns Hopkins Hospital's emergency room later that evening. The test that they ran did not show anything so they sent her home. Her mother said she woke up during the night and said she could not move. They took her back to the hospital and after further tests, discovered a tumor in her brain. They operated on her immediately and the operation was successful, but the hospital staff dropped her when they were moving her from the surgical table to a gurney. She never regained consciousness."

I dislodged myself from mom's embrace and got up to fix another cup of coffee since the other one had grown cold. Mom still had not spoken. We sat and shared our coffee with each of us lost in our own thoughts. I looked Mom in the face and she retuned my stare. "That's when I decided that life is not promised to any of us. I could spend the next ten years with Keith and be miserable or I could cut my losses and pick up the pieces. Can you understand that?" I asked.

"I understand that. But I don't understand why it took you six months to tell me that. You are my daughter and your pain is mine to share. How could you be so selfish and withhold that type of information from me?" she demanded.

I got a reprieve from responding when Keira and Kevin busted through the front door.

"Momma," they both yelled in unison. They bum rushed me, each pulling on a limb to get their kisses and hugs. I looked over their heads and smiled at Mom. We had reached a milestone and we both knew it.

"I'm sorry," I mouthed and she shook her head in understanding and forgiveness.

chapter 19

I opened the front door to find a naked Sammie and immediately pulled the door behind me to make sure the children did not see her.

"What the fuck?" I said before I could stop myself. Gazing into Sammie's vacant eyes, I knew that something bad had happened, but I didn't know what. I eased her onto the porch swing and ran inside for something to cover her up with.

She didn't speak as I wrapped the blanket around her and guided her into the house. I tucked Sammie into my bed and allowed her a few minutes to compose herself.

I didn't want Keira and Kevin to know that Sammie was there since she was in such a disoriented state. Several times I went to the bedroom to check up on Sammie and she continued to remain unresponsive. She never acknowledged me entering or leaving the room. And for the first time, I thought that maybe I should have dialed 911 instead of offering her a place to lay her head. I prepared a cup of hot tea for us and brought it into my bedroom.

"Honey," I coached, "you need to eat something. Here, sit up." I pulled on her arms until she managed to sit up in the bed. I reached behind her and used all my pillows to prop her up. She still had that vacant look in her eyes but at least she was cooperating. I had prepared some toast for her to nibble on.

I sat by the bed feeding her tea and toast while coaching her to tell me what happened.

"Sammie, where are your clothes? Did Jessie do this to you?" I asked.

"They took them," she responded.

"Who took them?" I asked. "Honey, you are not making any sense. Did Jessie do this to you?"

"No, he didn't do this," she said, looking down at her bruised body. "But if he was there, it would not have happened. I was raped, Marie, by two guys," she said, using the sheet to wipe her face. I handed her some napkins from my night-stand, which she accepted and quickly wadded up into a ball.

"When I left here, I went to my normal hangout. I was nervous 'cause I was the only one out there. I sat in the car for a full hour before getting out. Those young punks are the worst at hazing us. You never know if they are just kidding or trying to prove something to their gang friends," she said, pausing to blow her nose. She wasn't crying but I could tell she was having a hard time trying to keep it together. I patted her hand in encouragement.

"I was not on the corner long before this young guy, probably in his late twenties or early thirties, approached me. He had long processed hair, which he wore in a ponytail that fell to his shoulders. His face was kind and sweet. Marie, he had the nicest smile that I have seen in a long time. He looked like he just wanted some-one to hold him.

"I couldn't take him into the car, so the trick told me about a school not too far from the corner that they could go to and be alone. He was cute, so I went with him. We entered the school through the janitor's door, which was propped open and I followed him down some dark corridors until we got to the gym. It was poorly lit but definitely should and could be classified as a gym. I asked him how he found out about this place and that's when things got ugly."

Sammie said he led her into the gym. She was trying to get into the mood of the seductress and was finding it hard since she was not in an element of her own creation. Instead, she felt nervous and slightly afraid.

There were some mats already laid out on the floor. Sammie started tugging at her clothes eager to perform the sex and get back to the comfort of her car and the gun that she had concealed in it. She also wanted to hurry up and finish so that she could return to her corner just in case Jessie rolled around to check up on her. Lord knows that if he had chosen that moment to do a drive-by, it would have made things that much harder for her when she got home.

"What's the rush, sweetness," the trick said in a soothing voice—one that was echoed by another male voice coming from behind the petition wall.

"Yeah, what's the rush, sweetness?"

Sammie looked around and saw another guy approaching from the far side of the gym. Paralyzing fear consumed her limbs and crept up around her heart as she began to realize the severity of the situation. Not only was she away from her car and her gun, no one who cared about her knew where she was. Not to mention that there were two men against her. The second guy was short and stocky. Looking into his eyes was like gazing into empty sockets.

The original trick revealed a knife tucked in the waistband of his baggy pants. When Sammie looked into his face, he no longer had that sweet smile that persuaded her to come with him in the first place. Instead, it was replaced with an evil sneer that jeered at her.

"On your knees, hoe," the other guy barked. He was clearly older than the original trick and was much more sinister. There was such a strong resemblance between them that Sammie could tell that they were related. He had a nasty scar down the left side of his face as if he had been on the wrong end of an infected switchblade.

Guy number two also had a knife but his was open as he came towards Sammie. Silently, she dropped to her knees.

Crocodile tears formed in Sammie's eyes as she told me the rest of her story. The thing that tugged at my heartstrings the most was her confession that she was so tired of being scared. She had spent her entire life being scared of one thing or another and she prayed for release.

"Damn, bro, where did you find this fat bitch at?" the shorter guy complained. "Hell, we should have her paying *our* asses to fuck her!"

"Don't you even complain, nigga; the pickings were slim tonight. I guess Five-O scared the rest of the whores off the block when they did that sweep this morning. She is probably the only bitch that missed the sweep," he said, spitting a brown stream of spit in between Sammie's legs.

"Please don't hurt me," Sammie pleaded. "I will do anything that you want me to. Just please don't hurt me."

"Well, bitch, then you had better make it good," said the original trick. For the next two hours, Sammie sexed both men. They were plugged into her at both ends. Neither one of them let go of their knives the entire time they were having sex. When they were done with her, they took her clothes and left her in the school.

Sammie said she lost all concept of time during the event. All she kept thinking about was whether or not she was going to die and how badly Jessie was going to hurt her if she came home with no money after being gone so long.

She said that she walked through the streets to her car butt-naked. She did not even attempt to cover herself up as she drove home. Sammie was in shock but that was not enough to wipe away her fear of facing Jessie with no money. Briefly she had considered trying to stay on the corner to earn enough money to satisfy Jessie, but without clothes, she only would have winded up in jail.

She said she had driven to my house in a trance. Too scared to go home and having nowhere else to go she headed my way.

It was while I was fixing breakfast that I heard a story on the news about a drug addict getting beat up and molested. Instantly I thought it might be Jessie but quickly dismissed the thought as wishful thinking. When I saw his name flash across the television screen I ran into the bedroom to turn up the television. We listened in disbelief as the newscaster told of the arrest of a man they found in an alley behind the Sam's Club.

According to the reporter, the police arrested Jessie Alexander after they found him bludgeoned and left for dead. He was taken to Grady Hospital where he was being treated for his injuries. Stunned, we just stared at each other. Finally, I broke the silence.

"You need to go home. If they have Jessie, I am sure he is going to call you and until you know what is going on, it would be better for you to be home," I said.

"You're right," she said, getting out of the bed. She flashed me and I turned away. Seeing Sammie naked twice in one day was enough for me. That was more than I ever wanted to see of Sammie. I handed her a sheet for her to cover up with.

"Girl, I don't have anything that will fit you, and the children can't see you in this sheet!" I declared. I checked to make sure that the kids were still in their rooms and ushered a jubilant Sammie out of the house. She even gave me a faint smile as she left. Dazed by all the morning drama, I sat down on the sofa.

chapter 20

As the details of Jessie's arrest began pouring in, I could not wait to call Sammie back to gloat.

"Hello," Sammie said, clearly stopped up as if she had been crying.

"You heard for yourself, didn't you! They got that motherfucker," I said elated.

"Yeah, it was him," she simply stated. I could not understand why she was crying and not shouting for joy.

"What's wrong with you? He's in jail. You should be damn singing and doing the happy dance!"

"I'm happy for the moment but what happens to me when he gets out of jail. He's going to be pissed and when he's pissed I suffer for it," she whimpered.

"Look, I can't come over now. We are having breakfast, so why don't you come back over here and we can talk. Surely there is something that can be done to keep his ass in jail," I replied.

"I'm tired now. I'll get back to you later."

"NO, damn it; get your ass over here now! You can't sleep this away; you have to make a plan of action." I hung up the phone before she could reply. I knew what she wanted to do. She was going to try to sleep her way out of her depression. This time, I was not going to let her go into her protective mode.

"Mommy, is Ms. Sammie coming over here today?" Keira said.

"Yes, sugar, so I need you and Kevin to hurry up and finish your breakfast and get dressed, okay?"

"Will she be crying again?" she asked.

Wow! I thought that Sammie and I did a good job of putting on a happy face whenever she was around my kids. I had no idea that they knew how unhappy Sammie's life really was.

"I hope not, sweetheart, but if she does this time, she will be crying 'cause she's got some good news," I said. This was not exactly a lie so I didn't feel too bad in saying this to Keira.

"Hurry up, baby; you don't want her to see you with your hair all over your head, do you? Do me a favor and call Kevin to eat so his food won't be cold."

I went back into the kitchen to pour juice for them. My hands were shaking as I filled the glasses, and I pondered just how much I was really keeping from Kevin and Keira.

By the time Sammie made it to the house, the news was all over the radio and TV. Jessie finally had gotten what he deserved.

He tried to stiff a nigger and in return got a serious ass whipping. The guy beat him to a pulp and left him for dead in the back of Sam's where they were supposed to be doing the wild thing. The trick rammed a stick so far up Jessie's ass that it had to be surgically removed. I wish I could have seen that shit. The police found him the next morning. They took him to the hospital and once he was treated, they locked his sorry ass up for drug possession. They did not have any suspects in their investigation and were asking the public to come forward if they had any information.

At Jessie's arraignment held later the next week, Sammie learned about his prior arrests for prostitution, assault, battery and drug possession. Sammie was stunned to find out that he would be serving the next ten to fifteen years in jail. Elated and afraid, she filed for divorce while he was in prison and closed a very unpleasant chapter in her life.

I just prayed that Jessie got bunked with a big guy named Bubba that liked his bitches skinny. Only goes to show you, what goes around comes around. I just wish I could have seen him so I could have done the happy dance in his face!

chapter 21

Sammie decided to become proactive while Jessie was incarcerated. She had given Jessie thirteen years of her life and had nothing to show for it. It was a really scary time for Sammie because it was the first time in her life that she was responsible for herself. Her first step was to reclaim her children from her mother, Althea. She and I both knew that it was not going to be easy since they had been living with her for most of their lives, but she had to try.

Althea did not give up the children easily. Sammie had to retain the same lawyer that she had used for her divorce to get temporary custody of her children. Luckily for Sammie, Althea never had filed the papers that Sammie had signed as a youth giving up her parental rights.

The conditions of the temporary custody agreement were that Sammie maintain a full-time job and a stable home environment for the children. Therefore, she had to give up her job with the temp service. Although she had been working fairly regularly as a temp, it did not provide the health benefits that she also needed to maintain for the children.

After three months of battling, Sammie was a mother. Kendall was now thirteen and Tyson was sixteen. Both were bitter towards Sammie and she fought hard to earn their love and respect. They did not want to come live with their mom and they made it crystal clear every opportunity they got. I felt sorry for Sammie but this was the bed she had made for herself.

We were having Easter dinner at my house. My mother and her new friend had just left and Sammie and the children were coming in. Tyson hit the door first, walking up to the table bumping up against chairs. Kendall meekly followed him, never raising her eyes from the floor.

"Don't you walk up in my house and disrespect me by not speaking," I said to Tyson. Kendall cringed and I lowered my tone.

"Hi," he mumbled under his breath. I shot Sammie a glance to find out what was going on. She simply shrugged her shoulders. Tyson and Kendall had been living with her for over a month and this was the first time that they were on my turf.

"Kendall, I want you to meet my daughter. Hold on and let me get her." I turned around and went to the steps to call Keira. She came bouncing down the steps and they became instant friends. Kendall was three years older then Keira but as they turned to walk away, I could tell it made no difference. Tyson looked up but he still had that sour look on his face.

Kevin ran down the stairs as they were going up and almost knocked both girls down.

"Hey, hold on, mister. You ain't outside," I said firmly.

"Sorry," he mumbled. He went right up to Tyson and asked him if he wanted to play one of his PlayStation games. It was like someone had flicked a light switch on Tyson's face. He jumped up from the table and quickly followed behind Kevin.

"What games you got?" Tyson asked as they headed up the steps.

"Hey, what about dinner?" I said to their retreating backs.

"Aw, man, he ain't hungry," Kevin said, answering for Tyson. The only other sound we heard was the closing of Kevin's bedroom door.

"So how is it going?" I asked Sammie now that we were alone.

"It's tough; I ain't going to lie. Tyson hates me and Kendall is afraid of her own shadow. I tried to get my mother to give me their clothes, but she is still being a bitch. She won't give me any of their things and I can't afford to buy them the things that they used to have!"

"Sammie, it's not about possessions. They are still children and they are having a problem with accepting you after all this time. Just continue to show them love. They will come around; I promise you."

Although I never met Althea, I learned to hate her just by observing the empty looks in the eyes of Tyson and Kendall. It was a look of someone who was desolate and beaten down. It was not a look you hoped to see in two teenage children with their whole lives ahead of them. I could tell that they had to fight every day of their lives to be who they were and that made me very sad.

Of the two, Kendall was worse. She was obviously in pain and would not let either Sammie or me in. She had questions about her father that Sammie could not or would not answer. She knew that her father still resided in California but had no way of contacting him without Sammie's help. Sammie didn't want to tell Kendall that her father denied paternity of her so she denied knowing his whereabouts.

Over the next few months, Kendall did develop a relationship with Keira. She pretended that Keira was her sister and enjoyed spending time with her at my house. Tyson, on the other hand, was totally belligerent and he made no attempt to disguise his contempt of Sammie.

Sammie tolerated this abuse at home but I would not allow it when they came to visit me. One day, I pulled Tyson aside and made it clear what I expected of him in my home.

"Look, you may not like some of the things that your mother has done, but the fact remains that she is still your mother and you can't change that," I said.

"I hate her!" he yelled, standing face-to-face with me. "Why couldn't she just leave us alone? We don't want to live in that funky apartment with her. We had our own rooms back at my real mother's house. Why couldn't she have left us alone?"

"Because she loves you," I yelled right back at him, forgetting that he was still a child. I wanted to ring his fucking neck but I had to remember that all of his animosity probably had come from Althea. Children rarely hate their mothers regardless of how wrong they are.

"She had a fucked-up way of showing it," he snarled. I snatched his narrow ass up by his arm and brought his face closer to mine so that we were facing each other nose-to-nose.

"Look, I told you once before that regardless of the circumstances, she is still your mother and therefore is entitled to your respect. She made some mistakes. I can't deny that, but she is trying to correct them! You will not disrespect her in my house and I better not hear of you disrespecting her in yours. Do I make myself clear, mister?" I asked, making sure I pinched his skin hard enough to cause it to welt. He snatched his arm away from me and raised his hand as if he were about to strike me.

"Don't even think about it buddy 'cause I will have your ass laid out on this floor before you can draw back the nubs!" Tears welled in his eyes but he would not let them fall. He still bucked at me and I swung hard enough to rattle his teeth. For a moment, we were both too stunned to move. Even though I did not mean to hit him, I knew I had slapped the taste out his mouth.

On impulse, I grabbed him again but this time to comfort him. He resisted my touch but I continued to hug and kiss him, telling him how sorry I was.

"I had no right to do that and I am truly sorry. You made me so angry. Don't you see your mother is trying? Can't you just give her a chance?" He did not answer me but he did not pull away from me either. We sat down together on the sofa.

"What are you so afraid of?" I whispered.

Very quietly he answered, "That she will leave us again and where will we go?"

"But don't you understand; your mother never had a choice. She was still a teenager when she had you. Your grandmother would not allow her to take you both away. Your mother did not leave you of her own free will."

He did not respond so I continued. "Could you give her a chance, please? It won't be easy—I know that, and I am not going to sit here and lie to you that it will be, but I'll be here for you and Kendall. If things get scary, call me. I can't fix everything but I will damn sure try."

At that point, Tyson and I formed a truce. Even though I still felt he didn't like me for hitting him I thought that he respected me enough to listen to what I had to say.

He agreed to go to school and to stop all the senseless fighting with his mother. It was not the best truce in the world, but it was a start.

chapter 22

After Sammie filed for divorce from Jessie, we became regular bar flies. We stayed in the clubs. That's not really anything to be proud of but we were still young, single, and we both loved to dance. We would start on Thursday night with ladies night at Chit-Chat on Candler Road in Decatur and would continue at various clubs until Sunday night for the All-Male Revue at Faces on Glenwood Road.

We didn't like going to the ritzier clubs 'cause number one, since they were too far away, we didn't want to get caught driving under the influence; and number two, the niggas in those other clubs acted like they were too cute to dance.

We made that mistake one night when we went to Hairston's in Stone Mountain. It wasn't far from our houses but the people were too stuck up for us. We came to party and that is what we did! Those perpetrators acted like they could not even work up a sweat. That's when we swore off the swankier clubs. Since most of the people there were pretending to be something that they were not.

Sammie met Curtis Brock at Chit-Chat one Friday night after about a month on the club circuit. That first night, he could not keep his hands off her. They danced to nearly every song, and he bought her a rose when the flower peddler came around. That was a first for Sammie. I occasionally got a rose or a teddy bear from an admirer but it had never happened to her and it opened her nose for real. Curtis was not necessarily handsome but he wasn't barf bag material either.

In short, he was an okay-looking man with a fairly decent body. He had a short Afro cut into a fade. His most striking feature was the peculiar shade of his brown eyes—we later learned were colored contacts.

I could not help but to mentally pick him apart but I didn't let Sammie know of my concerns. His clothes were rather ordinary and the soles of his shoes were run-down and badly needed new heels. His only saving grace in my opinion was the way he treated Sammie. I knew she needed to be pampered as a princess. This was what had been missing in her life for as long as I had known her. Coming so soon on the heels of Jessie, Curtis was just what the doctor ordered.

After watching those two carry on, I envisioned Sammie and Curtis going steady, courting, and eventually getting married and having 1.5 babies. I'll admit it, I got carried away with my fantasy for them, but Curtis was doing and saying all the right things and I liked it. He got an "E" for effort in my book. He was attentive to her needs all night long, and I did not have to worry about whether she was having a good time or not for a change.

Normally I would have to hold myself back from too much fun just so I could make sure she was having a good time. Because if Sammie got bored, then she would want to go home and if she was driving, that meant I would have to go home, too. I kept thinking, *Uh-oh, this might be the one to straighten her ass out.* But she fucked it up and took the nigger home. She broke the number one rule of dating: never take a man home on the first fucking night. I was pissed and she knew it, but that didn't stop her.

The next day, Sammie and I had a major falling-out about going to the club. In my heart, I knew that if she saw that nigga again, he would dis her and I would be left to pick up the pieces.

"What are you wearing tonight?" Sammie asked when I picked up the phone.

"Well, good evening to you, too," I sarcastically replied.

"Oh, my bad, girl. I guess I'm still tripping about last night."

"Yeah, you and me both." She did not catch on that I was truly irritated with her.

"I had so much fun last night! I can't wait to get back there. What are you wear-ing?" she asked again.

"I don't think I'm going out tonight," I responded.

"And why not?" she said, finally picking up on that attitude I had.

"If I do go out, I'm thinking about going somewhere different. We are wearing a hole in Chit-Chat's and I don't want to be labeled a 'regular.'"

"What's wrong with being a regular? It has its perks; half the time we don't have to pay." I could picture her sitting up in bed with her hands on her hips.

I knew that she was not out of the bed since chill was all Sammie did when she was at home.

"Nothing, really. I just don't want to be one."

"Oh, I think I detect a little hate-a-ration," she huffed.

"Hate? Oh no you didn't just say that to me. Why the hell do you think I'm hating on you?" I demanded.

"I just detected a little jealousy in your voice, that's all."

"Jealous, of what? Now you really are tripping!" I said, suddenly pissed.

"You know, about Curtis and all," she said with a tee-hee to take the sting out.

"Sammie, I am pleased as punch you found a man but I have absolutely no reason to be jealous of you." *Shit.* "Hey, I changed my mind. We will go back to Chat's tonight and see your 'man' but you are driving. Call me when you are ready to leave," I said and hung up the phone.

I stomped around my bedroom slinging clothes and talking to myself. She had suckered me into her plan to go to the club and I didn't even realize it until after I had hung up.

I was searching for the perfect outfit to wear that night. I was going to show that heifer just how bad she fucked up by sleeping with Curtis on the first night. Keira and Kevin were still at my mother's, and Tyson and Kendall were old enough to stay at home alone so the coast was clear.

I decided to let my shoulder-length hair hang down instead of pinning it up like I usually did. I picked a brown suede skirt outfit that clung to my hips and showed off my sexy legs and phat ass. I knew I looked good. Sammie came over and she was wearing a tired black cat suit that left nothing to the imagination.

One of these days, I was gonna tell Sammie that just 'cause designers made something in her size didn't mean she should wear it. But for right now I was going to keep my mouth shut. I was still pissed at her.

Even though I was upset with her, I didn't want to wish bad luck on Sammie. Before we left, I prayed that God would seal my lips from saying, 'I told you so' if Curtis decided to clown on her.

Sure enough, the nigga was clowning. You would have thought he never laid eyes on Sammie because he did not even acknowledge her presence. I mean nothing. Nada. He did not even nod to indicate that he even knew her in the first place. I was hot and I could only imagine how bad Sammie felt. To her credit, she kept her chin up and tried to have fun even though her eyes stayed glued to him all night long. That shit was foul. I even made a point to dance right next to his stank ass shooting him evil glares. He looked right through me as if I wasn't even on the same planet that he was on.

When the song was over I left my partner and returned to my seat. Sammie was rooted in place with this fake ass smile on her face still following Curtis' every move.

"Girl, fuck him," I said, trying to break her trance. She ignored me completely. After staring at her upturned face for a few seconds, I left the table in search of more fun. Curtis did not come around to speak to her until the club was closing and had the nerve to pretend that it was the first time he had noticed that Sammie was even there.

Shit, as big as Sammie had become, you could not miss her in a club—I don't give a fuck how much you had to drink. The last song was playing when he slipped up next to her.

"Hey, baby, when did you get here?" Curtis said with this stupid smirk.

"She's been here all fucking night, watching your dumb ass," I said before I could stop myself. Sammie shot me a look that said, *Shut the fuck up and let me do this!* Well, I could take a hint and she was right, so I sat back to watch my girl tear a piece out of the fucker's ass for real. As much as I liked to be proven right about situations, I hated, in this incident, that I had seen the writing on the wall.

"Hey, yourself," she said, batting her eyes and twirling her hair. Dumbstruck, you could have rolled me off the fucking chair I was so outdone. Curtis started whispering in her ear and kissing her neck and she was lapping it up. I guess she had forgotten the last four hours she'd spent watching his ass hump on all the other women in the club. It must have also slipped her mind that when she looked him dead in the eye that he turned away as if he didn't even see her.

When Sammie stood up and kissed that maggot I excused myself and went to the car. I would have left her ass, but she was driving. I stood outside for fifteen minutes before they finally came out of the club. Sammie knew that I hated being in the club when the lights came on, and she also knew that I hated waiting outside by myself, but none of that mattered to her that night.

They came out of the club all hugged up like they had just spent the night together dancing their cares away. I stood by the passenger door waiting for

Sammie to unlock it. When she got to the car, she looked at me for a moment as if she didn't remember I was even riding with her. In fact, she looked annoyed that I was still there. I threw an eat-shit-and-die look at Curtis and began to open the door.

"Uh. Marie, Curtis is going with us," Sammie said with a giggle. I shot Sammie that bitch-is-you-crazy look, but she promptly dismissed me. She reached over the seat, unlatched the back door and gestured with her eyes that I should get in the back seat. As Curtis squeezed past me to get to the front seat, he made sure he rubbed up against my ass. My head rocked back as if I had been slapped. I stepped quickly away from his groin towards the back of the car but I could not make myself grab the handle. I looked around to see if there was anyone I knew that would give me a ride 'cause just the thought of riding in a car with him or her made me sick.

I stepped away from the car. I would walk before I allowed her to treat me like a goddamned stranger. The deejay and I went way back and I knew that he was still inside. I decided to ask him for a ride 'cause I could not and would not ride home with those two. I knew there was a chance that I might have to fight the deejay off me by the time we got to my house since he had been trying to tap my ass for weeks, but I had my mace and was not afraid to use it.

"Sammie, my bad; I didn't know you would be having company. Three's a crowd so I'll holler at you later," I said while backing away from the car with my hands up in the air. A part of me was hoping that she was not going to let me go out like that, but she acted like nothing was wrong.

"All right then, I'll get with you tomorrow." Sammie got in the car and they pulled off leaving me in the dark parking lot alone. She did not even look in the rear-view mirror to see if I had waved or not. After her taillights disappeared, I had a true hissy fit complete with talking to myself and cussing a lot. I even kicked the tire of a nearby car, which damn near crippled me.

I looked towards the entrance of the club and noticed for the first time that most of the people who had been in the parking lot when I had come out were gone. I was alone with the exception of a few cars that had probably been left by their owners when they went home with someone else. I felt sure that the deejay was still inside but after I thought about it, I decided that I did not want to have to explain why I was still there with no ride home. It was painful enough without having to explain it to someone else so I walked to the curb and hailed the first cab I saw.

After I was seated in the cab, I decided that was the last time I would ride anywhere with Sammie. Having to pay my hard-earned dollars for a cab when I had a perfectly reliable car at home helped to stiffen my resolve. During the ride home, I thought long and hard about my friendship with Sammie and as bad as the night had been, I still was not ready to give up on her. I just needed to learn to put conditions on our friendship.

The next day, I waited for an apology from Sammie for her behavior the previous night but I got nothing. I don't know whether they spent half the night and the whole day fucking or what, but eventually I decided to go out and let my hair down. I was going to the club solo. Friday and Saturday night had been ruined by Sammie's trifling antics, but I was determined to make Sunday night my night to party and enjoy myself without her. I didn't mind going solo. I had done it before and from the looks of things, it was going to become a regular routine.

Before I got ready to go out, I called my mom to check on Keira and Kevin. Mom insisted on keeping them for the weekends and although I missed them I needed my down time, too. Since Dad had died, I had worried about her being in that big house alone. The kids kept her occupied and I was grateful for the time it gave me. She enjoyed it and didn't complain much—that is unless I took it to the ninth power and went overboard. Then she would go on strike until I cooled my ass down. After she and the kids assured me that they were having a good time, I started to get dressed.

While I was adding the final touches to my makeup, the phone rang. I looked at the caller ID and saw Sammie's name listed. For a brief moment, I contemplated not answering the phone but I was still expecting an apology so I answered just as the answering machine picked up. I told her to hold while I turned it off and made her wait a few additional minutes for good measure.

"Hey, girl, what's up?" Sammie said nonchalantly.

"You just caught me heading out the door." My voice was cool but hearing her voice reminded me of last night's ill feelings and I felt my anger rising again.

"And you didn't call me? Where are you going?" she asked, sounding hurt and defensive.

"The last time I talked to you, you were busy," I snapped. "It's Sunday; I'm going to Faces. I assumed you and what's his name were still knocking boots."

"Oh, Curtis, it's like that, huh," she fired back.

"Yeah, unfortunately it is. I didn't write the script; you did." If she knew what I was referring to she did not own up to it.

"Girl, he wasn't here that long. He just wanted to talk to me, that's all."

"Oh, in other words, he did a wham-bam-thank-you-ma'am on your ass," I said, trying not to laugh out loud. That's what she got for treating my ass like a second-class citizen. He hit it and quit it and told her to take him back to the parking lot so he could get his car. I would never put up with a man who thought he could use me and then ignore me until the next time his dick got hard, but she obviously did not have a problem with this since she seemed happy to oblige.

"Can I go?" she asked in her little-girl voice that she sometimes used when she was trying to get her way.

"It's a free county," I replied, refusing to be swayed by her childish tone.

"When are you leaving?" she asked. She was all business now that she knew I wasn't up for her bullshit tonight.

"Now. I'll save you a seat if you don't take too long," I said and hung up the phone. I said more than I wanted to but she got my drift. Whether or not it would do any good, I said my piece and only time would tell.

She showed up at the club and as luck would have it, a seat was still available. She did not offer me an apology for the way she acted the night before and I did not bring it up. I had never officially said that I would never ride with her again but I think she understood it without my having to say it. Though the circumstances had been unfortunate, I had learned a valuable lesson.

Sadly, I acknowledged that another line had been drawn in the sand in our friendship.

We continued for months going to the club like it was church in separate cars and meeting up inside. We still arrived at the same time 'cause we would get dressed at each other's houses. Much to my chagrin, Sammie continued to see Curtis. It was Friday night and we were preparing to go to Chit-Chat's.

"How's Dickweed?" I asked her just to see if she knew who I was talking about.

"Dickweed? Oh, Curtis," she said, laughing. "I knew you had given him a name but I wasn't sure what it was."

"Yeah, I thought it was fitting since his dick be growing out of a lot of different things."

149

"Well, you don't know that for sure. You are just guessing," she said in a huff.

"Come on, Sammie, wake up. He ignores you at the club. You have never been over his house. Do you even have a phone number for him?" I demanded.

"I got his pager number!" she declared, beginning to get mad.

"Pager, what does that tell you. That means either he is married or living with someone."

"Have you ever paged him in the middle of the night?"

"No."

"When you page him, does he call you right back?"

"Sometimes," she mumbled.

"Did you ask him why he never spends the night?"

"Yeah, he said that he can't sleep anywhere but his own bed."

"What about the time he called you at 4:00 in the morning and you went to pick him up and all he wanted was a blow job? I still can't believe you blew him in the parking lot!" Sammie did not say a word.

"Ok, I got just one more question for you and I will leave this alone. How come if sleeping in his own bed is such a priority to him, he doesn't ask you to come visit him?" Sammie was silent.

"I rest my case," I said, leaving her in the bedroom while I went in the bathroom to get dressed.

Sammie didn't speak as we each applied our makeup and final touches to our outfits. We arrived at the club at 11:15 to get a seat close to the dance floor. The new bouncer liked me so I did not have to pay tonight. He charged Sammie and that pissed her off even more. Normally I would have paid half of her admittance but I was still angry with her for being so stupid about Dickweed.

I wasted no time getting on the dance floor when we got in the club. I refused to ride the bar stool as Sammie had been doing for the past couple of months. No one asked Sammie to dance anymore so her only chance to dance was to join in the Electric Slide.

This shit continued even though Sammie knew that I didn't approve for a long time. For the most part, I tried to stay out of Sammie's sex life. We could talk about her kids and mine. Our jobs and even our mothers but that man was a forbidden subject. Once again, conditions were put on our friendship.

chapter 23

Sammie met a new man named Malcolm Warrens whom she nicknamed "N&P." It stood for new and promising. Since he had been making regular appearances at her door for the past three months, she felt she had a good thing going. She told me he was a truck driver and I was glad if it was going to get her away from Dickweed.

"Oh Lord. Does he know that you have this thing for truck drivers?" I asked her one night over cocktails at my house.

"No, I got him thinking it's his dick that has me imprisoned." She had this goofy ass smile on her face and I could not help laughing with her. They saw each other at least once or twice a week depending upon his load.

"Girl, he said he is looking for a good woman, one he can pamper and take care of, and I told him that I was the woman he's been searching for. Lord knows I need somebody to take care of me," she said. We both fell over laughing, reaching out to give each other high-fives.

"What about Kendall and Tyson? Have they met him?" I inquired.

"No, it seems like every time that he is in town they are here with you." She was right about that. They had taken to coming to my house when they got home from school and staying until practically bedtime. Most nights I didn't mind it because I wanted to keep an eye on them. Tyson continued to be a discipline problem at school, and Kendall was so withdrawn that the only person who could get through to her was Keira. I tried to push my thoughts about her kids' state of mind to the back of my head.

"You sure do need someone to take care of you," I said, pushing her lightly as we clinked glasses. It was good to see her smile again. Her eyes once again took on a special glow and I began to wonder whether Malcolm was okay after all. I was still skeptical but I was willing to wait and see.

"And guess what?" Sammie said with a hint of amusement.

"What?" I responded, catching my breath between my cheeks and knowing instinctively that I would not like what was coming next.

"He is getting me a car! It should be here this week." She was so happy she could barely sit still. Once again, bells started going off in my head but her obvious delight was catching. And girlfriend really needed a car.

"Get the hell out of here. You mean you are willing to part with the 'Flint-mobile'?" I could not stop laughing when I thought of her driving a car with real floorboards. Sammie had been driving that beat-up Buick since I'd met her and I just couldn't picture her in anything other than that.

"In a New York minute," she said.

"Remember that time I dropped my lighter and it fell right out the car onto Interstate 285 through the hole in the floor!" I said, laughing loudly.

"Yeah, that shit was so funny and you had the nerve to get mad at me."

"It's your car! But I tell you what; I feel safe when I ride in it. As long as it starts, you can be sure that anything you hit will crumble and we will be okay. That car is built like an armored tank," I said, raising my hand for a high-five.

"You ain't lying about that. These cars today, if you just bump something, you are talking one-thousand dollars in damages. But I'm ready to get me one of those 2002 models! I want to style and profile like you do," she said, smiling.

I got caught up in her fantasy and started feeling good about her life once more. She had been through so much in such a short period of time. I'm not saying that I believed all the hype that this guy was feeding her but she was looking good again. She was back to watching what she ate, taking hours to get dressed and was her old chatty self. I felt full. Sammie was back in charge of her life and I was feeling good about that. I was happy that she was happy.

"So, you mean to tell me you're only getting dicked down once a week and that's okay with you?" I was laughing as I said this but she did not join in. She started to get nervous and placed her drink on the coffee table.

"Uh...I've got a little something, something on the side," she mumbled.

"I knew it!" I exclaimed. "Who is he and what's his story?"

"Tried and True, you already know him."

"Girl, please, I can't keep up with the names, only the circumstances."

"Curtis."

"Dickweed? Oh hell no, please tell me that you are not still dealing with Dickweed!" I jumped to my feet and began pacing the room. I could feel the heat rise to my cheeks. "Here we fucking go again!"

"Marie, I know that you don't like him but the brother is hung like a race horse and knows exactly what to do with it. Don't hate on his dick," she replied. She refused to look me in the eye. All those cozy feelings that I had been experiencing since Sammie and I had started spending more time together again were evaporating into thin air.

"I don't give a rat's ass what kind of dick he got; the man is scum and he treats you like shit. Is he paying you for your services, is that it?" I demanded as I paced back and forth.

I knew that I had crossed the line with that remark but I was way past caring. I was wearing a hole in the floor. I really wanted to understand Sammie but I was having a hard time. I left myself open to the fact that maybe she didn't know any better. Maybe she was just doing what she had been taught to do. Regardless, it didn't make it any easier to swallow.

Although I knew full well that it was possible, I did not want to believe it. I knew that Sammie could and would at any given moment get enslaved by a dick, but I had hoped that her self-worth would prevail over this one.

"I'm dick-whipped; not much of an excuse, but it's the only one I have," she replied. "When I want to get dicked-down-proper, he is the one. Sorry if that offends you but it's the honest-to-God truth. But this time it's different; he is my dick on the side now and I call him only when I got to have it, not the other way around."

"And what about Malcolm? This man is about to buy you a car. What he is going to say when he finds out you still humping Dickweed?"

"He ain't going to find out!" she shouted, gathering her things to leave.

I just glared at her. I wanted her to see how truly dissatisfied I was with her, but she still refused to look me in the eye.

I was livid and just shook my head. Dickweed would be the straw to break the camel's back in our friendship if Sammie was not careful. I wouldn't have minded him so much if he showed my friend a small measure of respect, but he treated her just like she acted at times, like a whore. At that moment, I lost all respect for Sammie.

chapter 24

Sammie was working at Waffle House as a waitress. It may not have been the most glamorous job in the world but she had potential to make good money if she were in the right location. It also served another purpose; she met more men than she could shake a stick at.

"Girl, you need to bring your tired ass up to Waffle House and check out some of the men that be coming through there!" Sammie declared.

"I'll pass," I said, laughing. "I draw the line with men who think fine dining is found at the Waffle House."

"Ain't nothing wrong with WH," Sammie interjected with attitude. "We have steak, pork chops… it ain't all about breakfast; we have everything," Sammie said.

"Hey, don't get your panties all twisted. If it pays your rent and keeps food on your table, it's all good," I said, laughing.

There was something about Waffle House and the South that I had not gotten. Even though I could not see the attraction, that place stayed full at all hours of the night. Sammie only worked enough hours to meet her needs and spent the rest of her time sleeping and fucking. She would work a little harder when she got behind on her bills, but she basically relied upon her men folk to pay her bills. Every week, it was someone else stepping up to add some assistance. She would have any number of men stepping up to the plate to pay her bills and would spend her money on clothes and different hairdos. That was why it was especially hard for me to understand why Sammie still put up with Dickweed's broke ass.

One day she called me and told me that her lights were out. In the seven years that I had known her, she had never had anything turned off. She was constantly adding furniture to her apartment even though it was rent to own. I didn't ask her what she spent her bill money on and she didn't volunteer to tell me.

"Gurl, it is February. I thought that they would not turn off your lights in the wintertime! How much is your bill?" I asked her. I would have floated her a loan if I had had enough money to cover it.

"You don't even want to know," she said.

"That bad?" I asked. Her silence told me it was.

"I talked to Malcolm and he is going to send me some money in the mail this week," she answered.

"Yeah, but in the meantime, it's too damn cold to be in that apartment!" I didn't say anything for a few minutes as I was thinking. I did not really believe that Malcolm was going to come through since he still had not gotten that car he had promised Sammie a few months ago.

"You can come spend a few days with me until you get your shit together. I don't want Tyson and Kendall to get sick." She must have had her bags packed because they were at the front door in fifteen minutes.

"Thanks, girl, good looking out. We won't be here but a minute. I'm waiting for Malcolm, you know, my fiancé, to send a check and then we'll be okay," Sammie said.

I did not comment on the fact that she would not have a fiancé long if she kept hanging out with Dickweed but that was her business. She continued to juggle her men and somehow managed to keep them separate. Since her fiancé did not come to town often, it shouldn't have been too hard, but Dickweed had the tendency to call up late at night for a quickie. On the nights her fiancé was in town, Sammie would turn off the ringer on the phone and let her answering machine pick up.

This was a bold move since Dickweed felt that he had her so completely under his spell that he could just pop up at her house and it would be okay. I was waiting for the day that he showed up and she got caught. Mind you, I was not wishing that on her but it was bound to happen.

By agreeing to help Sammie in her time of need, I wasn't condoning her behavior. We had numerous conversations about the errors of her ways but she was quick to point out to me that she was a grown-ass woman. She would have to answer to all of her choices in the end, but I was not going to allow Tyson and Kendall to be cold. I felt confident that Sammie would pull a rabbit out of the hat any day and pay her bills, so I did not stress about it.

All things considered, I guess I had my own blinders on when it came to Sammie. Had I thought about it in any great detail, I might not have offered her a place to stay. I should have told her just the kids were welcome. She was relying on Malcolm to send her money to pay her bills but this was also the same man that had promised months ago to get her a car and she was still waiting for it.

I had a rather large three-bedroom house so I had the space, and at the time I thought that's what friends were for.

Sammie took Kevin's room with Kendall. His room was larger than Keira's. Tyson moved in Keira's room with Kevin. Keira moved into my room with me. Tyson, who had just turned fifteen, did not much like the fact that he was sharing a room with a nine-year-old and spent most of his time sleeping on my sofa in the living room. If Kendall minded sharing a room with her mother, she never voiced her objections.

Even though these arrangements were temporary, after a week, Sammie and her clan were wearing on my nerves. Kevin and Keira were completely outdone. They saw Tyson and Kendall doing things that they were not allowed to do and little by little they started to show out.

Tyson was like a human garbage disposal, eating me out of house and home. As if that wasn't bad enough, he threw his clothes everywhere and insisted upon eating in my living room. He left a trail of dirty dishes all over the place. While I was not anal about cleaning my house, I insisted that my kids pick up their toys after they finished playing with them. I also restricted their play area to their rooms. The living room, which was the first room you saw upon entering the house, was off limits except under my direct supervision. So you could imagine my annoyance with Tyson.

"Sammie, I am about to ring your child's neck!" I said completely frustrated.

"Join the crowd," she answered without asking for specifics. If she had threatened one of my kids I would've wanted to know why.

"This is serious, Sammie. I don't allow eating in my front room and Tyson refuses to accept that. If I find one more dish under the sofa I am gonna whip his ass. Now either you talk to him or the next time, it's gonna be on between us!"

"I told him what you said and he just looked at me like I was an alien speaking a foreign language," she said.

"That's 'cause you accept that dumb shit. When I climb on his ass, you better not say a damn thing 'cause I told you it was coming."

"Good luck. He listens to you more than me anyway. Every time I try to say something to him, he gives me this poof-be-gone look."

I did speak to Tyson and he became good about cleaning up as long as I was around but when I left to go to work it would be on. He would attempt to hide his mess when I came through the door by shoving dishes under the sofa. However, it never worked because the genius would leave half the plate sticking out so I could see it. Part of me felt that he was doing it for attention, but he really didn't want that type of attention 'cause I was ready to put it on his ass!

I was going to work every day and coming home to dishes in the sink and no food on the table. Sammie would wait until I got there and ask what was for dinner or she would call me at work and tell me what to bring home. That shit got old real quick.

Stressed out from the long week, I suggested we hit the club. We both got dressed and Tyson agreed to watch over things while we were gone. I had bought a fly dress at the mall earlier that day and was anxious to show it off. It was a shorty-short black dress, cut off on one shoulder and stopping right over my breast. The dress was positively suggestive and I looked good in it. I hooked it up with a rhinestone necklace and earrings. Sammie wore her old standby, a skin-tight white dress with a split straight down the middle that accentuated all her negatives.

It was the same dress she was wearing the night she met Dickweed. The dress was so tight that she couldn't wear panties. She insisted we stop at the grocery store so she could buy some pantyhose. I was pissed that she didn't get them earlier, especially since she'd been home all day, but there was nothing I could do at that point but go along with the program.

I pulled up next to her at the grocery store and crunk up the music. I was still applying my makeup and was anxious to get to the club. She opened her door with a loud creak and hauled her ass out of the car.

"Come on," she said.

"What?"

"You're coming with me, aren't you?"

"For what? I don't need stockings. Just hurry up; we might not get a seat if you take too long."

"I don't want to go in there alone."

Hell, I don't blame her, I thought, but I also didn't want to be seen with her in those bright lights 'cause people might think that we were hookers. My dress was not as raunchy as hers but it was definitely a party dress. Not to mention the fact that everybody's mother and father was usually in the store at that time of night and would be looking us up and down like we had one-way tickets to hell.

"Sammie, just go get the damn stockings and hurry up!" I really was having second thoughts about going to the club at that point. Yeah, I wanted to show off my new dress but I just didn't want to show it off in the damn grocery store. And with Sammie exposing all her wares, it would be especially embarrassing.

"No. If you won't go in with me then we might as well go home!" She pouted. I failed to realize it until I was in the store that if she had gotten mad and gone home, I still could have gone without her 'cause I was driving my own car.

I got out of the car fuming, making it a point to slam the door. Fortunately I did not lock it 'cause the keys were still in the ignition. I saw my coat on the back seat and quickly put it on. It was a short wool pea coat that made me appear like I was naked underneath since my dress was so short, but it was better than nothing.

I did my best to lag behind Sammie, pretending that I was not with her, but that was an exercise in futility since no one wore heels to the grocery store at 11:00 at night. I just wanted to crawl into a hole and pull the opening on top of me. We got the stockings amid several lewd looks and finally set out for the club.

I was determined not to let this little setback ruin my night. I was irritated, especially since I had to wait while Sammie put the stockings on in the car. But watching her trying to squirm into a pair of pantyhose behind the wheel of a car in that tight-ass dress made me loosen up. Now that was some funny shit.

I found a parking space right in front of the club but Sammie had to park across the street. Just punishment, I thought, for her making me go into the grocery store with her. Ditching the coat, I met her halfway across the street so that she would not have to walk all the way across by herself. I did not mind being seen in this attire in front of the club 'cause there were a lot of women dressed just like me. We could not get a seat at a table but found two seats at the bar.

I really didn't like bar seats because I hated for my legs to dangle, but beggars can't be choosey, and it sure beat standing up. The other thing that I hated about bar seats was the fact that every guy coming up to order a drink felt compelled to hit on you, and that night all the fowl-breathed stinky mother fuckers were stopping right next to me. I just could not understand how they could have left the house without brushing their teeth and putting on deodorant. I tried not to be rude but when this particularly funky brother ambled up to the bar, I pulled out my perfume and sprayed it right in his direction. He was so drunk that he failed to get the message. He proceeded to ask me to dance. I told him thanks but no thanks.

You had to be careful how you dissed niggas in the club these days. If you were too rude about it, they would get loud on you and start calling you every name but a child of God. I had seen a guy the previous week that just hauled off and smacked a sister 'cause she turned him down and I didn't want any of that drama happening to me. I slipped off the stool when I heard my song start to play and went in search of a partner. I was not like the other women in the club always waiting for a man to ask me to dance. Sometimes I went and found my own partner.

Dickweed came in about an hour later with a pretty, petite girl on his arm. I looked over at Sammie to gauge her reaction, but she acted like she did not even see him. I decided then and there to stop worrying about Sammie so I could get my groove on. I grabbed the first available man that passed my hygiene test and I was not disappointed. My partner was fine and could really move on the dance floor. We danced for three straight records before I had to beg out 'cause my feet were killing me. I liked him. His name was Norman Parker. I had seen him before but either he was tied up or I was. We always stared at each other but this was the first time that we actually had danced. He left me but promised to return later when I had a chance to rest up.

Sammie was still on the bar stool when I got back.

"What's up?" I said.

"This shit is lame tonight. I think I might go home."

Translation—she hadn't danced a lick and therefore the problem was the club, not her. Not to mention Dickweed was there with a fine young thing and wasn't paying her any attention as usual.

"The night is young," I shouted in her ear while bobbing my head to the beat. I was really getting the full effect of the music since I was seated near one of the speakers positioned on the floor.

"What are you drinking?" I asked, noticing for the first time the empty drink glasses in front of her.

"Rum and Coke," she responded while motioning to the bartender to bring her another one.

"That's a bit on the heavy side for you, ain't it? You usually stick to wine coolers."

"Tonight, I need this," was her response. I ordered a pina colada and turned my back to her and the bar as I continued to snap my fingers to the music. I was trying so hard not to let her dampen my good mood. I looked too good that night not to enjoy myself. I had been watching Norman for months and always had thought that I was not his type but that night I was on fire. Nothing was going to bring me down. I saw a couple of old partners enter the club but I was so far past them, I did not even break my stride.

In my case, when I say partners I mean dance partners but in Sammie's case, it more than likely meant fuck buddies. I saw one guy that I had slept with before but we both realized it was a mistake and maintained a cordial relationship. I didn't hate on him and he didn't hate on me. Almost every relationship that I had had ended on an amicable note. I still considered these people my friends and vice versa. The only exception to that rule would be my ex-husband. He said he still loved me but I wanted absolutely nothing to do with him. I had made that mistake once before and had no intentions of doing that again.

On the other hand, I didn't know what Sammie did to her men 'cause once they had had her, they became obsessed. I couldn't think of one of Sammie's former lovers that she still considered a friend. If she ended the relationship they either hated her and wanted her dead, or they continued to stalk her, making her wish she were dead. I just didn't understand. Sammie's ex-boyfriends just might've run her down crossing the street. So when another of her old fuck buddies came into the club, I started sweating.

Oh shit, I thought. Even though their relationship hadn't lasted longer than a few months, he was very bitter and vocal about the breakup. She had duped him out of $750 and he wanted his money back. He felt like Sammie had just used him for his money and left him when things got tough which is essentially what she did. If he decided to nut up, I did not want to be in the way. I didn't think he saw her but I wasn't taking any chances.

Feeling the need to put space between them and me, I jumped off my stool and went off in search of Norman. I was so determined to find out what was really going on between us. All this staring and smiling was working on my nerves and I just had to know if he found me as attractive as I found him. I didn't care what he was doing when I found him. He was going to be with me and that was it. As it turned out, he was alone, nursing a drink and welcomed the opportunity to dance again. We danced for the next hour and after we were through, we went off to a corner to get to know each other. I positioned myself so I could still see Sammie but I tried to tune her out as best I could.

Norman was thirty-three and single with a little girl named Allison. He said he was still on speaking terms with his baby's mamma and that he actively participated in Allison's life.

"So what does active participation mean?" I asked so that there would be no misunderstanding on my part.

"I get her every other weekend and one month during the summer," he replied. "Does that bother you that I have a child?"

"Quite the contrary. I like men who spend time in the life of their children. I have two kids myself, Keira and Kevin. I hate men that act like once the relationship is over with the mother, the relationship with the children has to end. It takes a special man, in my opinion, to continue a relationship with the child after the love or lust, is gone for the mother."

"And your children's father, is he still in the picture?" he inquired.

"Barely. He lives in Baltimore. When we were there, he put conditions around seeing the children."

"Conditions, I don't understand."

"He only wanted to see them when I was around. Since we moved to Atlanta, he has been here twice. My problem is that he calls and makes all these promises to the children and I have to look into their faces when they realize it is all a lie. I hate that shit. I would rather he not call at all if he is going to continue to set them up for disappointment."

Norman nodded his head as if he could understand exactly where I was coming from. I didn't want to get this deep and personal with him but it felt natural.

"Dang, it's like that, huh?" he said, laughing and trying to lighten the mood.

"It's really not funny when you are talking about your life. When we were first separated, he just wanted to come over to my house and hang out all damn day. I had enough of that when I was married to him. Although I didn't keep him from the kids, I felt that if they were more of a priority to him, he would have made more of an effort before we left!"

"How long have you been in Atlanta?" he asked.

"We have been here since 1995. We got here right before the summer Olympic games so I guess that makes it six years!"

Thinking about my ex caused me to zone out of the conversation I was trying to have with Norman and I had to shake myself and regain my focus. Besides, this was not the time, nor the place to be having this type of discussion. We were already yelling to be heard over the music. I switched gears and tried to put the focus on him.

"Well, you sure haven't been lonely 'cause every time I've seen you, you've been with a different female," I said.

"Only 'cause I could not get with you."

"Touché," I said, laughing. "But there have been times when I was alone."

"Tell the truth, those times were few and far between I didn't notice. Plus, you never gave me any indication that you knew I existed. You seem so above all of this. When you enter the room, you look around and take inventory and if a brother does not have it together, you dismiss him. I've been watching you," he said while waving his hand around the club.

I was busted and I could not even fake the funk. His comments made me take a good, hard look at myself. People often said that I appeared uppity and snobbish.

"That's a club persona. I'm not like that once you get to know me."

"Is that an invitation?" he slyly asked. He was so damn good-looking I had a hard time concentrating on what I was trying to say. I kept looking at his thick lips and wondering how they would feel against my body. That is what prolonged celibacy will do to a person. Make you equate everything that a man says to sex.

I ignored his question and continued to babble about nothing.

"The way my face is structured, if I'm not smiling I'm often told I look mean. But people couldn't very well expect me to go around smiling all the time. I would look silly." I tried explaining that to Norman but I don't know if he really bought my story.

"You still did not answer my question. Is that an invitation?" he restated.

"If you want it to be," I answered.

"So, are you going to give me your phone number if I ask for it?"

"Well, that depends on if you're asking for it to use it or just to say you got the digits and then add them to your black book collection."

"If you give it to me, I assure you, I will use it," he quickly replied, showing all of his teeth in the process. I gave him my number and told him I would speak with him later. Under his gaze, I felt as though I was wrapped in a blanket of euphoria. Suddenly, I realized I hadn't been paying attention to Sammie. I felt compelled to return to her side, fearing the worst.

Sammie was on the same stool I had left her on but my seat was taken. She was scanning the crowd looking for someone, I assumed Dickweed. I regained my seat just before her song, the Electric Slide, came on. This was the fat-girl-anonymous call to dance and she damn near knocked me over trying to get to the floor. She made a beeline to where Dickweed and his date were standing and stood right behind him. Every time she dipped down to the beat, she would grind her hips into his ass. I was embarrassed for Sammie and the girl he was with was livid. Dickweed did not even stumble while Sammie was grinding him and he was grinding the other girl. The shit would have been funny if I hadn't known the principals. Sammie was oblivious to this girl's attitude and did not miss a step in her moves. She acted like she was there with Dickweed, and the other girl had just magically appeared.

Sammie was in her element, what she lived for—chaos, conflict and confusion. The three C's.

From where I was sitting, I went through a whole range of emotions. I looked around to see who was watching this spectacle and noticed with great dismay that

Sammie's second husband, Stanley, finally had noticed that she was in the club. And if that wasn't bad enough, the girl Dickweed was with was seething. Obviously she was not used to sharing a man. She looked Sammie up and down as if to size her up and judging from the look on her face, she had decided she did not want any part of her. Sammie outweighed her 10 to 1 so she quickly stepped off. Instead of directing her anger toward Sammie she took it out on Dickweed. I was glad, too, 'cause I really was not in the fighting mood. I was not much of a fighter, but I would not let my girl get trashed if I could help it. That was just the code among friends the way I saw it. I would have jumped in throwing something other than punches if the situation got too ugly. Fortunately, girlfriend cussed out Dickweed and left the club leaving only Sammie and Dickweed on the floor.

I looked to my right and saw that Norman was standing right beside me. I didn't even remember leaving my bar stool. He did not tap my arm or do anything to let me know that he was there but I appreciated his valor. Meanwhile, Dickweed was losing his fucking mind.

"Bitch, are you crazy?" he yelled at Sammie while getting all close up on her as if she was one of his boys on the basketball court and they were about to fight over a missed shot. I glanced to the right and saw that her ex-husband was nudging his way to the front of the crowd that was gathering around Sammie and Dickweed. Those words, "Bitch, are you crazy," ignited a fire in me. I felt as though I had just been electrocuted. I did not even wait for Sammie to respond; I jumped right in.

"Who the fuck is you calling crazy bitch? She's been *Your Bitch* for the past year so what does that make you, motherfucker? You slimy sack of shit!" I could feel pressure on my arm and looked down and saw that Norman was trying to restrain me because I was about to get straight-up ghetto on Dickweed. Sammie's eyes were so big and round, I could tell just by the expression on her face that I was totally out of control and steadily losing ground. I was so far out there I was jumping around as if I was in the boxing ring about to knock a motherfucker out. I did not even notice the crowd as it swelled, anxious for the first punch or shot to be fired.

Acknowledging yet another squeeze on my arm, my sanity returned. Public outbursts were so not like me that I had to take a virtual step back from my own damn self. I asked myself why in the hell was I concerned; that motherfucker didn't disrespect me. I loved Sammie but was it worth publicly embarrassing myself over her shit? I thought not.

"Look, I'm sorry," I said to Dickweed. "This isn't my fight. If Sammie wants to put up with your sorry broke ass, that's on her." I turned to Sammie and said, "I'm out, see you at the house."

I turned and walked away. Norman was right beside me. The crowd that had gathered around us made it difficult to leave the area, but I just kept elbowing my way out of the circle and out of the club. Norman pulled me aside.

"Could you hold up for a minute? I really would like to see you again, all bullshit aside. I like what I see," he said.

"After the way I just behaved?" I exclaimed already feeling deeply ashamed of myself.

"Now more so than ever," he simply stated. "I was always attracted to you on a physical level but tonight you showed a fire in you that I have been looking for in a woman. I don't like the kind of women that allow men to walk all over them. I want a woman that will stand up for what she believes. Marie, I definitely want to see where this leads." He grabbed my hand and kissed my palm. Now I had had guys kiss my hand before but never my palm. It sent goose bumps up my spine and started my pussy to twitching. I sent my pussy an instant message and told it to chill the fuck out. There would be no playing tonight! It had been a while since my pussy had a good workout so I could relate to it acting that way, but I did not want to make a mistake with a club junkie that I would regret.

Men thought that they were the only ones who thought about sex. They would be surprised to know that we thought about it just as much or more as they did.

Norman was in for a challenge 'cause I didn't go for the okie-doke like some of my female counterparts. If he wanted to get to know me, he was going to have to be prepared to deal with me. When it came to men, I was strictly on the up and up and I demanded the same thing that I gave out and then some.

He walked me to my car and we slid inside out of the cold night air and we talked for the next thirty minutes. The conversation was so nice, and he applied no pressure. He acted like he really wanted to get to know me. I started the car to take the chill off.

Eventually Sammie came out of the club with Dickweed in tow. I rolled my eyes at him and tried to stare Sammie down to make her come to her senses.

She stopped by my car before leaving the parking lot. "Marie, I'm taking him to my house. I'll see you later," she said as if nothing had happened inside of the club.

"In the dark?" I questioned, surprised again at the lengths Sammie would go to get that dick. It was downright disgusting.

"We don't need any lights for what we are going to do." She giggled.

The fact that this whole conversation had taken place in front of Norman really had pissed me off. It was bad enough that I almost had gotten into an all-out brawl with Dickweed 'cause he was disrespecting her trifling ass, but to have had it take place in front of a strange man had added insult to injury.

"Well, I'll just be damned!" I said in complete awe. Norman gently squeezed my hand, cutting off the low blow that I was about to throw at her departing figure.

"Whatever, heifer, holler at you later." I watched her drive away with tears pricking the corners of my eyes. She was a grown-ass woman and there was nothing I could do about her behavior, but it still hurt me. She was not only disrespecting herself, damn it; she disrespected me and I did not play that shit.

I turned to Norman with tears brimming in my eyes. They did not fall but they were there. He kissed his fingers and put them up close to my eye. It was so sweet of him not to try to take advantage of the moment.

I cleared my throat and said, "You know what, she's my friend and I love her dearly but sometimes I really don't like her! You don't know that man. He really treats her like warmed-over shit but her dumb ass keeps coming back for more. I just can't understand it and for some reason that causes me a great amount of pain." I tried to get the words out in between sniffles.

"That's what makes you so special to me," Norman said. "You have compassion for other people. You are not just out there thinking of yourself. I could see it in the way you defended your friend even though she's acting like a fucking idiot, excuse my French. And you're right, I don't know the guy that she left with but I have seen him before plenty of times and this does not surprise me. The only thing that I'm thinking about is that if you can love her with all her flaws, imagine how we could learn to love each other." Norman surprised me with his insight and I was touched.

Norman and I spoke for another fifteen minutes but my heart wasn't really in it. I think he sensed it, too, 'cause he gently kissed me on the cheek and said goodnight. I drove home in deep thought about the events of the night and others in the recent past. In the end, I made a firm resolve to never go out with Sammie again. That shit was just too dangerous for me and if I wasn't careful, I could wind up getting hurt.

chapter 25

Sammie's car was in the driveway blocking my entrance. I started to get mad all over again. She knew not to park there unless she was behind me 'cause when I pulled behind her big-ass car, the back of my car stuck out into the street and I hated that shit. She was just a non-rent-paying visitor so she should not have been in my space. I parked on the street with every intention of waking Sammie up and making her move her damn car out of my spot.

I assumed that the two-minute brother had come and gone since she was there so early. It was late but the kids were still up playing Nintendo when I opened the door. Tyson and Kendall were draped over the sofa as if it were the afternoon instead of three o'clock in the fucking morning. I was pissed that Tyson had allowed my kids to stay up that late. I was about to give him a piece of my mind when I heard moaning sounds coming from Kevin's room.

Although the sound registered as those made while fucking, I could not get a clear picture of what was going on. Slowly it dawned on me. Someone was getting busy and that someone was Sammie. I raced down the hallway like a woman on fire. I pounded on the door like a demented bitch. I contemplated knocking down the damn door but I knew that she could not afford to replace it. Kevin and Keira, scared by the wild look on my face, were clinging to my legs and crying. I was so hurt that Sammie would deliberately disregard my feelings for Dickweed and bring him into my home. My kids were too young to know what was really going on but her kids knew what time it was. Obviously they had been down this road before 'cause all they did was snicker.

With tears streaming down my face, I continued to beat on the door. At first, they stopped making noise as if I hadn't heard them in the first place. As I continued to pound on the door, I could hear them whispering but I could not make out all of their words. What I could hear was Dickweed urging Sammie to finish what she had started since he was almost there. This incited me even more and I began to pound the door with both my feet and hands. I did not stop banging on the door until it was opened and a half-naked Sammie peeped her head out.

If I had thought to grab a weapon, I would have cold cocked her ass and snatched the weave off her head.

"You low-down dirty bitch! How could you bring that piece of trash into my house!" I screamed. "What the fuck have I ever done to you to make you treat me like this? All I ever wanted to do was to help your sorry ass, and this is the thanks that I get! I want you and that slimy motherfucker to get the fuck out of my house!" I screeched.

For a moment, Sammie did not move and she looked as if she were truly afraid of me.

"Now, bitch, or I'm calling the fucking police. If you don't believe me, then keep your fat ass right there and see what happens! You've got ten seconds to get out!" I was screaming and spitting in her face.

From behind the door, I could hear Dickweed asking her if I had a gun.

"I don't want to get shot in the back by this simple-ass bitch," Dickweed continued. Sammie shut the door and there was further rustling as they continued to get dressed. I put my ear up against the door so I could hear what was being said.

"She does not have a gun; I would know that shit. Just get dressed so she will stop yelling," she hissed at him. Unfortunately, I did not detect any remorse in her voice.

Sammie came out first with Dickweed super-glued to her backside, using her as a shield. I would not look at Sammie but I did steal a look at Dickweed. He had a shit-eating grin on his face that just made me want to go Mike Tyson on his ass! I was so upset that I was shaking. Twice in one night they had pushed me beyond my limits. I ordered my kids to go to their rooms and get into bed. They did not want to, but they could tell from the tone of my voice that they had better not challenge me.

I took a deep breath and in the most normal voice that I could muster, I spoke to Sammie and Dickweed. She was looking at the floor, and Tyson and Kendall's eyes kept darting back and forth between their mother and me. Dickweed was still grinning like that shit didn't mean anything to him and in reality it probably didn't 'cause he had gotten what he had come for.

"Sammie, tell your fucking friend to get out of my house now before I have to hurt him!" I said this through clenched teeth and she knew that I meant business. My fingers were curled around the neck of a beer bottle that I had grabbed out of the refrigerator and I was ready to launch it at his head.

"Wait by the car," she said to Dickweed under her breath. He sauntered out of the door, leaving it open, but not before he instructed her not to keep him waiting too long. He had the nerve to blow a kiss in my direction and I threw the bottle barely missing his head. The bottle exploded, splattering beer and glass all over the walls and carpet.

Sammie did not flinch. I stood there staring at her for a full five minutes willing her to say something to me to make the situation better. With a heavy sigh, I told Tyson and Kendall to get their stuff 'cause they were leaving along with their trifling mother. They went into the kids' rooms to gather the stuff that they had managed to move in during the course of their stay. I stopped them both out of hearing range of their mother. "Tyson and Kendall, if you ever need me, I'm just a phone call away. I am not abandoning you two; I just can't be a friend to your mother. Do you understand that?" They both nodded. "I love you both; please remember that," I added.

"Then why are you kicking us out, too?" Tyson said, always the bold one.

"'Cause I can't legally keep you. I could get in more trouble if I did that. Your mother's responsible for you, not me." Watching their faces as they prepared to leave was tearing my heart to pieces but I could not help it. Sammie had caused all the drama.

Back at the front door Sammie waited while she shifted her weight from foot to foot as if she had to go to the bathroom. She did not say anything and for a while, I was tempted to just leave it at that.

"You need to get your stuff, too. You crossed the line today and you are no longer welcome in my home—ever." I was still crying but I was not yelling anymore. I was too drained and hurt. She turned to go get her stuff but I stopped her. From the look on her face, I believed she thought that I was changing my mind.

"Sammie, just tell me one thing. Why? What did I ever do to you that would make you hurt me this way? Make me understand, please, so that one day, I can look back on our friendship and say something good about it." I was pleading with her to try to salvage some part of our friendship. She opened her mouth to speak but nothing came out. She looked at me briefly but lowered her eyes and turned to go get her things. I heard a horn blow from outside and assumed that it was Dickweed. It just didn't make any sense to me. She got her things and after several trips to the car, they were ready to go. I stopped her from shutting the door with my foot and requested my keys back. She looked as if I had slapped her but she gave them to me. She walked out the door without answering my question or bothering to offer any explanation for her actions. Even after witnessing my hurt and anger, and watching the tears fall from my eyes, she never even said that she was sorry.

I spent the entire day cleansing Sammie out of my life. I didn't want any visible evidence of her stay. I found several items that they had left behind, and I packed them up and dropped them off at Sammie's apartment on our way to the grocery store. I did not want to knock so I just left the package outside her door. When we got back, I crawled into bed with Kevin and Keira and we took a long nap. Sammie and I did not speak for one year. She would call, but when I saw her name on the caller ID, I refused to answer the phone. Sammie had hurt me too bad. It was as though she had created an open wound and now it was infected.

I still kept in contact with Tyson. Kendall was too shy to call but I saw her around. Tyson told me that Sammie spent most of her days sleeping and the others just barely getting out of bed. If he had told me this to get me to forgive his mother, it did not work. Sammie had created the rift, not me.

chapter 26

Norman and I began speaking on a regular basis. I told him what Sammie had done and how it was affecting me. He listened to me as if he really cared about what I was going through. He seemed truly sincere and I liked the words of comfort that he whispered to me when I broke down into tears while recanting what had transpired.

"Marie, I know it doesn't feel that way but things are going to be okay," Norman said.

"I know but it's still a touchy situation as far as I am concerned. I am afraid for Kendall and Tyson 'cause I know Sammie. She will just hide from the world and the only ones that will suffer are Kendall and Tyson," I said.

"If you feel this strongly, why don't you do an intervention?" he asked.

"Two reasons, really; I hope that this will wake her ass up and two, her children need to learn to rely on her, not me. I have my own that I am responsible for," I said.

"True, you do but if it is going to worry the hell out of you, then you just can't push it under the rug."

Norman had a good point. I was making myself sick worrying about what was going on behind their closed doors.

Norman was different from the average guy. He proclaimed that he was not just interested in getting into my panties, and he was showing it by taking an active interest in the things that concerned me. Needless to say, I was intrigued. Although I had not seen him since the night we'd met, he called me every morning to wake me up, and he was the last person I spoke to every night.

That was unusual because most guys didn't like to talk on the phone unless they absolutely had to and they kept it quick and to the point. Not to mention, I was not much of a phone person either.

Norman would ask me about my kids and even remembered their names. This was a good sign to me 'cause most men talking to a woman with kids tried to ignore the children or pretend they did not exist.

"I would like to see you this weekend. Do you think we could get together and maybe watch a movie?" he asked. I was open to that suggestion and offered to cook for him but he said that he would pick up something on the way. I gave him directions and we set a time that would have him at my front door by eight o'clock Friday evening.

I was nervous about seeing him in my home without the club gear that he was used to seeing me in but if this "friendship" were going to grow into anything else, we would have to pass this moment. I was also taller at the club due to the high heels that I always wore. When I went out, I usually wore very short-form fitting dresses showing off my sexy legs with four-inch heels. But that night I was toned way down in some Tommy jeans and a V-neck sweater. I had chosen the sweater 'cause it molded my upper body showing off my big breasts. My hair and makeup were tight so in all I thought that I looked fly and if the brother didn't like it, shame on him.

To add to my anxiety about seeing Norman again, my mother was tripping about watching the kids and she waited until the last minute to tell me. She started to clown when I told her I might have a date and then began to complain about all the things that she had to do that evening. Any other time I would have had to fight with her just to take the kids home with me, but all of a sudden, she had things to do. She had their bags packed and waiting when I pulled up to her door and was ushering them out to the car as if the house were on fire. Imagine that, my own mother hating and blocking on me. In a way I couldn't blame her. In the long run I thought that it would be okay for the kids to meet Norman since he acted like he was going to be around for more than a minute. But that called for plan two, to make the kids so tired that they would be anxious to go to bed on time.

I was not sure how my kids were going to react to a man in the house since I never entertained men in the house. I never wanted to confuse them by seeing a lot of different men, but I felt like Norman would be an exception. Since my move to Atlanta, I had only dated two other guys and they never made it to my house nor did I to theirs. Plus, the kids' bedtime was 9:00 so if things didn't go that well, it would only be an hour before they would be heading off to sleep.

Norman arrived promptly at 8:00 with two big bags. Since he had not asked me what I had wanted, I was surprised to see that they were from one of my favorite restaurants, the Olive Garden, and he had ordered my usual dish of seafood alfredo. The restaurant was near my house so the food was still hot.

"Are you psychic?" I inquired as I emptied the contents of the bags he'd brought in.

"What do you mean?" he replied.

"I'm just saying, how did you know that this was my favorite dish? Plus Olive Garden has the best salad in the world and the breadsticks aren't bad either." He gave me the sweetest smile that heated up my insides.

"Baby, I wish I could take credit for pulling a rabbit out of a hat on this but I can't. I just got my favorite dish and hoped that you would like it. I should have called to confirm but I really did want to surprise you," he said with a sheepish grin. "I'm glad it pleased you, though. I didn't know what you wanted to drink so I got some beer for me, some grape soda for the kids, and a bottle of the house wine for you. Will that be all right?"

I kissed him right on the tip of his nose. "Yes, that was very sweet of you." He blushed and I found that refreshing. It had been too long since I had spent time alone with a man and I found myself having that woman-to-pussy conversation again. I told Norman to go into the living room and make himself comfortable.

After I had a chance to put the food away I peeped in and was stunned. Norman was on the floor with my son playing with his PlayStation 2. My daughter was curled up right next to him and for a minute I thought I had peeked in someone else's living room. To my surprise, they appeared extremely comfortable with each other. I wanted them to get along but damn, I was not ready for this. My son did not take to strangers well at all. He would have to know someone for at least a month in order to speak to them and he never let anyone play on his Play Station, not even his sister. Hell, he got an attitude when I tried to play with him and I bought the damn thing! Normally I would wait until he went to sleep so I could play as long as I liked and he would not be the wiser. He was nine and the concept of sharing had not entered into his brain yet. Everything was his and you had better know it.

My daughter, on the other hand, was more affectionate so I was not too surprised by her closeness to Norman but oh my goodness, she was snuggled up to him like she had known him all of her life. I tried to keep the astonishment off my face as I came in and sat down on the sofa to join them.

"I see you've met Keira and Kevin," I said.

"Yeah, great kids."

"Are you ready to eat yet?"

"Aw, Mom, we're playing here. Do you want me to mess up?" Kevin said with a touch of attitude.

"Give me a chance to catch up. Kevin is kicking my butt," Norman replied.

"Ok, I'm going to pour myself a glass of wine. Are you ready for a beer?" I asked.

"In a minute, I'll take one with dinner." He did not even look up from his game and I had to suppress a chuckle. I got caught up in the games, too, on the rare times I had a chance to play. I would get to fussing at the television, like it could hear me, when I lost or it did something that I did not like. I was so engrossed in my musing I forgot to get up until I looked over at Norman and caught him looking over at me. Our eyes locked making my knees weak. If I had read his gaze correctly, it said, *It could be like this all of the time, baby, that is, if you want it to be.* Damn, this brother was deep and my antenna went up. I was going to have to be very careful how I handled him.

My, my, my, I thought. I got up and headed to the kitchen to get myself together. My thoughts went straight from the Hallmark moment in the living room to a raunchy bedroom fantasy straight out of *Penthouse* magazine that I should not have been thinking about at all. He'd just arrived and all I really wanted to do was run my fingers through his chest hairs that I peeped poking up through his partially unbuttoned shirt. I could see myself doing a series of tongue dances with him.

I could hear Kevin and Norman yelling at the television in the living room, acting like they had been friends for years. I poured myself a glass of wine and sat down at the kitchen table to gain some composure. I didn't know whether to get horny or misty-eyed. Talk about confused! I wished at that moment that I could call Sammie to tell her how well things were going. I'd had a little bit of time to heal since the incident with Dickweed but I still ached over it. And during moments when I should have been happy, I was saddened because I couldn't share my life with her. It ain't like I would have asked her advice regarding whether I should sleep with him or not but I still would have liked to share my observations of him. Sure, I had other friends like Leah and Angie, but Sammie and I had recent history. She knew my dirt and I knew hers. The only difference was that the last time Sammie had thrown her dirt on me, and I was unwilling to forget that shit.

Even though Sammie wasn't around to share the news of my good fortune, I was still happy that I had found Norman. Truth be told, I needed a good man in my life. I had endured all the bullshit and drama that one woman could stand in a lifetime and I was ready for the real deal. I felt that if God was finally sending me one good man, I needed to take a few moments to thank him.

Two glasses of wine later, I was still alone in the kitchen, and Norman and the kids were still involved in the game. I looked at the clock and realized it was 9:30 and that I was going to have to be the bad guy and put an end to their fun for the night, if I wanted to spend any time with Norman.

When I walked into the living room, I found Keira asleep. I woke her up and pushed her to her room. I tucked her in and gave her a kiss but she did not even feel it 'cause she was down for the count. Next came the hard part—getting Kevin to turn off the game. I dragged my feet getting back to the living room 'cause I could just hear Kevin's mouth.

But when I returned, the television was off and the room was empty. I looked around but did not see Norman or Kevin anywhere. I backtracked upstairs and found that Norman was tucking Kevin into bed. I almost hit the floor. There were no temper tantrums nor any crying, yelling or slamming of objects. He simply had climbed into bed, and was waiting patiently for his kiss goodnight. When I leaned down to kiss him, he whispered in my ear, "I like him. Can he come play with me again tomorrow?" He said it so quietly, I had to strain to hear him but I shook my head yes and fought to keep the tears from falling down my face.

"Go to sleep, my little man. Have pleasant dreams," I said, quickly kissing him and turning out his lights. Norman had already left the room so I did not immediately have to face him. I knew that he did not hear what my son had said 'cause I had to strain to hear it, but it opened another floodgate of emotions that I was not ready to deal with. Did my son know something that I did not know? Were my children telling me that Norman was the one? I felt so confused.

Going down the stairs, my heart was racing and I was not sure why. I was plagued with questions and no answers. Was my son so starved for male companionship or was his radar better than mine? I really didn't have an answer to that one. Both of my children behaved like model children that night and that's something that rarely happened when I wanted to make a good impression on someone. Up until that moment, I did not realize how much I had wanted Norman to like my kids and me. I shot God another thank you and went to find Norman.

He was back in the living room but this time, he had a beer in his hand. He grabbed my hand and pulled me down to the sofa with him.

"I like your kids," he said. "Especially your son; that little man is a trip. Do you know that he asked me to come back and play with him tomorrow?" he quietly said. *Damn, so much for him not knowing what my son said.* He was in like Flynn and he knew it and there was nothing for me to say!

"Are you ready to chow down or what," I asked, trying to change the subject and put a little distance between us. As it was, I had settled next to him shoulder to shoulder on the sofa and the close contact was not helping my befuddled brain. I was feeling way too comfortable and I was glad to have somewhere to go when I jumped up to see about the food. I was in the kitchen before I even heard his reply.

"I'm ready when you are. You have a nice place, too, and did I tell you how beautiful you look tonight?" he said. Stunned and at a loss for words, I managed to tell him thanks and asked him to turn on the radio. He opted for the local jazz station for some sultry dinner music. I liked his choice.

"The food should be ready in about half an hour. You can't rush pasta or it won't be any good at all. We can start with the salad," I said. Since it was a pasta dish, I put the tins into the oven and turned the temperature on low.

He came into the kitchen quietly, scaring me.

"Don't sneak up on me like that. I watch too many scary movies." Not to mention the multi-media entertainment center I called a brain was working overtime, causing me to be more antsy than usual. My body was on fire and the wine that I had consumed was helping to fuel it. Norman wrapped his arms around my waist and pulled me gently back against his chest. We stayed that way for several minutes and I could feel the swell of his dick against my butt. It was all I could do not to push back on it to let him know that I was just as eager as he appeared to be.

He turned me around and placed a gentle kiss on my forehead and said, "Relax baby, I want this as much as you do." Was I that transparent? I was having such a hard time thinking with him so close to me. He brought his lips down to mine and gave me yet another gentle kiss. He did not seek my tongue and I did not offer it. It felt so good to be held that I just wanted to savor the moment. He gently rubbed my back and my neck muscles. We stayed that way for at least ten minutes. He pulled me closer and after a few seconds, firmly pushed me away. I immediately regretted the distance but I tried to recover. He was rock hard and my nipples were standing at attention. He rubbed his hands along the side of his pants legs to ease the electric pulsations that had filled the room, and I bowed out to get plates for the salad.

Neither of us spoke while we enjoyed the meal. It was not a strained silence; it was a silence born of comfort. Remarkably he was at ease and so was I. After we ate, he helped me clean up the dishes and we went together into the living room to watch the movies he had brought. Although it was getting late and the wine was making me a little sleepy, I did not want the night to end. He had a long drive ahead of him and I would have understood if he had chosen to leave, but he did not seem to be in any hurry to get going. I got the bag of movies to see what he had brought and was pleased to see that we had some similar tastes in movies as well as food.

I liked to be scared and I liked to laugh. He had brought *The Ring*, a movie that I had not seen before but wanted to; and *Barbershop*, a comedy that had caused a lot of controversy in the black community.

"Can we watch the scary one first? I love scary movies but hate to watch them alone."

"Sure, it's your night; do what makes you happy," he replied. *Was that an invitation to jump his bones 'cause that shit would sure make me happy*, I thought. I shook my head to clear the sexual fantasies. I put in the movie and adjusted the sound. I had the serious hook-up with my big-screen television and surround-sound speakers. I lowered the lights and took a seat next to him on the sofa. I was not yet comfortable enough to just slip into his arms but before the opening credits were finished, he had me snuggled up next to him. We fit like we had been together for years. We wound up lying down on the sofa with him in the back and me in the front. He kept his hands on my shoulders or my waist. He never attempted to touch my nipples, which were screaming out to be held, nor did his hands wander down to my forbidden triangle. Don't ask me what happened during the movie 'cause it wasn't long before we both fell asleep. He went to sleep first, snoring softly in my ear, which was as soothing as a lullaby to me. I wasn't far behind. Sometime after two o'clock he woke up, turned me over and we had our first serious kiss. He got aroused and since I was already there, I became more aroused. We kissed passionately for the next fifteen minutes or so complete with all the bumping and grinding, and it felt so good but at the same time, it was torture.

"I need to go," he whispered into my ear while gently nibbling on my earlobe. I was so hot that I was not thinking straight. Part of me wanted to beg him to stay and the practical part of my brain said, *Bitch, don't blow it by sleeping with him on the first date.*

He removed me from his chest and we sat side by side. I got up to take the DVD from the player.

"Don't," he said, halting my movements. "I'd like to come back tomorrow if it is all right with you. We can get an earlier start and maybe get to actually see both movies."

"Sure, that's fine 'cause I really want to see both of them. But I kind of promised the kids to take them to the zoo tomorrow. I can call you when we get back," I said.

"Oh, can I come along, too?" he asked, waving his arms around like a kid waiting to be picked at school.

Laughing, I said, "Yes. I'm sure Kevin would like that, too," as I walked him to the door. We shared another magical kiss and he was gone.

I was so elated, I wanted to call some damn body and tell them about my date, but there was no one who would feel me like Sammie would. Leah briefly came to mind but she and Kentée had tied the knot and who knew what they would be up to at this time of the night. If Angie were up, she would either be out on the town or screwing. Dejected, I went upstairs and pulled out my trusty vibrator. I got the nut out of my system and took a hot shower before falling into bed. That night I went to sleep a happy woman full of anticipation and dreams of a promising future with Norman.

chapter 27

Norman called at 10:00 to say that he would be over by 11. I jumped out of the bed and ran to wake up the kids to start getting dressed. I forgot to wrap my hair so I had some serious work to do to be presentable in one hour.

Out of habit, I didn't tell Kevin or Keira that Norman was joining us. My past relationships had taught me to never tell a child something unless you are sure it is going to happen. So, when the doorbell rang, I told Kevin to open the door. It was a true Kodak moment. Kevin's whole face lit up when he saw that Norman was back.

"You came back," Kevin exclaimed, hardly able to contain his excitement. He was so excited he did not know whether to shit or go blind. It was comical but again I felt the pull on my heartstrings. Was my son really that starved for male attention?

"Sure I did, little buddy; didn't I tell you I would be back?" he said, smiling, making light of the emotional situation brewing. Keira hid behind my legs until he began to look around for her. I knew that he had seen her 'cause he winked at me and started calling out her name like he could not see her. She kept hiding behind me, giggling the whole time. She waited a few minutes more before she bum rushed him. She wrapped her arms around his legs and said, "Here I am!" It was such a special moment I could not help but join in the laughter.

Norman did not kiss me in front of the kids, which I was thankful for, but I wanted a special greeting as well. He patted my ass while the children were not looking and it shocked me so much, I almost walked into the wall. I got the kids' jackets and we were off. I had to fight with Norman to allow me to pay for our admission into the zoo but in the end, he was a good sport about it as long as I let him pay for lunch.

We had a wonderful time. Even though it was cold, he did not rush through the zoo like the average man would, trying to get it behind him. He appeared to be just as excited about seeing the animals as the children were, and he was patient and stopped every time the kids wanted to stop. After the zoo, we went to the playground where we took turns pushing each other on the swings. We all felt comfortable with each other and I was beginning to like having a man around. It was a scary thought 'cause I had adjusted to the fact that I was destined to be alone forever.

It was after 4:00 when we left the park and by then we were all starving. We went to McDonald's and each had Happy Meals. I wished that I had been the one that created the concept of fast food 'cause Mickey Dee's, as we were fond of calling McDonald's, was making a mint. I didn't know one kid that didn't like a Happy Meal and the fries were good enough to make you wanna slap your momma!

"You are going to be satisfied with a Happy Meal?" I asked Norman.

"Yeah, I like the burgers. Plus, if you open the trunk, you will see all the little toys that I have been collecting. One day, they are going to be worth a fortune," he said, laughing, and I joined in. Norman was indeed a special case.

By the time we got back to the house, the children were asleep. Norman helped me get them inside and put them down for a nap. I wanted a nap, too, 'cause I was tired from all the walking but I was so enjoying his company and I didn't want the date to end. We settled on the sofa and watched the rest of *The Ring*. This time, I was too excited to go to sleep and I think he felt the same way. The movie was scary but it challenged you to think.

I used the movie as an excuse to get right up next to him, and he did not object. I was nervous but still confident 'cause he seemed like he was enjoying himself as well. After the movie was over, we talked for a while about what we were doing and where we wanted things to go from that point.

"Marie, I like you and your family. I think we have a chance at something special, but I don't want to rush it," Norman said.

"I agree one hundred percent that we need to take our time. I took a big step by introducing you to my children, which is something I rarely do. I only did that 'cause I felt like you would be around for a minute." I said all that out loud but my greedy ass was ready for more.

Sooner than I wanted, he told me that he had to leave. It was only 7:00 on a Saturday night and the kids were wide awake asking for dinner. I asked him if he wanted to stay but he said that he had to go. I walked him to the car after he said good-bye to the kids. They did not want him to leave either and made no attempt to hide it but he was very firm. Short of falling on the hood of his car or lying underneath his tires, there was nothing I could or would do to stop him.

At the car, we kissed for the first time that day. It was sweet and sensual and it gave me a hint of the pleasures to come if I would just be patient. After a few more kisses, I pulled away from him and started back to the house. This time I was the one who ended the encounter. I wanted him to crave me back in his arms instead of the other way around. He was in the car before I remembered the tapes and I yelled at him to wait while I ran inside to get them. My return led to more kisses and finally half an hour later, he left. He promised to call me when he got home.

Norman lived with his mother, a situation I normally frowned upon. He told me that he moved back to help take care of his mother, and I thought that his actions were honorable. She'd recently had one of her legs amputated as a result of diabetes and was having a tough time getting around and caring for herself.

"It was a good thing that I left when I did," Norman said when he called me later that night.

"Why's that?" I asked, thinking he was going to say something about making love to me.

"Momma got her chair stuck and she was crying when I got there."

"Oh, I am so sorry. How did she get stuck?" I asked, suddenly ashamed of my sexy thoughts.

"She still hasn't built up her upper-body strength and she could not get out of the kitchen!"

"Is she okay now?"

"Yeah, she's okay. I thought my sister was going to stay with her until I got back. She was upset 'cause she could not reach the phone and needed to go to the bathroom."

"Awh," I said not knowing what else to say. There was a brief silence on both of our ends.

"This is going to get better, Marie; it's just going to take some time," he said with a sigh.

"Of course it will. Take your time and work it out. I'm not going anywhere," I told him.

"You mean that?" he whispered, sending chills down my spine.

"Of course I do," I answered honestly. Norman was a good man; I could feel it in everything that he did. I was looking forward to getting to know him better. It was just going to be difficult. But nothing that comes easy is really worth it. The good things in life you had to work for.

"Well, goodnight, sweetheart. I just wanted to hear your voice before I fell asleep."

"Sweet dreams," I said, smiling.

"Of course they will be; I'll be thinking of you."

"Nite," I said, hanging up the phone. I went upstairs to my room and showered. My thoughts were on Norman and a chance at happiness. I turned on the TV and before I knew it, it was watching me.

chapter 28

Norman and I continued to see each other and developed a comfortable relationship. He would either come over my house or we would get together at the club where we had met. I still had not seen his daughter Allison but I talked to her several times over the phone. She appeared to be very grown for her age and asked me when she was going to get the chance to come over to my house. I told her to ask her daddy to set it up 'cause I would've loved to see her.

"Hey, sweetness," Norman said when he called me. I had just gotten in from a very hard day at work. I was under a lot of pressure and just wanted to take a hot bath and go to sleep. The partners of my firm were literally fighting over me. I had so much work to do I could not see straight and the other paralegals were getting pissed at me. I had planned to meet with the office manager in the morning to discuss my assignments 'cause it was getting to be too much.

"Hey, yourself," I answered back sort of distracted. I had so much stuff to do if I wanted to turn in early. The kids had stayed at Mom's 'cause I had told her what was going on at work.

"What's wrong, baby?" she had asked.

"Just work; they are pulling me in a million and one directions and it's getting old. Each partner is trying to pull rank and I'm stuck in the middle. Especially Mr. Miller. He is a senior partner and does not want me working for anyone else but him. He is giving me so much I can't keep up with my other duties."

"I'm sorry; is there something that I could do to make your day?" he asked. He was being suggestive again but I was not in the mood. We had been dating for about four months and still no sex.

"Listen, my mom is throwing together a little dinner party this weekend for the family and I wanted to know if you wanted to come," he inquired.

Oh shit, I thought, *meeting the family.*

"Sure," I said, even though I didn't mean it. I had not thought about meeting his family yet. I wanted to meet his daughter, but I wasn't sure about his mom. In my head I thought it was too soon to meet the family, but our relationship had been on a steady track since the first night we had talked so I ignored that notion. I was feeling a little nervous but I felt confident that Norman would be mine regardless of what his mother or his family had to say. Besides, I thought, at that point I had not invested too much in the relationship and if it went badly, I wouldn't have to see any of them again.

Norman told me that they lived in the country in Conyers, Georgia, about twenty-five minutes from my house. He said that he had two dogs and that they had a large piece of land. I had pictures of a big stately home in the countryside dancing in my head and was anxious to see it.

Norman had three older sisters: Kia, Kenya and Kim. He told me that they would also be there for dinner that weekend. I had seen Kenya at the club with Norman and she seemed nice. She was one of the women that I used to see him with and I had assumed she was a girlfriend.

Norman was the baby of the bunch and the only male so I could tell that he was spoiled, but I did not have a problem with that. I liked to spoil my men, too!

The week just seemed to drag by. I wanted to see Norman again and he hadn't come to visit all week. I spent the days entertaining the notion that he did not care for me as much as I cared for him or he would have taken the drive to see me at least by Wednesday. But he made me suffer quoting a lyric from an old commercial: *anticipation, anticipation is making me wait, blah blah blah*. Stupid ass commercial!

We still talked on the phone at least twice a day and sometimes he would surprise me by calling me at work. But what I really wanted was a flesh-to-flesh visit where I could reach out and touch a nigga. I did not call him at work 'cause he was often out in the field. He was a surveyor and would typically be out of the office for the entire day so when he showed up at my job for lunch on Friday I was ecstatic.

The receptionist called and told me I had a visitor in the lobby that wanted to see me. I didn't know what I was thinking when I went to the lobby 'cause any other time someone came to see me, the receptionist just sent them upstairs to my office. I must have been preoccupied not to think much of a request to come downstairs. I caught the elevator down two floors and when the doors opened, Norman was there, bearing flowers in his arms. I was floored. I understood why the receptionist had wanted me to come down. She had wanted to see my reaction to the flowers and she probably had desired to continue to look at Norman with his fine self.

He was dressed in a suit and tie, something that I had never seen him in, and he looked as delicious as a big chocolate bar with nuts and honey. I could have eaten him up right then and there but I had to play it cool 'cause we had witnesses.

"Norman, what are you doing here?" I said with a shit-eating grin on my face. I was so glad that I had taken the time to really dress up. Sometimes, depending on my mood, I would just wear jeans to the office, but that day, for some reason, I felt compelled to dress to impress. I had on a killer red suit with matching shoes and scarf. Hell, I even painted my fingernails the same fire-engine red color, which is something I rarely did. I normally prefer to pay someone else to do that mundane shit 'cause I usually mess the shit up with my impatience.

"I missed you, baby, and I was in the neighborhood so I dropped by hoping I would catch you in," he said, trying his best to hide his own stupid grin.

"Bullshit; your work does not bring you downtown. But, I'm so glad that you came anyway," I said. I looked over at Pam, the receptionist, and noticed that she was eating up every word that we said. I grabbed Norman's hand and pulled him toward the elevator doors rapidly pushing the up button so that we could finish our conversation in the privacy of my office.

I silently prayed that he understood that I did not like the people at work all up in my business. I peeped back over my shoulder as the elevator doors opened and I could see Pam checking out Norman's ass. I could not help but feel proud *'cause the brother belonged to me.* I winked at her and pulled him into the elevator laughing.

"Are those flowers for me?" I asked since he did not immediately hand them over.

"No, I just like carrying around two dozen roses just for the hell of it," he said with a smile. I could not help myself as I fell into his arms as the elevator doors closed. We were still kissing when they opened on my floor and I took him back to my office. Luckily, no one saw this public display of affection. Once behind the closed door of my office, we finished what we had started in the elevator.

"Do you have time to have lunch with me or what?" Norman said. "I need to get back home to help Momma with dinner, but I wanted to make sure that you would not chicken out about tonight. You are still coming, aren't you?"

"God, you really know me well. I was tempted to chicken out, but yes, I will be there and yes, we can do lunch. Just let me put these roses in some water," I replied. I pulled a vase from under my desk and excused myself while I went to get some water from the bathroom down the hall. I was so happy I could have shit on myself and not minded one bit. When I got back, I buzzed Pam and told her that I would be going to lunch.

We went to the Hilton, which was right next door to my office, and we ate lunch on the top floor as it revolved giving us a 360-degree tour of the city. This was not necessarily the best place to go on my lunch hour, but I think he was trying to impress me. It was beautiful but to be honest, I was so nervous I did not even pay attention to the decor. I knew the restaurant existed and it was on my to-do list, but today was not the day. We ordered cheeseburgers and he promised to bring me back when I had a chance to appreciate the restaurant and all its splendor.

"What are you trying to do to me?" I seriously asked him.

"Whatever do you mean?" he responded, avoiding the direct stare that I gave him and any further questions about his intentions.

"Are you trying to make me fall in love with you or what?" I could not believe that I so frankly asked the question that had been on my mind since we met. He was so smooth I did not want to make any incorrect assumptions regarding his intentions. I felt that I should just put it on the table then, so I didn't get my feelings hurt later. He did not directly answer my question.

"I have never brought any other woman to my mother's house other than the mother of my child, and that was only after I learned that she was pregnant and had no intentions of aborting the baby. Oh God, forgive me, I know that sounded wrong. I love my daughter; don't misunderstand me, but her mother and I were young and totally unprepared to be parents. That should tell you something about the way that I feel about you." He did not say anything else and my happy ass was content with that answer. He protected his mother from a bunch of riff-raff just like I protected my kids.

"Speaking of kids, when am I going to meet your daughter?" This was another question that I thought I would never ask but I was on a roll.

"It's my weekend so she will be there at dinner, too," he quickly answered. "I won't be able to come back to your house after dinner, but I am sure you understand that, don't you?"

Damn, I wanted to meet his daughter but in a one-on-one setting where she would not feel pressured in any way, sort of like the way that he had met my kids. His family just might have a notion to gang up on my ass and I was not comfortable with being the odd woman out.

"Don't you think it would be more appropriate for us to meet one on one? Hell, I'm gonna feel like I am on some kind of display and I don't know if I like that," I honestly answered.

"Baby, you will be fine. If I thought there would be a problem, I would not put you through it. My peeps know that I am in love with you. They just want to meet you," he said as if that would resolve all my doubts and indecisions.

I drained my glass of tea to cover my silence while I thought of a response.

"Norman, are you sure that this is a good idea?" I despised the whining tone of my voice but felt helpless to change it.

"It is important to me that all the women in my life get to know each other and in this case, the sooner the better 'cause you are an intricate part of my life now. Did I tell you that you look simply breathtaking today, not that you don't look beautiful all the time, but I love red on you?" He effectively changed the subject and I tried to shake off my feelings of apprehension.

"No, Mr. Parker, you did not say anything but thank you and I must admit I am liking what I see as well, you sexy thang you!" I said. I was fighting to hold back a smile. He grinned and nodded his head accepting the compliment. Norman got me back from lunch on time. He insisted on riding up in the elevator with me to my office. My co-workers were about to break their damn necks trying see who I was with, and I had to admit that it felt good to have a *fyne* man on my arm.

Before he left, Norman gave me detailed directions to his house and kissed me goodbye. I told him that I would be at his house by 7:00 which would give me enough time to go home, pack a bag for the kids and drop it off at my mom's. She picked them up from school so I didn't have to worry about that.

I arrived at Mom's house ahead of schedule and spent a few minutes with the kids hearing how their day went. I didn't tell my mother I was going to meet Norman's mother but she already knew, thanks to my big-mouthed son. I needed to have a serious talk with him about spreading my business.

She gave me a look of displeasure. Clearly she was miffed at me for not telling her but I could not do anything about it at that point. She offered her cheek to me when I told her that I had to go.

"Enjoy your date," she said as I closed the screen door behind me.

"Mom, no offense, I'm just not ready to talk about this yet. I love you and trust me, if it is something that you need to know about, I will tell you, okay?"

My mother could be real nosey and I didn't want her in my business until I was ready to invite her in. I thanked her and waved goodbye. She stood in the doorway until I was safely in the car and down the street. I did not have to look back because I knew she was there at the door just like I knew she loved me.

chapter 29

I had never been to Conyers even though it was only about half an hour from my house in Stone Mountain. Driving was not my forte and I only went places where I absolutely had to go when I was behind the wheel. I had this great propensity for getting lost so I had my map next to me on the seat. The funny thing was that I didn't know how to read the motherfucker so I could have left the shit at home and it would not have made a damn bit of difference.

The directions said to take Interstate 20 towards Conyers and to the best of my knowledge I was going in the right direction. Despite the uncertainty that awaited me, I was feeling good. I had the music cranked up and was not paying attention to the road that I was traveling on until I looked at the clock. I had been traveling for about forty-five minutes and I realized something was very wrong. I was in the country true enough but according to my calculations, I should have been seeing some of the landmarks that Norman had given me in his directions. I pulled out my cell phone and called Norman to tell him that I was lost.

"Where are you?"

"I don't even know. Wait, I'm approaching a sign." I slowed down the car to read it.

"Walton County," I said, stifling a cry.

"Calm down, you messed up somewhere. Let me get my map." He put the phone down and I pulled over to the side of the road to compose myself. I lit a cigarette and inhaled deeply. "That's why I hate driving," I said out loud, pounding the steering wheel. Norman got back on the line.

"I think you are on State Route 81. I need you to turn around and look for State Route 20. There will be an Eckerd's drugstore on the right. Turn right and I will meet you at the Texaco station."

Shit, I exclaimed to myself when I found out he wanted me to take State Route 20, which I could have picked up by just going straight down Sigmund Road. Norman assumed that I knew where the hell I was going.

Now instead of being early for dinner, I would just make it or worse yet, I would be late. I hated being late more than anything in the world. The second most-hated thing for me was being lost and I was truly lost. I drove and drove and drove and finally had to park the car and wait for Norman to come find me. By this time, I was crying and had messed up my makeup. It was dark and I was out in the middle of fucking nowhere and not a happy camper. It took him almost thirty minutes to get to me and by that time, dinner was long done and over with.

I followed him to his mother's house and I swear to God his directions would have never led me to the place he eventually took me. Even accounting for the fact that we were approaching it from a different angle, it was almost as if he messed up the directions to seal my fate with his family. Hell, I would have never found it on my own. It was way back on a small dirt road, deep into the woods.

When we arrived, I got mad at him for even thinking that I could have found it on my own since he knew my bad sense of direction.

He apologized for not making it clear that I should have been on State Route 20 instead of I-20 and while part of me accepted his apology, the other part of me that got lost was still pissed. I had wanted to make a good impression on his peeps, but now, I looked like an idiot that could not follow simple-ass directions.

The house he resided in, and I use the term loosely, was nothing more than a doublewide trailer. It was on a large lot of land as Norman previously stated, but it could not be considered "farm land" because the only thing that appeared to be growing on it was junk. I tried not to let the shock register on my face as I entered the rickety trailer but I am not that great of an actress.

The floor was sinking so badly that I was leaning to the right in my heels. I lost my footing and stumbled into the kitchen giving the appearance that I was drunk. I was mortified. Now I understood how his mother could get stuck in the kitchen. He should have warned me to wear sneakers instead of dressing to impress his family. As I looked around the group that was assembled at the table,

I was the only one that had dressed up for the event. I felt about two feet tall.

His family was seated around the table finishing up supper and I just wanted to go back home and cry. The table was not very big but it was loaded with food and since the trailer was so small, it took up the entire room. Eating was the farthest thing from my mind since my entire fantasy was ruined. I had to make two of his sisters get up just so I could get a seat.

"Mom, I would like for you to meet Marie," Norman said. His mother smiled at me. It was not the fake happy-to-meet-you smile but a genuine one felt from the heart. This made me feel much better.

"Hi, Ms. Parker. Sorry about being late," I said, beaming back at her.

"And this is Kia, Kenya and Kim," he said, pointing to each of his beautiful sisters. They appeared to be real close in age.

"Hi," they said in unison. I nodded to each of them as I continued smiling and growing more and more uncomfortable by the minute. He saved the final introduction to his daughter for last.

"And this little lady is Allison," he said while pulling out a chair for me. Allison was at the far end of the table and barely visible over the top. She was the cutest little girl that I had seen in a while, with the exception of my own daughter, of course. She was only four and from what they had told me, she refused to sit in a high chair 'cause she wanted to sit up just like the grown folks. As the only grandchild, I knew that this little lady would be a handful. She had a whole room full of people at her beck and call and I could tell that she already knew that at her tender age.

His family did their best to make me feel comfortable and I tried my best to get over my anxiety over being late and my disbelief of the sinkhole he had just brought me to. I was worried about finding my way home and I could not get over how different his house was from the way that he had described it.

Not that it made much difference to me that he lived in a shack instead of a house; it was more like he saw things differently than I did. For example, he drove a Lexus, which was easily worth $40,000 and his mother was living in a sinking pit. I had a problem with that on the real tip. He was a surveyor and his salary was at least $80,000 in a bad year. I didn't even know what his paychecks looked like but I knew the business.

The question became why hadn't he done something about his mother's home, and it kept nagging at my soul. If he had moved back in (that is if he had ever left) to help his mother, why hadn't he fixed the fucking floor? That had to be hell on the wheels of her portable chair.

I made it through dinner though I did not even taste the food that I ate nor did I recall one word of the conversation.

"Please, let me help with the clean-up," I said as I choked down the last forkful. I wanted to tidy up so I could get the hell out of there.

"Nonsense, we got this," Kia said as I tried to help wash the dishes but all the while I just wanted to go home and sort everything out.

Kia offered to show me back to Interstate 20, which was a real blessing 'cause I was so confused as to where I was, it would have taken me a week to find it on my own. I wanted to kiss her but did not know how she would take that shit! She said she was going to Chitchat and asked me if I wanted to go. I told her thanks but no thanks. Part of me wanted to take her up on the offer since I had not been dancing in a long time but one, I was not dressed for Chitchat and two, it would have probably given off the wrong impression to his family.

I just wanted help to get back to the highway and the safety of my house so I could think. I kissed Norman on the cheek and followed Kia's car to the highway. She pulled up next to me and told me how great it was to see me again. She also told me that she thought her brother really liked me. I told her thanks and said that he was special to me as well. In restrospect, my heart wasn't in my response to her.

chapter 30

The next day, Norman came over around 5:00. He was bearing flowers and my heart started to melt a little bit. He was looking too good in his black FUBU shirt with matching FUBU jeans and black Timberland boots. I had to give points to the man 'cause he sure knew how to dress. It wasn't that he was sporting designer gear; it was the way the clothes hung on his frame. It got me to thinking, what was he guilty of, living off his momma? Hell, she allowed it and that did not necessarily mean that he would try to move in with me and live off of me, did it?

He came through the door and kicked it shut with his foot. He pulled me to his chest and gave me the most powerful kiss that I had had in a long time. When we were done, I was breathless.

"What was that for?" I asked still trying to catch my breath.

"I just wanted you to know how very much I missed you over the past week and to tell you how proud I was to introduce you to my family as my lady. They loved you," he said. He had a wrapped box with him that he presented to me.

"Ohhh, I love surprises," I squealed. The box was small enough for a bracelet. I eagerly grabbed it and started to unwrap it. "Take your time, sweetheart; I won't take it back." I tried to compose myself and act as if I were used to receiving presents outside of birthdays and Christmas. But I just could not take it. I got the paper off and threw it to the floor. Norman just laughed at me. I opened the box, which he had taped down as well, and saw that it contained a watch. "Wow, it's a *Timex*," I said to cover my dismay. Not that I had so much against Timex but damn! It even had one of those stretch bands on it that just collected dirt and caused your arm to change colors. I tried to keep those thoughts from registering on my face. After all, it was the thought that counted.

Part of me wanted to get pissed. I was not a superficial type of woman but I would not give a Timex to my children. If Norman had bothered to look at my arm, he would have seen what a real watch should look like. The watch I was wearing had twelve diamonds on its face and it didn't have the stupid stretch band. I put his watch on next to my own and held it out for his inspection. If he noticed how badly his watch compared to mine he didn't say anything. While he was busy being pleased with himself I tried to get over my initial disgust.

"It's waterproof, too!" he declared.

I was at a loss for words. I pulled him into the living room and asked him what he wanted to do for the evening. Since I was so used to the *no pressure, I don't have to have sex* routine, I was shocked when he backed me into the corner and started playing with my nipples. He did not give me a chance to object either 'cause he covered my mouth with his and tried to suck away my very breath. At that point, my brain shut down and my hormones took over. *Fuck the Timex!* I thought. *We are about to get busy.*

He pulled one of my legs up off the floor and wrapped it around his body. He then proceeded to grind his body into mine against the wall. I could not have escaped if I had wanted to and believe me when I say, I did not want to. He broke away from my lips and started planting kisses along my neck alternating between biting and sucking my neck and throat. I was moaning and totally out of control. This was the most pleasure that I had received from another person in a long time. It had been too long since I had a man, I could hardly think straight. He was as hard as a brick and he was trying to get it in there despite the fact that we were both still fully clothed.

Norman pushed away from me, looked deep into my eyes and said, "I need you," and that was all he needed to say. If I was a genie, I would have blinked our clothes away, but we had to do it the old-fashioned way.

He picked me up and carried me upstairs to my room. He gently lowered me onto my bed and proceeded to do a striptease dance for me. He stopped when he got to his bikini underwear. Damn, the brother had it going on! Hell, I thought he looked good with his clothes on but Lawd have mercy, near naked was off the chain.

"Would you undress for me?" he asked.

I'll admit at that point my brain became disconnected. I was not in control anymore. It had been a long time since I had been this close to a near naked man and I was having a hard time staying focused. His upper body was chiseled and reminded me of the dancers at Faces on Sunday night.

I started grabbing at my clothes like a woman who had been stuck in the desert for months without anything to drink. I tore at my clothes the same way that I had with the wrapping paper on his present. That was how bad it was! I stripped down to my g-string before he could even blink an eye. I threw clothes everywhere and just lay there for his inspection.

That was by no means a striptease and I wanted to apologize but since he didn't complain, fuck it. I guess he liked what he saw 'cause he turned around so I could get a rear view of the beautiful ass I had a spotted in his jeans so many times before we had gotten to this point. I could not wait until he turned around so I could get a glimpse of the cucumber that was between his legs. The same large member that kept me hung up on the dance floor and pinned against the wall earlier that night.

I was so excited I was panting and we had not even done anything yet! He told me over his shoulder that he loved my breasts. He said that was the first thing that had attracted him to me aside from my juicy ass! I was creaming and waiting for him to turn around. I assumed for all the fumbling he was doing that he was putting on a raincoat 'cause without a coat, wasn't shit happening up in my camp! He kept talking about the different outfits he had seen me in and how they had made him feel, and I was just eating it up.

I began to rub my nipples getting them hard so when he did turn around they would be standing at attention. I was so ready for this lovemaking that I was about to pop without him even touching me!

And then, he turned around! My eyes traveled down the length of his body and got stuck on his dick or lack there of. He had switched the cucumber with a Sweet Pickle!

Shit, I'll bet Kevin is bigger than he is, I thought. His shit was so small it looked like my pinkie finger sticking straight out. What in the hell was I supposed to do with that?

My initial inclination was to jump off the bed and run for cover. I looked around for the big dick that had rubbed against my clit but he must have stuck it in his underwear when he took them off. Got damn, no wonder this motherfucker wanted to wait so long to have sex. He wasn't packing shit! Don't get me wrong; I have had some small guys before but they knew they were small and as a result, compensated for their shortcomings. This motherfucker was still under the impression that the cucumber was still in place and jumped me humping and bumping like he was doing something. IF he penetrated, I'm here to tell you I didn't feel a damn thing. It was over so quickly; my thoughts could not keep up with the action. Just like that, he was through.

He rolled over on his side and the nigga was asleep before I could figure out what the hell was really going on. I was so deeply disappointed that I did not know whether to cry or to laugh. If I weren't so horny, this shit would have been too funny but since I was, I failed to see the comical side of the situation. I nudged him to stop him from snoring but the brother did not move. I got out of the bed and went to get my real man, an eight-inch vibrator that had helped me get through many sleepless nights before.

I took the vibrator back to the bathroom and positioned myself up on the counter and took care of my own pleasure. This was the type of man I was beginning to think I needed. I did not have to do anything to my vibrator but plug him up. He did not require any special attention; all I had to do was wipe him off and he was ready to go again! My vibrator did not eat every damn thing in sight and he didn't talk back, alas the perfect man. After I was finished, I ran a shower and got in the bed.

As I crawled into bed, the words to a song by TLC came rushing to my head. *First he came, and then he went, right to sleep so fast; I could not believe...he pulled a quickie on me.* Norman slept for a couple of hours and got up to go home. I had already figured out that he could not or would not spend the night at my house, which was just as well because I was ready for him to go. I should have won an award for the performance I put on before he left. I urged him not to go while he was steadily talking about how wonderful the lovemaking was. He did not call it sex, 'cause to him it was the most beautiful experience of his life. He kept kissing me on my hands, my face and neck, telling me over and over again how I had rocked his world. I gave him my key and told him to lock the door on his way out.

I had a lot to think about and I did not need him around to cloud my judgment. Before climbing back in bed, I checked under it to see if he had put the fake dick that he came into my house with under the bed, but he must have stuffed it back in his pocket and taken it with him. I could not wait to call Angie and tell her that shit. Before I could reach for the phone, Norman called.

"Hello," I answered, pretending sleep.

"It's me baby and all I can say is damn, girl!"

"I know what you mean," I said, "but you got me so tired I have to get some rest. I will call you later."

"All right, sweetness, think of me as you sleep as I will be thinking of you," he replied.

The bile rose in my throat. Was this guy serious? Did he really believe that he had it like that? Suddenly the shit became funny and I laughed myself back to sleep.

I slept for a few hours more and went to the grocery store. The phone was ringing when I got back to the house. I looked at the caller ID and saw that it was Norman again. This was the third call that I had had from him that day and it was only 1:00. He had called first thing that morning waking me up after I finally fell asleep; he was on my caller ID again around 11:00; and now he was on the phone again.

Pissed, I answered the phone. "Hello."

"Damn, baby, sounds like you need a little tender love and care. Do you want me to come over?" he said.

Only if you bring a friend, I thought.

"Can I come back and get into bed with you?" he asked. I had to refrain from asking him if his mother would let him come out and play.

"I'm pooped, baby. Maybe tomorrow," I lied as I hung up the phone. I was going to have to deal with this situation sooner or later but I still had not decided what bothered me most—the fact that he was living with his momma in a run-down shack or the fact that he perpetrated on his dick! I pulled out a chair at the kitchen table and sat down to weigh the situation.

I drew two columns on a piece of paper and at the top of one column, I wrote "Reasons to Be With Norman." On the other column I wrote, "Dump the

Dwarfed Penis." I cautioned myself to think positively and to fill out the reasons-to-stay column first 'cause up until I had gone to his house, I was very much on the way to falling in love with Norman. In the plus column, I listed the fact that my kids loved him; he was very good-looking; he had a nice upper body (I could not say his whole body was nice anymore now that I had gotten a look at the goods); he had a great sense of humor; we liked the same movies, and some of the same foods; he was a great dancer; and he knew how to treat a woman.

In the negative column I listed first and foremost, his little dick; the house that he lived in with his momma; the fact that he could be moody sometimes; demanding, pushy, critical, egotistical and spoiled; he liked sports; had a tendency to hog the remote; and the fact that he gave me a fucking Timex.

After the list writing was done, I studied everything in the negative column and asked myself what, if any, of those things could I change and learn to accept. He was stuck with the little dick; God gave it to him and if it hadn't grown to full size yet chances were good that it would never grow up. But I could teach him that there were other things that he could do to please me to make me forget about his little dick, at least for a little while. Hell, I could even show him how to use my vibrator on me!

The deal with the house was really not my problem. If his mother chose to live in the house, then what could I say? I could've asked him why didn't he and his sisters contribute some money to fix the house up but I did not want to broach that situation unless I decided to keep him. The reality was that if the house continued to be an issue, I never had to go back there again. If there was another function that we had involving his family, I could have it at my house.

With regard to his being pushy, demanding, and egotistical, I was just going to have to decide how much of that shit I was going to take and have a serious heart-to-heart with him about that. I knew that if he caught me on a day when my tolerance level was low, I was more than likely to put him in his place real quick so that did not appear to be a real big issue. Finally with regard to the remote, if he got too damn happy with the shit I would just turn the damn set off 'cause after all, it was my TV!

Logically I had resolved all the issues I had with Norman with the exception of the watch; I simply would not wear it. I would put it back in its box and maybe give it to someone that I didn't like for Christmas.

chapter 31

In the end, after going over my list and checking it twice, I was not ready to be single again and Norman did have a lot of pluses in his box. I had been single for so long that I thought my minor problems with Norman could be worked out for at least a little while. We had only been dating for a little over eight months and we had only had sex once so maybe I was being a little too harsh.

I agreed to let Norman come over that night and this time I said I would cook for him.

Tyson called me at work. I didn't know he had my number but I just assumed that Sammie had given it to him.

"Hello, Tyson, how have you been?" I asked. He did not sound quite right. I heard noises in the background but I could not tell from the sounds. I glanced at my watch and realized that it was only 10:00 a.m. *He should be at school assuming that he still went*, I thought. I wanted to ask about his mother but something would not let those words out.

"Ms. Marie," he started but did not continue. I could hear him crying.

"Tyson, what's wrong? You're scaring me!" I tried to keep my voice down but all kinds of thoughts went through my head. He still didn't answer me because he was having a hard time catching his breath.

"Are you in trouble? Are you hurt?" I quickly asked him.

"It's not me," he wailed. Cold clammy fingers pricked my spine. "Tyson, tell me, please. Is it Sammie?" I had not spoken her name aloud in months and the word seemed foreign to my tongue. I had not forgotten her but I didn't dwell on her either.

"It's Kendall. She's in the hospital," he said, gaining some control.

"What happened?"

"She tried to kill herself!"

For a moment I could not speak. Visions of the lonely child flashed before my eyes. I shook my head to clear the images.

"Is she okay?" I whispered, fearing the worst. "Where are you?"

"I don't know yet. I found her this morning. She would not get up when I knocked on her door for school. I went in and found her on the floor with a bottle of Mom's pills lying beside her." He was crying again. "She stopped breathing on the way over here. We are at DeKalb Medical. Can you come?"

"Where's your mother?" Not that it mattered 'cause I was already grabbing my things.

"I don't know," he replied. "Will you still come?" he said.

"Of course, I'm on my way. If you need me before I can get there, call me on my cell phone. The number is 404-555-5175. Did you get it? Make sure you write it down but I'm on the way."

"Hurry, Ms. Marie. I'm scared," he said.

"Me, too, baby. Hold on, I'm coming." I called my supervisor and informed her that I had a medical emergency and had to leave. She tried to get nosey but I told her that I didn't have time to answer her questions. I said I would call them back later when I knew more. I ran down the hallway with my coat flapping behind me. As luck would have it, I did not drive that day and had to depend on MARTA to take me to my car. My moods switched between fear and anger. Fear that Kendall could die and anger at Sammie for making Tyson face this alone.

The elevator did not move fast enough and when it finally stopped on the first floor I took off running. I had on high heels but you would have thought I had on sneakers the way I was moving. People turned to watch me run but mostly got out of my way. I'm sure that I was a sight to behold.

I had two blocks to run to get to the MARTA station. By the second block, all those years of smoking caught up with me. I did not stop but my breathing was very labored. I looked down to make sure that I grabbed my purse. I would have been pissed if I had made it all the way to my car only to discover that I had no keys. Thankfully it was on my shoulder but my lungs hurt so bad I could not feel the added weight.

When I got to the escalator, I finally stopped running. I could have rushed down those steps as well but I was so winded that I probably would have had a massive heart attack. Sweat was pouring down my face and in my eyes. I used the sleeve of my coat to wipe my face staining it with my makeup. I had not started crying yet 'cause if I had I didn't think I would be able to stop.

The stairs moved so slowly I started trotting down them. I arrived at the MARTA platform as the train was attempting to leave. I ran full tilt into the closing doors screeching for someone to hold them open. For once, a Good Samaritan did me a favor. I jumped on the train and collapsed into the first seat I found. Everyone on the train was staring at me and I didn't blame them. I was sure my hair was all over my head and my eyes were wild.

I tried to compose myself while searching my purse for a Kleenex to wipe my face. I still was trying to catch my breath so I raised both hands up over my head hoping to expand my lungs. This appeared to work and after a few minutes I could finally shut my mouth and breathe through my nose. I searched for the guy that held the door and thanked him. He smiled and nodded his head at me. I looked around and everyone else quickly averted his or her eyes from me.

I again started digging through my purse so I would have my keys in hand and to find my cell phone. I thumbed through my directory until I found Sammie's cell number. I called her and got her stupid voice mail. I put in my number and put 9-1-1 behind it. I didn't know whether Tyson had tried her number or not but it was worth a shot. Chances were that if they had to pump Kendall's stomach I was so sure they would need parental consent before they did. If necessary, I would lie and fill out the forms my damn self.

chapter 32

Tyson was waiting by the emergency room door when I arrived at the hospital. Since I couldn't park in the emergency room entrance, I signaled to him that I would go park the car. I ran the entire way back to Tyson and held my arms out to him. He came towards me with no hesitation and his slim shoulders convulsed against mine. I was afraid to ask him how Kendall was but I knew I had to.

I raised his face to look him in the eyes. He blinked but held my gaze.

"Any news yet?" My heart practically stopped beating as I waited for his response.

"No, nothing. I'm so scared, Ms. Marie. I don't know what to do," he said again.

"I know, baby, me too. Have you heard anything from your mother yet?" He shook his head no.

"Listen to me," I said, grabbing his face sternly once again. "If anyone asks you, I'm your mother. Do you understand?"

"I wish you were!" he said.

"Stop that," I admonished. "Let's just get through this. If they need to do anything to your sister, someone will have to sign for it. I'm willing to do that but you have got to back me up!" He nodded his head in agreement. Together we walked through the emergency room doors.

"I'd like some information, please. My daughter, Kendall Davis, was brought in a couple of hours ago. Can you tell me where she is, and how she's doing?"

"Spell the name, please," the attendant curtly responded.

I wanted to snatch that heifer across the desk but I knew it would not help the situation. "K-e-n-d-a-l-l- D-a-v-i-s," I repeated, slowly enunciating each syllable.

She punched something in the computer, hesitated and looked me directly in the face for the first time. Once again I felt the icy grip of fear. Tyson, whose arm was still around my waist, drew me closer.

"They have not updated her condition yet. I will let the doctors know that you are here. Please have a seat." A single tear slid down my face. I turned to guide Tyson to the nearest row of chairs. He was crying all over again. I held him until he could speak.

"Tyson, do you know why Kendall did this?" He mumbled something and I told him that I could not hear him.

"The kids at school are always teasing her. They call her Frankenstein. She doesn't say anything to anybody; she just takes it." I knew firsthand how cruel children could be. Kendall was built just like her mother. She was almost as tall as Sammie.

"How old is Kendall now?"

"She just turned fourteen," he said.

"She has not even had a chance to grow into her body yet. It will change and once she starts to fill out she will have all the boys looking at her just like her momma." I meant those words to be of comfort but Tyson turned his nose up in disgust.

"She don't want those boys looking at her. That is the point! They have been hounding her since her breasts started to grow. They call her names like slut and whore! I hear her crying at night but she won't talk to me," he said.

"Did she tell Sammie?"

"I don't know. I haven't been around the house much since you two stopped hanging together. I've got my own place now but I stop by to make sure that Kendall is OK when I know her mother ain't there."

"She's your mother, too! You're still seventeen; what do you mean that you have your own place?"

"It's like I said. I'm all right," he angrily declared. I was not trying to get him pissed but I was so confused.

"Are you still in school?" I inquired.

"Not day school; I'm taking classes at night to get my GED. I work during the day." So much had happened in so little time.

"Why didn't you call me, Tyson?" I asked.

"For what? You've been cleaning up Mom's shit for years. I'm a man now and it's time I look out for myself. I know I'll do a damn better job than she ever did!" he said as he swiped fresh tears from his face.

I could not deny anything that he had said. It hurt me that I couldn't fix this for him. When I put Sammie out I didn't think it would come to this. I thought it would make her silly ass grow up but obviously it didn't.

"When we left your house she got worse and worse. She knew she fucked up with you but wouldn't admit it."

"Look, grown man or not, you are not going to sit here and cuss like a sailor. Cussing is my job, damn it," I said with conviction in my voice and a tender smile on my lips.

He looked up confused to see if I was really mad but my smile told him I wasn't. "I'm sorry," he said and for the first time, I felt he truly meant it. I patted his hand for him to continue. He had not let me go since we sat down.

"Mom stays in bed all day. She wouldn't eat and wouldn't fix anything for us either. She finally went to a doctor and he gave her all kinds of pills. She said she was a manic something or another. Those are the pills that Kendall took."

"Sweet Jesus." I could not think of anything else to say. "What about your grandmother; have you called her yet?"

"I ain't calling that heifer." He looked at me and offered another apology. "She would only make a bad situation worse and Kendall is fuc...uh, messed up enough as it is."

From what I knew of Althea I could only agree with him. I struggled between what I thought was good for the kids and my moral responsibility as an adult. I opted for the kids. "Look, I will be right back. I need to call my mother to make sure that she goes and gets Keira and Kevin. I don't want them coming home to an empty house. Stay right here," I instructed.

I went to a pay phone anxiously eyeing the attendant to see if she would give me more information now that I was alone. She ignored me and I fought the urge again to snatch her skinny ass over the desk. I called Mom and briefly explained the situation. She said she understood and that she would see me when I was done.

"I'll be praying for her, too," she said as she hung up the phone. I also called my job and told them that my niece had been rushed to the hospital and I was waiting to speak to a doctor. My boss acted like she wanted to get an attitude but I told her my sister was out of town and I was the next of kin. She backed up immediately. White people make you lie to them! I also tried Sammie's cell again but she still didn't answer.

"Damn!" I shouted at the phone as I slammed it back on the receiver. I was so angry with Sammie I could have run her over with my car. I was also very scared. I didn't want to have to make any decision regarding Kendall, but I would if I had to. I went back to Tyson and together we waited for news from the doctor. It was the longest two hours of my life and when he came out, it was written all over his face that the news was not good.

"Are you Ms. Davis?" he asked. I stood and nodded my head.

"This is Tyson, her brother. How is she?" A very large knot grew in my throat and I didn't think I would be able to swallow the spit that was pooling in my mouth. My hands were shaking and I tried to hide them behind my back but Tyson would not let my hand go.

"My name is Dr. Phillips and I was the attending physician when they brought your daughter in," he said.

"*Was?*" I said, squeezing Tyson's hand tighter. The tears began all over again as I looked at Tyson to see if he had heard what I did.

"I'm sorry; I mean I *am* her attending physician." My knees started to buckle. He noticed and gently guided me back to my original seat. He took the seat between Tyson and me, breaking the bond that was holding us both together. For a moment, he did not say anything further. The silence was so thick you could have cut it with a knife. He was giving us an opportunity to get ourselves together and briefly I appreciated it.

"Do you have any idea what type of pills she took?" Dr. Phillips asked. I looked over his head trying to make eye contact with Tyson. He just shook his head. I realized that I could not keep up the pretense of being Kendall's mother.

"Dr. Phillips, I have to be honest with you. I'm not really Kendall's mother. She is the daughter of my best friend and I can't seem to get in touch with her. This is her brother and he phoned me when he found his sister."

"I see." He turned to Tyson and said, "Do you know how long ago she took these pills?" Again, Tyson just shook his head.

"How old are you, son?" he inquired.

"Almost eighteen, sir," Tyson respectfully answered.

"How close is almost?"

"Within the month."

"Ms. Uhm...?"

"Morgan," I replied.

"Yes, by rights, Ms. Morgan, I cannot discuss Kendall with you. I can, however, talk to Tyson as her next of kin and if you so happen to provide him with some advice I can pretend that I didn't hear it from you. Agreed?"

"Yes," I promptly agreed. I looked at him for the first time. He reminded me of a younger Marcus Welby who used to have a show on TV when I was much younger. He had the softest blue eyes that I had ever seen and had a very kind smile. He took my hand and gently patted it.

"Okay then. Kendall is unconscious. We have pumped her stomach but without knowing how long she was out and exactly what she took I can't make you any promises. The next forty-eight hours will be critical. If she can make it through that, she has a good chance of pulling through."

Tyson and I both breathed easier for a moment.

"She has a lot of positive things on her side—for one, her age and apparent health. However, I don't want to fill you both with false hope. We almost lost her twice since she was brought in. We won't know if there was brain damage until she wakes up. I'm sorry the news is not better, but I want to assure you that I will do everything I can to help her. Do you have any questions?" he asked, directing his attention to both of us. I shook my head no 'cause I did not know what else to say. He stood up and was turning to leave.

"Wait, can we see her?" I begged with tears running down my face.

"No, I'm sorry. She will remain in ICU for the next forty-eight hours. She is on a respirator and we will be keeping a close eye on her. There really is nothing else that you can do tonight except maybe find her mother."

Those words burned a hole in my heart. He instructed me to leave my contact information at the front desk. He also wanted a number for Tyson, but I told him that Tyson would be staying with me. He promised to call us if her condition changed in any way.

Tyson didn't want to leave the hospital but I made him realize that we had done all we could do for the moment. We were hopeful but still scared. I tried Sammie's phone once more before heading out, and this time I left her a message.

"I don't know where the fuck you are but your daughter is fighting for her life at DeKalb Medical, so I suggest you get off your fucking ass and come to the hospital immediately!" I regretted leaving such a harsh message on her cell phone but she left me no choice. I was not Kendall's mother and that was who she needed. I debated again about whether or not to call Althea, but I decided to wait at least until tomorrow. Basically, she could not do any more than I had done, and I had not signed any type of form that would hold me legally account-able if her condition did not improve. I just did not feel like sparring with Althea; plus Tyson looked like he could really use some sleep.

I made one other call and that was to my mother.

"Mom, it's me."

"How is she, baby?" she responded.

"I don't know. She is still unconscious and the doctor said the next forty-eight hours would tell. I have Tyson and I am taking him to my house. Can Kevin and Keira stay with you tonight? I don't know if I will have to come back to the hos-pital tonight and it would be easier if I don't have to bring them along with me."

"Of course they can. I have enough clothes here for the weekend and if we run out, then I'll just wash them," she said.

"I know you will. Thanks, Mom. I will call them later after I get Tyson settled. I love you."

"I love you, too, sweetheart," she said.

I led Tyson to my car unsure of what to say to make him feel better. A part of me wanted to take the blame for Sammie's actions but she was an adult. I just hated the fact that two innocent lives were caught up in her trifling shit.

"Tyson, can I ask you a question?" I meekly said once both car doors were closed and locked. He didn't reply, forcing me to look over at him. He was trying to keep the tears inside and losing the battle. He sniffled and said, "Yeah."

"Do you think Kendall would have done this if she still lived with your grand-mother?" He took his time answering me and for a moment I thought that he was going to totally shut me out.

"I really don't know, Ms. Marie. I would like to blame this on my mother but it probably would have happened wherever we lived. Kendall has always been unhappy. I can count her smiles on my two hands. Mom might have made it better if she had noticed, but the results might have been the same."

I did not know how to respond to that so I changed the subject. "Will you come to my house and spend the night?"

"Yeah, I would like that but I need to stop by my house to let my girl know what is going on. We don't have a phone yet and she will surely trip if I don't come home tonight."

"You mean you are living with your girlfriend?" I said shocked again at how fast he was growing up. "Does your mother know this?" I asked while pulling out of the parking space.

"She knows but there ain't a damn thing she can do about it." He gave me directions to his apartment and I waited outside while he went in and explained Kendall's situation. He came back out about twenty minutes later carrying a small overnight bag. He looked like he was holding the weight of the world on his shoulders.

Tyson refused my attempts to feed him and opted for turning in early. I think he just didn't want to talk anymore and I did not press him. I told him he could take Kevin's room and I would see him in the morning.

I found it difficult to get to sleep. I was plagued with fears for Kendall and Sammie. In my heart, I did not believe that Sammie was injured but this could not be confirmed until I spoke with her. I kept calling her cell phone every two hours hoping she would finally answer. It amazed me that she would allow her home phone to be cut off while her cell phone remained connected. I finally fell asleep around 3:00 a.m., holding the phone firmly in my hand. I forgot all about my dinner date with Norman and didn't even check my messages when I got home.

Surprisingly, I did not wake up until 9:30. It was not the phone nor Tyson knocking at the door that caused my sleeping body to get out of bed. It was an urgent call from Mother Nature, which insisted that I get up. With nature's business behind me, I called the hospital to check on Kendall's condition. The lady who answered the phone said that her condition remained critical. I tried Sammie again before I got in the shower but still received no answer.

Norman had called several times during the night and I phoned him to let him know what was going on.

"Look, I'm sorry about dinner. I had an emergency. My girlfriend's daughter is in the hospital and it does not look good," I said.

"I'm so sorry. I was wondering why you had me come all the way over there and would not answer the door. Which girlfriend?" he asked.

"Sammie," I responded not feeling the need to say anything more.

"Oh damn," he responded. "Let me know if there is something I can do."

"I will, but I got to get back to the hospital. I have Tyson here with me and we have not found Sammie yet."

"Okay, baby, take care and I will talk to you later." Whew, that was easier than I thought. I didn't want to have to explain where the hell Sammie was 'cause I was having enough problems with that myself.

Tyson was in the kitchen and already dressed when I entered to start the coffee pot. To my surprise, he already had it hot.

"I remembered that you needed your java to start your day," he replied with a sheepish grin. I smiled at him and gave him a kiss on the forehead. I went to the cabinets and pulled down a cup. I turned to Tyson to see if he wanted one since he was all grown up. He anticipated my question and said, "I'll just have a glass of OJ." He got up as I handed him the glass and pointed to the refrigerator.

After my first soothing sip of coffee, I looked Tyson fully in the face. He had looked older and wiser since the last time I had seen him less than twenty-four hours ago and no longer looked like the little boy that I remembered. He had dark circles under his eyes that matched mine but I concealed mine with makeup.

"As much as I hate to do this, Tyson, we are going to have to call your grandmother," I said. Tyson dropped his head to his chest and he took a deep breath.

"I know," he said with a heavy sigh.

"You are not going to fight me on this?" I said, not bothering to hide my surprise.

"My mother left you no choice. If you don't tell my grandmother and something happens to Kendall, she will come after you like the devil chasing a fresh soul!"

A brief cartoon played out in my head with Althea chasing me in a red suit with a giant pitchfork. If the situation wasn't so grave, I would have shared that visual with him but instead I got up to get the phone with him close on my heels. I didn't know the number and Tyson had me try several different numbers before Althea finally answered the phone.

"Hello," she snapped as if I had just peed in her cornflakes.

"Mrs. Davis, this is Marie Morgan, Sammie's friend," I started but she cut me off.

"She ain't here," she barked, clearly agitated that I was calling. "I ain't seen her nor those kids of hers in about a year." I was getting pissed but I tried to regain my composure.

"I'm sorry about that but I was not calling you to find Sammie. I have some unpleasant news for you."

"What's that heifer gone and done now?" she demanded. I was tempted to hang the phone up and would have if Tyson hadn't reached across the table and grabbed my hand. I took a deep breath and continued.

"Kendall is in the hospital. She tried to kill herself." For the moment Althea didn't have anything to say. "Ms. Davis, her condition is very serious and I can't find Sammie. I wanted you to know. Tyson is with me and we will be going back to DeKalb Medical shortly."

"What do you mean you can't get a hold of Sammie? Where in the hell is she?" Althea's voice continued to rise as she fired questions at me that I could not or would not answer. "Why the fuck didn't Tyson call me?" It was then that I snapped.

"Look, Ms. Davis, I am trying to be respectful. I know you are upset but yelling at me is not going to change the situation. Now if you want to meet us at the hospital fine. If not, that's fine, too. I just thought you would want to know." I slammed the phone down before she could utter a response. I was so mad that I could feel the steam pouring from my ears. I knew the woman was a bitch but that was the first time that I had to experience it and I didn't like it.

I wanted to tell her ass a few things but didn't want to do it with Tyson hanging on to every word I said.

"She's pissed, ain't she?" he said.

"That's an understatement!" I responded. "Come on, kiddo. Let's get to the hospital before she gets there and starts clowning." I called my mother before we left to tell her that we were going back to the hospital. It was a good thing that it was a Saturday, and I didn't have the added problem of calling into work.

We drove to the hospital in silence, each deep in our own thoughts. Luckily, Althea was not at the hospital when we got there. We stopped at the registration desk to let Dr. Phillips know that we were back. The nurse informed us that he was with Kendall, and she promised to let him know that we were there.

We settled down to wait for the doctor. I had given up on Sammie since she had not returned any of my calls. I was beginning to believe that something must have happened to her 'cause she never went anywhere without her phone. Sammie was the only person that I knew who could not stand to just let a phone ring without knowing who called. Just seeing my name on the caller ID should have been enough for her to get right back to me. Surely my last few messages to her should have alerted her about the urgency of the situation. The waiting was almost unbearable but it gave Tyson and me more time to really get to know each other.

"When this is done, I'm leaving," Tyson said under his breath but still talking to me. His eyes were looking at the floor but I could tell he was scared.

"What do you mean leaving?" I said with fear mounting in my heart.

"I'm going into the army. I have already signed the paperwork and am waiting to hear from my recruitment officer for a report date."

"You can't go into the army; you are still a minor," I said.

"Mom signed my papers. Don't you see? I can't stay around her any longer; she won't do nothing but pull me down! If I stay, she will ruin my life. She will keep sucking me in like she did you. I can't take it. No, I won't take it."

What the hell was I supposed to say to him? Hang in there; it would get better. He and I both knew that was bullshit. If I was honest with myself, he was doing the only thing that he could for himself.

"Will you keep in contact with me?" I asked.

"Sure. You never did me any harm. Thanks for being there when I needed you." I gave him a hug. What happened next was a bit bleary. Sammie and Althea appeared almost at the same time.

Sammie was charging down one hallway and Althea down another. Sammie appeared haggard but still dressed to the nines. Althea looked like a raging bull. They locked eyes with each other and without even stopping to see how Kendall was doing, they immediately started screaming at each other.

When Tyson and I got to the hospital, we were the only ones in the waiting room but others had drifted in while we were talking. I glanced around the room and saw the looks of complete surprise on the faces in the room. I started to get up to stop them from making further spectacles of themselves but Tyson pulled me back in my chair.

"What the hell are you doing here, Althea," Sammie demanded.

"I'm here because your trifling ass was nowhere to be found. Someone had to be here for that baby," she said, throwing her shoulders back and raising her head.

"I have told you before, I'm her mother, not you; and she is hardly a baby."

"When you start acting like a mother, then I will treat you as one." I felt that blow as if she had physically struck me.

Tyson tightened the grip that he had on my hand but did nothing to stop their cat fight.

"I'm here now so you can just leave," Sammie shouted, placing her hands on her massive hips. In the background, I heard this constant tapping on the floor. I looked around to see where the noise was coming from and I saw a man, barely 5 feet tall coming up to stand next to Sammie.

Althea was still blessing Sammie out and neither of them paid attention to the little man. I looked at Tyson to see if he knew who this character was and he shook his head.

The registration nurse came rushing over to calm Sammie and Althea. I stood up then to take over the situation. This time, Tyson let me.

"Sammie and Althea, you are about to get thrown out of this hospital if you don't keep your voices down." I waved my hands around the room for emphasis and said, "This ain't about you and your problems. It's about Kendall!"

The nurse reached us as the wind was sucked out of both Althea's and Sammie's sails. I wanted to ask Sammie where the hell she had been but I didn't want to light a fire under Althea again.

Pissed, Althea turned around and left without even saying hello to Tyson or kiss my ass to me. Tyson sighed in relief and I sank back down to my chair. Sammie was still standing over us with the strange man holding her hand.

Dejected, I said, "Sammie, where have you been? I have been calling you all night."

"Vegas. I got married!" she announced.

I felt like I had been sucker punched. I looked at Tyson and he had a look of disgust on his face. I turned back around and looked at the man by Sammie's side. For the first time, I noticed the cane that the man carried and it occurred to me that he was blind.

Sammie was smiling and looked like she was waiting for us to congratulate her. I could not decide whether to head-butt her in the stomach or throw up. The little man just smiled.

Any further conversation was interrupted when Dr. Phillips joined our group. I jumped to my feet and introduced him to Sammie.

"Dr. Phillips, this is Kendall's mother," I said relieved to have something else other than Sammie's marriage to discuss.

Dr. Phillips acknowledged Tyson and me with a nod and turned to Sammie. Sammie was scantily clad and he turned his nose up at her. I think she forgot why she was there but Dr. Phillips quickly reminded her.

"Your daughter attempted suicide by taking a massive overdose of pills. We pumped her stomach and she spent the night on a respirator. She was showing signs of improvement until a few hours ago. I'm sorry to tell you that she died approximately ten minutes ago. I'm so sorry. We did everything we could for her."

I sat in my chair speechless. I knew that Kendall was in critical condition but I never entertained the fact that she would die. Warm tears flowed down my cheeks and I clutched Tyson to my chest, squeezing him so tightly I thought he would pop. He was softly moaning.

Sammie fainted, falling on top of her blind husband. If the situation weren't so dire, it would have been funny. The entire waiting room shook when she hit the floor and everyone appeared to be running in our direction. For me, time was suspended. I could not move, and frames of our lives kept flashing before me.

chapter 33

The next few days passed in a blur. Mom was still watching the kids as I tried to patch up Tyson's life. He was very bitter towards his mother and I was a bit miffed myself.

She did not have the money to bury Kendall and let me make the arrangements. Secretly, I blamed Sammie for Kendall's death and could not forget it let alone forgive it. After all, it was her drugs that Kendall had taken. If Sammie had been more attentive to Kendall, she would have noticed the signs but she was so focused on her own life, she did not see the pain that Kendall was obviously feeling. I also blamed myself for not going the extra mile to take her under my wing.

Norman was a constant source of help during those hectic days. He did not complain when I told him that I would be unavailable until I got things straight for Kendall. Tyson moved in with me and was scheduled to go into the armed services the day after we buried his sister. He still had not spoken to his mother and I did not try to force him to.

Sammie checked herself in to the mental ward at Charter Peachtree. She claimed to be suffering from depression but I did not buy it. More than likely, she was suffering from guilt. Although she did attend the gravesite services, she was so doped up I doubt if she really knew why she was there. Althea did not show up at all. Kendall went out of this world as quietly as she had come into it.

Momma came and brought Keira and Kevin. Leah, my co-worker, and her new husband came to the services along with Norman. I appreciated all of their support. I hadn't spoken to Leah since she had gotten married but I noticed she was either getting fat or was pregnant. A few of Kendall's classmates came as well. We all stood over her grave and prayed silent prayers. Sammie sat throughout the services dry-eyed. I knew the drugs were keeping her quiet but to others, she appeared to be uncaring.

Tyson took it the worst. He clung to his girlfriend the entire time stealing hateful stares with his mother. He waited until the first pile of dirt was thrown on his sister's grave before he approached Sammie. He did not scream or yell at her; in fact, he was almost respectful.

"This is your fault. You know that, don't you?" he said and spun around and left. That was the last time I saw Tyson in person. He kept in contact over the phone and through letters, but he never came back to Atlanta as far as I know.

I gathered my children to me and we prepared to go home. "Thanks, Mom. I appreciate your taking care of them for me but I need to be alone with them for a minute. We will call you later, okay?" I said, hoping she would understand.

"Sure, baby. Take your time. If you need me, just call."

I paused in front of Sammie but I still didn't have anything to say to her. Surprisingly, her new husband was nowhere to be found.

I stopped by to thank Leah for coming and we cried together. As I pulled away from her, I asked, "Do you have something to tell me?"

"Yes, we are expecting," she said. I was happy for her because despite my earlier misgivings, her husband appeared to be on the up and up. Leah had quit her job and was attending school full time.

"I better be the godmother," I said half-joking.

"And you know this!" she replied. We hugged again and followed the crowd of people back to their cars. I was reminded of the last time that I had been at that cemetery and I started to cry again. Before we got in the car, I took the children by my Daddy's grave and we said a prayer for him and asked him to watch over Kendall.

t had been three months since Kendall had died and I still had not heard from Sammie. When I arrived at my door one day, Sammie had left a potted plant on my porch with a note. When I saw it, I thought that Norman had left it so I immediately carried it into the house. It was a pot of tulips that I could plant in my yard, and my heart swelled at his thoughtfulness. But when I read the card I discovered it was from Sammie. I fought the urge to throw them in the trash. Sammie hadn't even sent me a thank-you card for burying her only daughter.

The note read, "I messed up. I never had a friend before so I did not know how to treat you. I took your friendship for granted and probably ruined the best part of my life. I don't know how I can make it without you. I was totally wrong bringing that fool into your house, especially since you were doing me a favor by letting me stay there, coupled with the fact that I knew you hated his ass. In hindsight, I can see where I was wrong and will understand if you don't forgive me but I still have to ask, can you forgive me? I am truly sorry and I miss you. I Love You, Sammie."

She didn't even mention Kendall, I thought. Knowing Sammie like I did, she was probably still in denial. I was still touched by her letter and truth be told, I missed her, too. We had not spoken in over a year and a half and even though I still hated what she did, I was willing to let that go.

Sammie didn't give me a chance to figure out what I was going to do because she called me as I was wiping away the trail of tears that had slipped down my cheeks. I reached for the phone and pulled it to my ear without even looking at the caller ID. I could hear Sammie crying in the background.

"Damn, damn, damn, damn, damn," I exclaimed. "What did you do, camp out across the street to see when I got the flowers?" I asked her angrily. She caught me in a vulnerable moment and I did not want to talk to her when I was weak. I still needed answers 'cause in my heart I believed that if she were a real friend, she never would have done what she did.

"Not really. I was parked around the corner and followed you to the house. I saw you pick up the flowers and gave you enough time to read the letter and decided to phone you just in case you had a change of heart. I don't think my heart could have withstood your hanging up on me so I just came over. I am so sorry." She sniffled.

"You still didn't tell me why," I quietly said. A lot of time had passed since Sammie had brought that asshole over my house, but it still hurt. Then it dawned on me, "Came over?"

"Yeah, I'm outside," she replied. She continued speaking on the phone even though she was on my front porch. I was not ready to face her yet so I did not open the door.

"Marie, you had it all and a large part of me was jealous," she continued. "I let Dickweed get into my head and I figured if I let him think that I had it going on like you do, he would stop treating me like some cheap-ass trick!"

"Did it help and was it worth it?" I assumed that was why Sammie had chosen to do what she did, but it was still painful to think that she had brought that low-down dirty bastard into my house.

"No, it didn't; he just ridiculed me even more. Marie, I need for you to believe me. I never knew that I was jealous of you until I stopped at your house instead of mine. It was not a premeditated thought. As we were driving, I told him that I moved and that I wanted him to see my new place. I did not want him to know that my lights had been cut off or that I was living in the same old one-bedroom dump, so I brought him to your house."

"But what about the children, Sammie; didn't you even think about how they would feel!" I shouted angrily. "Shit, my children were young but yours...how could you?"

"Marie, if I could go back and rewrite the script of that day, I would, but the bottom line is I can't. I will have to live with the consequences of that day for the rest of my life. I lost both of my children and the only friend that I ever had! I have been through extensive therapy and I feel like I am ready to be a friend; that is, if you let me," she declared.

She was opening up a canister of emotions that I hadn't felt since Kendall had died. Part of me wanted to run screaming from the room but the other part of me needed to know what drove her to do the things that she did. I needed to understand why her fourteen-year-old daughter had to die and her son had to run off to the military. I also wanted to know who the hell the short blind guy was who came to the hospital.

I was not going to beat a dead horse. The things that happened before that night were water under the bridge and nothing could be done to change them. Switching subjects, I asked, "Why were your lights out in the first place?"

"That requires a cup of coffee. Can an old friend get some?" she asked.

I opened the door but told her that this did not mean that I had forgiven her. She said she understood where I was coming from. We went into the kitchen and I put the water on to boil. I got down two cups and put two blueberry muffins in the microwave.

"Malcolm was in jail. I was hiding that from you," she began. I sat down at the table to hear her story.

"He claimed that his truck got searched and they found drugs in it. He said that he used a friend's rig 'cause his was in the shop and didn't check it. He was calling me collect several times a day and my phone was about to be cut off."

"Damn," I said, shaking my head.

"I used the light-bill money to pay the phone. To make matters worse, all the checks that he had been giving me turned out to be stolen. He had me giving him my cash and he would write checks for me. It all came crashing down on me at once," she said as tears fell down her face.

"Damn, girl, you get your ass in more shit!" I said to her. "So where is Malcolm now?" I asked.

"He is still in jail. I pressed charges against him after I found out about the checks. They were about to evict me 'cause my rent checks bounced, too."

"Is he still calling you collect?" I asked.

"Nah, he stopped," she said, laughing. Sammie never stopped amazing me with her antics. I had not forgiven her yet but we were talking and that was a start.

"Oh, where is your husband?"

"We had it annulled. I damn near broke his leg when I fell on him!" she said howling. We both fell over on the table laughing.

"That shit was too funny. Was he blind?" I asked with tears rolling down my face.

"Yep," she said, still laughing.

I filled Sammie in on some details of my life with Norman.

"So are you all in love?" she asked.

"I'm in; put it like that. He is great with the kids and is such a compassionate and caring man."

"You're in luv, child. I can see it on your face," she said and we both laughed. This felt good joking with Sammie again.

chapter 35

was on my way out the house rushing to get to work when the phone rang, thinking that Norman was calling back with some last-minute term of endearment. I answered. I was wrong. It was Sammie.

"Gurl, I'm glad I caught you. They let Jessie out of jail last night," she said.

"Oh shit! How did you find out and why the fuck did they let him go?" I screamed.

"He appealed his case and the officers could not produce the drugs that he had when he was arrested. They had to throw the case out for lack of evidence. The prosecuting attorney called me saying I had a right to know." I could tell by the tone of Sammie's voice that she was scared. I was, too, but not for myself, only for her.

"Has he called you?" I inquired.

"He can't; my phone is turned off again."

"Thank God for small favors," I said. The kids were pulling my hand and I really needed to go but I was still curious. "Wait, I don't understand. How did the attorney get you if your phone is off?"

"My phone was not turned off until this morning; he left a message last night. I did not get it until this morning and when I tried to call you, I found out that it was not working. I used my cell phone to call and check my messages," she said.

"Where are you calling me from?"

"I am at the gas station around the corner from the house."

"You should get your number changed," I said.

"Yeah, you are so right. I think I will do that. I'm also going to buy a gun!" She laughed but I could feel her fear.

"Damn." That was all that I could think to say. I didn't want her toting a gun 'cause her silly ass might fuck up and shoot her own self but I could not say anything.

"Watch your back, girl," she said, as she was ready to hang up.

"Why should I have to watch my back?" I asked, not quite catching the connection.

"He blames you for my divorcing him," she said.

"Wait, hold the fuck up? Why the hell does he think that I had something to do with that? Look, I can't talk right now. I really got to get on the expressway before I-20 gets backed up. Give me a couple of hours and call me at work, okay?"

"Yeah, I'll call you when I get back from the phone company."

"Damn. More fucking drama," I said to myself as I hung up the phone.

I was upset but in my heart I did not feel that Jessie was a threat to me unless Sammie was at my house when he decided to make his move on her. I was nervous but the nigga would have to be straight-up crazy to fuck with me so soon after being released from jail. I would make sure that if the nigga so much as breathed on me he would go to jail and stay there!

I was so anxious waiting for Sammie to call me, I could hardly concentrate on my work. Every time my phone rang I jumped to get it as if my secretary could possibly know what was going on in my personal life. I went to great measures to keep my private life just that—private.

She took her sweet time calling, too; it was almost 3:00 before she got back to me. She said that it took her all afternoon to get a gun permit and she had to prove that she knew how to use it. I wanted to cut to the chase and find out why she thought that Jessie would come anywhere near me.

"Jessie claims that I would have never had the nerve to divorce him unless you put me up to it. He used to say that when I was accepting his calls, that that bitch was going to get hers." I had prayed that he had gotten Sammie and the drugs out of his system while he was in jail and had been smart enough to pick up the threads of his life and leave the both of us alone.

When I got home from work, Norman's car was in the driveway. I did not see him sitting on the porch. I opened the door and could hear the TV blaring in the living room. That was when I remembered the key. That nigga had crossed two lines at one time. One, he came over without calling and I thought back to our conversation of the night before and realized, with a sinking feeling, that I never did get around to telling him that I didn't play that drop-by unannounced or uninvited shit!

He was stretched out on my sofa as if he made the monthly payments on it. He had taken off his shoes and socks and they were lying on the living-room floor. I guess the nigga wasn't full-blown crazy, just a tad touched in the head! He didn't even bother to get up; he just hollered at me, "Hey, baby," and continued to watch the *Jerry Springer Show*. Little did he know that if he didn't get his funky feet off my white sofa, it was about to be a Jerry Springer show right in my living room!

"What are you doing here? I don't remember *inviting* you over here tonight," I said. I stood directly in front of him blocking his view of the television.

He raised his eyebrows and gave me this crazy look like I had switched the script and didn't tell him about the revisions.

"You gave me the key," he stuttered.

I waited until the kids went upstairs before I answered him. They did not have to hear what I was about to say. I really didn't need this shit given the bad day that I had had. I prayed for strength and wisdom from God. I asked God to help me so that I would be able to phrase what I had to say to Norman in a diplomatic way.

"Norman, look, I let you use my key the time you were here so you could lock up 'cause I was too tired to come down and do it myself. It was not to be used at will like a gold card with expanded privileges. Please don't take this the wrong way, 'cause I like you, but you still need to respect me enough to call me before you come over, and you also need to return my key."

He flinched and put both his feet on the floor. He started looking around for his shoes and socks as if he were going to leave, which was fine by me 'cause I needed to set him straight before it got too far out of control.

"You know what, girl, your ass is a trip! Just when I think I understand you and we start to click, you throw a monkey wrench in the works. I don't understand you," he said as he was lacing up his shoes.

He was mad and made no attempt to hide it. I knew that I was losing this fight but because it was so important to me, I just kept coming.

"I don't see what is so hard to understand. Yes, we are dating but we aren't married. I don't just drop by your house and you can't just come dropping by mine. It's a matter of showing respect. Hell, they did not give me the key to this place until I started making monthly payments on this bitch, so what makes you think that you can have a key?"

Uh-oh. I knew that I pushed the bar with that last remark but I was tired of pussyfooting around the issue. It was a bad day that was steadily getting worse.

"Oh, so this shit is about money; you want me to pay your rent, is that it?" he angrily declared.

"Hell no, I don't want you paying my *mortgage*. Get it right, nigga; it ain't rent. I can pay my own damn bills but you need to respect the fact that this is my house and you are just a visitor. And visitors get invited, you get it!" I was doing every-thing I could to keep my voice down but with all his slamming and shuffling, it was clear to my kids that we were fighting.

That's the part that I hated the most. My kids had already been through the drama of all that fighting when my ex and I were together. They did not have to go through that shit again and neither did I for that matter. If Simple Simon could not comprehend why I needed my privacy that was his problem, not mine. Fortunately, the kids did not come downstairs while we were fussing. Norman was busy collecting the shit that he had spread out in the living room and shooting me evil glances. At the door, he said to me over his shoulder that I was making it real difficult. He shut the door and it took me a full two seconds before I realized that he did not give me my key back.

I ran out the door at break-neck speed and managed to catch him before he cleared the subdivision. He must have thought that I had come after him to beg him to return, but I just held out my hand. Slowly comprehension dawned on him as to why I was really there and it showed on his face. He threw his car into park, turned off the ignition and took my key off his ring. I looked at his ring while he was fumbling with the keys trying to find out if a copy had been made, but I could not really tell. I made a mental note to replace the lock with a dead-bolt that could be locked from the outside so that I would never have to wonder about that.

Before he left I tried to explain why I had to be the way that I was. Right there in the middle of the street, I told him that my ex-husband had taken me through the ringer about the key to my house. I let him have it one day when he had to bring the kids home early while I was still at work. He stayed until I got home but would not return my key. For months, I had to put up with him showing up in my bedroom after I had gone to sleep. I told him that I would not go through that shit again. If he understood my position he did not reveal it to me. He pealed off down the street burning rubber, leaving me to only assume that he was through with me.

Once I got back inside I had to have a long conversation with myself to determine whether or not I was right to nip that shit in the bud or let it continue. I concluded that hell yeah, I was right and if the motherfucker could not deal with it, fuck him! I went in and checked on the kids. They were going about their normal daily routines but they appeared to be subdued and distant. I could tell without questioning them, that they had overheard the argument between Norman and me. It was rough to be a single custodial parent 'cause your life was laid open like a book for your children to judge.

Although I thought I did a good job of keeping the petty shit away from them, lately it seemed like I was losing control. I decided it was time for a family meeting. I did not know what was happening between Norman and me, but I wanted them to know that they were secure.

"Family meeting in my bedroom in ten minutes," I yelled up the stairs loud enough for both of them to hear. I stopped by the phone and switched on the answering machine 'cause I wanted to talk to my kids without being interrupted.

chapter 36

"**H**ey, girl," Sammie said when I picked up the phone. I had just returned from the mall so I told her to hold on while I put down my bags. It had been a few weeks since we last talked and I had a lot to tell her.

"I'm stressed. I did the naked mambo with Norman and I'm not in luv no more," I replied. "I still like him but I am not feeling him like that."

"What happened to the compassionate man that wasn't all about the panties?" she inquired.

"Girl, I don't even know. I feel like he was switched with his evil twin. This man comes over here like he's running shit up in this camp!"

"What, it can't be that bad?" Sammie said with feigned annoyance.

"Yes it is; he wants to tell me how to cook, what to fix and then dictate what we watch on television and you know I don't be giving up the remote on no bullshit."

"He ain't trying to watch sports on your TV, is he?" she said, laughing. Sammie knew how much I detested men and their sports.

"Oh girl, it's worse than that. He wants to have dinner served in front of the TV while he watches them. I made the mistake of leaving the remote on the arm of the sofa and that son of a bitch called me out of the kitchen to hand it to him. I don't know how much more of this I can take."

"What about the dick? Is he putting it down proper; that's what I want to know?"

"Hell no, this little-dick brother gives new meaning to the words two-minute brother! First, I thought he was just excited 'cause I made him wait so long. But damn girl, he's been hitting it for over two weeks and the shit ain't getting no better. Hell, I'd rather watch a football game than have him fumbling with my shit. And you know how much I hate football!"

"You is crazy, girl. Did you tell him?"

"Not yet, but I'm telling you, I'm at my limit. Luckily, he is staying at his house tonight but our days are numbered. I would have kicked his ass to the curb weeks ago if he did not have such a good relationship with my son. But the way I look at it, my son does not have to sleep with him so the brother is history! Not to mention the fact that his sisters keep calling me, welcoming me to the family like I was their new sister-in-law. They are just trying to get rid of him so they don't have to fool with his ass. That's what I think and that's my story and I'm sticking with it!"

"Well, maybe that means that I will get my road dawg back and we can start hanging again," Sammie said.

"I don't think so; my clubbing days are over. I have not found anything in the clubs that I can't find peeping in the gutter. I can sift through garbage right here in my house; I don't need to go out and pay for it. Look, that's my other line. I'll holler at you later." I was just about to answer the phone when I peeped at the caller ID and saw that Norman was beeping through. Part of me just wanted to go back to my conversation with Sammie, but I had worked myself up to a little attitude and decided now was as good a time as any to end this mess.

"Hey, baby, what's up?" Norman inquired. He sounded so sweet on the telephone that I almost wanted to change my mind but I knew that once he got to my house, he would turn into Adolph Hitler. We didn't talk about the fight we had the day before.

"I'm just getting in from the store," I said.

"Were you on the phone just now? It sure took you a long time to pick up." He said it like he was joking but I knew better. It was at that exact moment that I lost all the cool my mother had given me and decided the only way to exorcise this demon was to go gutter foul on him.

"Excuse me?" I said, feigning like I did not hear the words coming out his mouth.

"Uh, I was just checking to see that you were all right. I wanted to make sure that I didn't have to dash over there and help you out." He quickly tried to clean up his mistake but it was too late; I was on a roll. I'd had enough and wanted my life to return to normal no matter how boring that was. In hindsight, I felt like kicking my damn self. I was doing fine all by myself but I had to complicate my shit and add someone else. I was even under pressure from my mother to bring Norman around to meet her, thanks to Kevin's big mouth.

"Norman, I wasn't going to have this conversation with you over the phone but I think we need to talk," I said.

"Oh Lord, it must be your time of the month," he said. I could hear the smug, condescending tone of his voice and I just straight up lost it. I tried to keep an even tone to my voice and my blood pressure down to a minimum, but to me that was the lowest blow that a man could serve a woman.

"Oh, so what are you trying to say; since I want to talk to you I must be on my cycle? Nigga, please! You are lucky that I ain't on my cycle 'cause I would tell you where you could stick that little-ass dick of yours." Norman did not say anything so I guess I had his full and undivided attention.

"You do not have to check up on me. I am a grown-ass woman and I don't appreciate your tone of voice."

"Look, I didn't mean anything about my earlier comment; I was just making a joke," he said.

"Norman, save it. I don't believe that you make jokes about things like that. I think that you are trying to be controlling and I'm here to tell you, I am *not* the one."

"Wait, you are blowing this all out of proportion! All I said was what took you so long to answer the phone. What is wrong with that?"

"Everything. I just don't like where this whole thing is headed."

"What whole thing?"

"This relationship," I said quietly. Norman did not respond. For a moment, I thought that he had hung up the phone. I waited for his response but for once, he was at a loss for words.

"I would like for us to remain friends but if you can't handle that, I understand. I wish all the best for you and hope you have the best of luck in the future." I was ready to hang the phone up when I heard him yell for me to wait.

"You are going to end us, just like that? I was falling in love with you, Marie. Did you meet someone else? Is that what this is about?"

"Why does it have to be about someone else? Why can't it just be about us?"

"I thought you were happy," he said.

His quiet demeanor brought me down a decibel. I regretted calling his dick little, at least to his face, and I regretted flying off the handle. Basically, I was not a bitch at heart but I had been through so much with men, my tolerance level was non-existent.

Acknowledging my slip-up, I said, "I'm sorry. I was not deliberately trying to hurt you. I get crazy when guys say stupid stuff about a woman's monthly cycle. Hell, a menstrual cycle is bad enough without the bad PR men give it. It's so sexist!"

"I'm sorry, too. I'll try to be more sensitive."

Was he trying to be condescending? The problem with Norman was that he was so arrogant that he thought his shit didn't stink. At times, he treated me like he was doing me a favor by being with me and I did not appreciate that one bit.

"What I'm trying to say Norman is that I'm not ready for a 'relationship' like the one you apparently want. I need a friend more than I need a lover. Can you understand that?" I said.

"Yeah, I understand all right."

I detected attitude in his clipped response and I was weary of taking the easy approach with him. Norman was obviously one of those men whose ego I would have to crush in order to get my own life back. He asked me if he could come over 'cause he really needed a hug, but I begged off telling him I was tired. I agreed to speak with him the next day and told him goodnight. I was emotionally drained. I would have never thought that our blooming romance would end so badly and so quickly, but he was the obsessive type and that could become a problem if not stopped. Despite the way it ended, I felt I did the right thing. But that did not take away the emptiness in my heart.

The only reason why he wanted to come over was 'cause he thought that we would wind up falling in bed like the last time we had an argument. Why is it that men think that all ills in a relationship can be cured by a fuck? When I'm mad, the last thing that I want to do is have sex. But men think it's a cure-all. They feel like if they sex you just right, you will forget whatever it is that made you upset. That's bullshit!

I was so tired of starting over. While I really didn't want to be alone for the rest of my life, I was sick and tired of playing the games that men and women play with each other. I had made an exception to my rule by letting Norman into my home and the life of my kids. That was the biggest regret that I had. I didn't feel like explaining to my children why they would not see Norman again. My head was so heavy and my eyes were burning. I gave up all pretense of keeping it together and had myself a good old-fashioned cry.

I cried for all my failed relationships. I cried for the other single women out there just like me. I cried for those sorry men that had been spoiled by their mothers, making them utterly useless to a good woman. I cried for my son for the lack of a positive role model in his life.

After I finished sobbing, I started planning. I vowed to not let another day go by without my finding a male role model for my son. Prior to meeting Norman, I thought that I was adequately filling all the roles in my son's life but obviously I was wrong. It was evident in the way that my son bonded with Norman that I needed to do something different for Kevin. I would apply to the Big Brothers of America, an organization that I had heard about that sponsored kids without parents to help them grow to be well-rounded individuals. I would do whatever I had to do to protect and help Kevin be a real man. I made a promise to him that night to make him my priority.

I dragged myself upstairs to take a soothing bath. It had been a very long day and I wanted to wash my cares away if it was at all possible. I ran the water while I took off my clothes. While I was at it, I decided to give myself a facial and work on my nails. I put the scrub on my face but I just did not have the energy for the nails. They would have to wait until I was feeling better or I paid someone else to do it. I stayed in the tub until the water turned cold. After drying myself off, I climbed into the bed and switched off the light. I was asleep before my head hit the pillow.

I was awakened at 3:30 a.m. by the ringing of the phone. At first, I thought it was a part of my dream. I tried to ignore it but it just kept ringing. I reached out to my nightstand trying to grope the phone without opening my eyes. I answered it after several failed attempts. The first two times, I was talking to a bottle of lotion and finally after pushing the phone to the floor I answered it. It was Norman.

"Do you know that it is after three in the fucking morning? Somebody better be dead or dying," I said, making no attempt to hide my irritation.

"Listen, I know it's late but I need to ask you a favor," he pleaded. For a moment, I thought that he might be having car trouble and for one terrible moment, I thought something was wrong with his mother or possibly his daughter.

"Norman, what's the matter?" I asked, sitting upright in the bed.

"Can I claim one of your children as a dependent on my income tax return this year?" he whispered.

All remnants of sleep quickly vanished. Surely he was joking, I thought.

"I beg your pardon, come again?" I stuttered trying to keep from choking on the bile that had risen in my throat. All kinds of thoughts were flying through my head and none of them were making any sense.

"I need an additional deduction for my taxes and I wanted to know if I could claim one of your kids so I won't owe this year." He did not appear to be slurring his words so I assumed he was sober. And if he was sober and still asked me that question, then the nigga was certifiably crazy.

"Are you on crack? Why in the hell would I do something like that?" I screamed into the phone. My headache came back twofold. This man was totally demented if he thought that I would possibly say yes.

"I just did my return and the numbers don't look good. I'm going to owe a lot of money and I hoped that you might be willing to help me out," he calmly stated. "You don't have to give me an answer tonight. Just think about it and I'll talk to you about it in the morning."

"Hold on," I said and placed the phone down to go into the bathroom to run some water over my face. I looked in the mirror to see if "Doctor Dumb Ass" was written all over my face 'cause that was just how he made me feel. Who in the hell did he think he was dealing with? I purposely left him on hold for about fifteen minutes before going back to the phone.

As politely as I could, I said, "There is nothing to think about. Hell No!"

"You really must hate me, don't you?"

I shook my head. Norman was one sick puppy. Obviously he was not hearing me. He tried to turn every situation to his advantage to make me look like the bad guy. He had missed his calling. He should have been a used car salesman. I tried a different approach.

"Why don't you claim your own child," I asked, still trying to remain calm despite how angry he was making me.

"Her mother won't let me. That heifer lied to me for a whole year. She told me that if I increased the support I was giving her over the year she would allow me to deduct her," he said angrily.

"Why does she have to be a heifer? She is the mother of your child," I declared.

"'Cause her ass lied to me."

"Well, did you ever think that the little bit of money that you pay in support is not enough to take care of a child? Do you know how hard it is to raise a child on one salary? Do you?"

"I give her plenty of money."

"Do you pay her health insurance? What about day care?"

"I give her enough but she probably is spending it on herself instead of Allison."

"When is it enough when you have children? You have got some nerve. OK, I'll give you credit because at least you claim to be paying child support and you do keep your daughter every other weekend. But how could you twist your lips to ask me for one of my dependents? You know that I am doing this all by myself and I'm the bad guy for saying no?"

"Look," he said. "Just think about it. You don't have to answer me until you have had a chance to think about it."

"There is nothing to think about, you fucking moron. You have not done a damn thing for my kids and you want me to risk going to jail for tax fraud for you? Get a fucking grip!" Norman interrupted my tirade.

"You fucking bitch! My mother told me not to get involved with you. She said you would suck me dry and she was right. You will get yours, bitch!" he said and hung up the phone.

I was so upset I was trembling. Did he just threaten me? I hung up the phone and called Sammie at work. She would be just getting off so I was not worried about calling her so late. She answered right away and said she would come by the house on her way home. Over coffee, we discussed filing a restraining order against Norman. I was spooked and didn't mind admitting it. Even in my darkest hour, I had never had a man go off on me like that.

Now not only did we have to contend with Jessie's stupid ass, Norman was nutting up! Of the two, Jessie scared me more 'cause Norman never displayed any violent outbursts that I knew of. I wanted to call his sister Val to see if I could feel her out but Norman was such a good manipulator, he probably had already turned her against me. Needless to say, I would not be going into work in the morning.

Sammie stayed with me while I slept off and on. I woke up shortly before 8:00 and got dressed to go to the police department to file the order. I called into work since Sammie had agreed to watch the kids. I needed to have them near me 'cause I was feeling so bad. I fed them breakfast and kissed each of them on the forehead. I thanked Sammie for coming to my rescue the night before and I grabbed my stuff and headed for the door.

chapter 37

I don't recall the moments just before the bullet pierced my lung. I only remember a slight burn as it entered my body, and the feeling of my legs giving way as I crumbled onto the steps. Everything that they say in the movies is true. My whole life flashed before my very eyes. I could not turn away from the bitter moments nor could I rejoice in the happy ones. I was powerless. I could feel my body react to the lack of air but I was helpless to do anything about it.

I fought to hold on. I knew that I was mortally wounded but I had so much to do. Sammie ran out of the house and cupped my head in her lap. She was crying but I could not say or do anything. I hoped my eyes expressed what I was feeling. I wanted her to let my children know that I loved them. I wanted her to be there and let them know who I was and to tell them that I would always be around looking out for them. I willed her to tell them that they could achieve anything and that I would always be there right behind them pushing them on.

Norman walked up the steps with the gun still pointed at me. Sammie scooted back against the porch rail allowing my head to hit the concrete floor. It didn't hurt since my main focus was on trying to breathe. He was smiling as he approached me.

"What, bitch? Ain't talking now, are you? Cat got your tongue?" He leered at me with this demented look on his face. I could not believe that Norman was going to actually kill me on the front porch of my house in the presence of my kids. How could I have possibly misjudged him like that?

I could hear the children inside the house screaming and I prayed that they would not come out to see what was going on. Sammie was wailing as if she had been shot her damn self. I heard the second shot but my vision had failed. I was still aware of my surroundings but I could not see the players anymore. I prayed that Norman would not shoot Sammie, too, since she was a witness to the crime. Luckily for me, I did not feel the bullet that entered my head and it did not stop my mind from working. I was unable to move but my thoughts were still clear. I was yelling at Norman and for Sammie to call the police but neither responded since they could not hear me.

I did not hear the third and final shot. I was already dead but I could still see what was going on around me. Norman administered that bullet to his own head on the front steps of my house. He fell right on top of me. I wanted so badly to push his ass off but I could not move.

I stayed with Sammie as long as I could. I saw the white light but refused to run toward it. I was so afraid. Not of dying 'cause that was done already, but of living in the hereafter without my kids. I think I would have tried to stay longer, that is if I didn't see Norman reaching out a hand to me from the depths of hell. It was time to go.

THE END

about the author

Tina Brooks McKinney was born in Baltimore, Maryland.
She moved to Atlanta, Georgia in 1996 with her two children,
Shannan and Estrell. Once in Atlanta, she met and married her loving,
supportive husband, William. Tina has mad love for Atlanta, but Baltimore
will always be home. Her love for writing is evident in her debut novel,
All That Drama. The characters are vivid and somehow familiar as
they take the reader on a wild ride through domestic dysfunction.